ACCLAIM FOR KATHLEEN FULLER

"Fuller's inspirational tale portrays complex characters facing real-world problems and finding love where they least expected or wanted it to be."

—BOOKLIST, STARRED REVIEW, ON *A RELUCTANT BRIDE*

"Fuller has an amazing capacity for creating damaged characters and giving insights into their brokenness. One of the better voices in the Amish fiction genre."

—*CBA RETAILERS + RESOURCES* ON *A RELUCTANT BRIDE*

"This promising series debut from Fuller is edgier than most Amish novels, dealing with difficult and dark issues and featuring well-drawn characters who are tougher than the usual gentle souls found in this genre. Recommended for Amish fiction fans who might like a different flavor."

—*LIBRARY JOURNAL* ON *A RELUCTANT BRIDE*

"Sadie and Aden's love is both sweet and hard-won, and Aden's patience is touching as he wrestles not only with Sadie's dilemma, but his own abusive past. Birch Creek is weighed down by the Troyer family's dark secrets, and readers will be interested to see how secondary characters' lives unfold as the series continues."

—*RT BOOK REVIEWS*, 4 STARS, ON *A RELUCTANT BRIDE*

"Kathleen Fuller's *A Reluctant Bride* tells the story of two Amish families whose lives have collided through tragedy. Sadie Schrock's stoic resolve will touch and inspire Fuller's fans, as will the story's concluding triumph of redemption."

—SUZANNE WOODS FISHER, BESTSELLING
AUTHOR OF *ANNA'S CROSSING*

"Kathleen Fuller's *A Reluctant Bride* is a beautiful story of faith, hope, and second chances. Her characters and descriptions are captivating, bringing the story to life with the turn of every page."

—AMY CLIPSTON, BESTSELLING AUTHOR OF *A SIMPLE PRAYER* AND THE KAUFFMAN AMISH BAKERY SERIES

"The latest offering in the Middlefield Family series is a sweet love story, with perfectly crafted characters. Fuller's Amish novels are written with the utmost respect for their way of living. Readers are given a glimpse of what it is like to live the simple life."

—*RT BOOK REVIEWS*, 4 STARS, ON *LETTERS TO KATIE*

"Fuller's second Amish series entry is a sweet romance with a strong sense of place that will attract readers of Wanda Brunstetter and Cindy Woodsmall."

—*LIBRARY JOURNAL* ON *FAITHFUL TO LAURA*

"Well-drawn characters and a homespun feel will make this Amish romance a sure bet for fans of Beverly Lewis and Jerry S. Eicher."

—*LIBRARY JOURNAL* ON *TREASURING EMMA*

"*Treasuring Emma* is a heartwarming story filled with real-life situations and well-developed characters. I rooted for Emma and Adam until the very last page. Fans of Amish fiction and those seeking an endearing romance will enjoy this love story. Highly recommended."

—BETH WISEMAN, BESTSELLING AUTHOR OF *HER BROTHER'S KEEPER* AND THE DAUGHTERS OF THE PROMISE SERIES

"*Treasuring Emma* is a charming, emotionally layered story of the value of friendship in love and discovering the truth of the heart. A true treasure of a read!"

—KELLY LONG, AUTHOR OF THE PATCH OF HEAVEN SERIES

LETTERS TO

Katie

ALSO BY KATHLEEN FULLER

THE AMISH OF BIRCH CREEK

A Reluctant Bride
An Unbroken Heart
A Love Made New (available September 2016)

THE MIDDLEFIELD AMISH NOVELS

A Faith of Her Own

THE MIDDLEFIELD FAMILY NOVELS

Treasuring Emma
Faithful to Laura
Letters to Katie

THE HEARTS OF MIDDLEFIELD NOVELS

A Man of His Word
An Honest Love
A Hand to Hold

NOVELLAS INCLUDED IN

An Amish Christmas—A Miracle for Miriam
An Amish Gathering—A Place of His Own
An Amish Love—What the Heart Sees
An Amish Wedding—A Perfect Match
An Amish Garden—Flowers for Rachael
An Amish Second Christmas—A Gift for Anne Marie
An Amish Cradle—A Heart Full of Love
An Amish Market—A Bid for Love
An Amish Harvest—A Quiet Love (available August 2016)

THE MYSTERIES OF MIDDLEFIELD SERIES FOR YOUNG READERS

A Summer Secret
The Secrets Beneath
Hide and Secret

LETTERS TO

A
MIDDLEFIELD
FAMILY
NOVEL

KATHLEEN FULLER

THOMAS NELSON
Since 1798

Published in Nashville, Tennessee, by Thomas Nelson. Thomas Nelson is a registered trademark of HarperCollins Christian Publishing, Inc.

Thomas Nelson titles may be purchased in bulk for educational, business, fund-raising, or sales promotional use. For information, please e-mail SpecialMarkets@ThomasNelson.com.

Scripture quotations are from the King James Version of the Bible.

ISBN 978-0-7180-8278-9 (Repack)

Library of Congress Control Number: 2013932913

ISBN 978-1-59554-777-4

Printed in the United States of America

16 17 18 19 20 21 RRD 6 5 4 3 2 1

For everyone seeking God's will

PENNSYLVANIA DUTCH GLOSSARY

ab im kopp: addled in the head

aenti: aunt

appeditlich: delicious

boppli: baby

bruder(s): brother(s)

bu: boy

buwe: boys

daag: day

daed: dad, father

danki: thank you

dawdi haus: grandparents' house

Dietsch: Pennsylvania Dutch, the language spoken by the Amish

dochder: daughter

dumm: dumb

dummkopf: dummy

Dutch Blitz: Amish card game

Englisch: English, i.e., non-Amish

familye: family

frau: wife, woman

freind: friend

geh: go

grosskinskind: great-grandchild

grossmammi/grossmudder: grandmother

gross-sohn: grandson

grossvadder: grandfather

gude mariye: good morning

gut: good

guten nacht: good night

hallo: hello

haus: house

Herr: Mr.

hochmut: pride

hungerich: hungry

kaffee: coffee

kapp: prayer covering worn by women

kinn: child

kinner: children

kumme: come

lieb: love, sweetheart

maed: girls

maedel: girl

mamm, mammi: mother, mom

mann: man

mariye-esse: breakfast

mei: my

meidung: shunning

menner: men

mudder: mother

nee: no

nix: nothing

onkel: uncle

Ordnung: the Amish rule of life (unwritten)

rumspringa: literally, "running around"; the period of time (around age sixteen) when Amish youth defy conventions and experience life in the "Yankee world" before making the decision to be baptized and commit to the Amish life.

schee: pretty, handsome

schweschder: sister

schwoger: brother-in-law

seltsam: strange, unnatural

sohn: son

vadder: father

wie gehts: how are you?

willkum: welcome

ya: yes

yung: young

CHAPTER 1

"Oh, Katherine. This is so *schee*."

Katherine Yoder smiled at her best friend, Mary Beth Shetler. She'd spent hours working on the baby quilt, making sure the tiny stitches were as perfect as possible for Mary Beth's new baby. "I'm glad you like it."

"Of course I do." Mary Beth touched the soft flannel quilt, running her fingers over the pale yellow, blue, and peach blocks. Each block had a ragged edge, a new pattern she hadn't attempted before. The simple style was well suited for a baby, and Mary Beth's was due in a few weeks.

"I love it." Mary Beth folded the quilt and placed it on her knees, her expanded belly barely allowing the space. "*Danki* for such a beautiful gift. Although I don't see how you have the time, working so many hours at the restaurant."

All I have is time. She pushed the self-pity aside and managed a smile. She didn't want to ruin the moment between them with jealousy. Unlike Mary Beth Shetler, Katherine didn't have a husband—and soon a child—to take care of. Outside of working

1

at Mary Yoder's and helping her parents at home, her only other pursuits were her sewing and needlework. She was always busy yet longed for something different. Something more.

Apparently God had other plans.

Mary Beth managed to rise from the chair in her tiny kitchen. Her husband, Chris, had built the four-room home behind Mary Beth's parents' property. The dwelling resembled a *dawdi haus*, and likely would be used as such once the rest of Mary Beth's siblings—Johnny, Caleb, Micah, and Eli—married and left home. But for now, the tidy, cozy home was enough.

And more than Katherine had.

Mary Beth placed the quilt on the table. "I'm glad you came over. Since I've gotten so big, I haven't gotten out much." Her light blue dress draped over her bulging belly.

Katherine's eyes widened. "Are you sure you're not having twins?"

"*Nee.*" Her friend laughed. "But I look like I am." With a waddling gait she moved to the cabinet. "Do you want anything to drink?"

Katherine shook her head. "I can't stay too long. I wanted to make sure you got the quilt before the *boppli* arrived. I have to work later today."

"Maybe just a few minutes?" Mary Beth went back to the table and sat down. She reached for Katherine's hand. "It's been so long since we talked."

"We've both been busy." She squeezed her friend's hand. "And you'll be even busier in a few weeks."

"*Ya.*" A radiant glow appeared on Mary Beth's cheeks. "But I don't want us to drift apart. You're *mei* best friend."

Katherine released her hand. "And I promise I'll be the best *aenti* to your *boppli*."

"The baby has plenty of *onkels*, that's for sure." Her smile dimmed a little.

Katherine frowned. "What's wrong? It's not the *boppli*, is it?"

"*Nee.*"

"Chris?"

"Chris is fine too. We're happier than we've ever been."

"Then what is it?"

Mary Beth sighed, but she didn't reply.

"You know you can tell me anything. If something's troubling you, I want to help."

Her friend looked at Katherine. "It's Johnny."

Katherine's heart twisted itself into a knot. She glanced away before steeling her emotions. "What about Johnny?"

"Are you sure you want to talk about him?"

"I've accepted that there's no future for us. What I felt for Johnny was a childhood crush."

A crush. The truth was, Katherine had loved Mary Beth's twin brother, Johnny, for as long as she could remember. For years she held out hope for a chance, however small, however remote. She had clung to that dream as if she were drowning and it was her only lifeline.

But not anymore.

She sat straight in the chair, brightened her smile, and said, "What's going on with him?"

"He's been acting . . . different."

"What do you mean?"

"Distant. Partly because he's been working so many hours

at the buggy shop. *Mamm* said she barely sees him except for church service. He leaves early in the morning and comes home late. But when he is around, he's quiet."

"That doesn't sound like him," Katherine said. "Do you think he's keeping something from your *familye*?"

Something . . . or *someone*?

Despite Katherine's vow not to care, her heart constricted again at the thought.

"I don't know." Mary Beth's brown eyes had lost the warmth they'd held moments ago. "He's becoming like a stranger to me. To all of us. We've drifted apart." Her smile faded. "Like you and I have."

Katherine shook her head in protest. "You know I'm always here for you."

Tears welled in Mary Beth's eyes.

Katherine drew back. "I'm so sorry. I didn't mean to make you cry."

"I'm always crying." Mary Beth wiped her eyes. "It makes Chris *ab im kopp*. Hormones, I'm sure." She sniffed, wiping her eyes. "I'm glad we're still best friends."

Katherine hugged Mary Beth. "We always will be."

Johnny Mullet put his hands on his hips and surveyed his new property. Four acres, a small house, and an even smaller barn. All his.

The sad little farm didn't look like much. But by the time

he finished fixing everything up, no one would recognize it. He glanced at the empty pasture on the left side of the house. Tall grass, green and dense, swayed against a southerly breeze. He planned to purchase that acreage too. Expand and make his horse farm something he could be proud of.

If only *Daed* could see . . .

At the thought of his father, the grin faded from his face.

Hochmut, his father would say. Pride.

The worst character flaw any Amish could have.

But was there something wrong with feeling satisfied after hard work? After a job well done?

This wasn't about pride. It was about independence. Making a good living. He'd seen his family struggle. He didn't want that for his future. A future that, God willing, wouldn't include only him.

With the hazy orange sun dipping below the horizon, Johnny hopped into his buggy and headed home. Ten minutes later he arrived at his parents' house. He was late for supper. Again. He quickly put up his horse and hurried into the house, sliding into his seat just as his father closed his eyes for grace.

After prayer, his mother passed his father a platter of ham. He speared a slice with his fork, peering at Johnny as he did. "Long day at work again?"

Johnny picked up a roll from the basket on the table. He drew in a deep breath. *"Nee."*

"Then why are you late?"

"I bought a farm."

Silence. Johnny glanced around the table. Caleb's mouth

dropped open, and Micah's fork was poised in midair. Even six-year-old Eli gave him a funny look. "You what?" His mother's eyes went wide with shock.

"You know that house down the road a piece? The one with the barn in the back?"

"You mean that shack?" Caleb shook his head.

Micah scooped up a forkful of green beans. "Calling it a shack is a stretch."

Their father cleared his throat. The boys ducked their heads and kept eating. He turned to Johnny. "When did you do this?"

"Signed the paperwork yesterday."

"Where did you get the money?"

He was already tired of the third degree, but he had expected no less. "Savings. From my job at Gideon Bender's."

"You must have gotten it for a song," Caleb added. "Or less than a song. Maybe just a note." He chuckled.

"Caleb." His father shot him a silencing look before turning to Johnny again. "I wish you had consulted me first."

"I'm an adult, *Daed*. I didn't think I had to." Seeing the flash of hurt in his father's eyes, he added, "Trust me. I know what I'm doing."

"I hope so."

"Maybe you two could discuss this after supper?" *Mamm's* lips pinched into a thin line. "The food is getting cold."

Daed nodded and dug into his food. No one said anything for the rest of the meal. But all Johnny could think about was the disappointed look on his father's face.

Cora Easley gripped the smartphone in her hand. "The doctor wants me to do what?"

"He'd like to see you again," the nurse repeated in a crisp, emotionless tone. "As soon as possible."

"Why?"

"He'd like to run a few more tests."

"How many more tests does he need?" Cora looked down at the bruise on her arm from the blood draw she'd received a few days ago. For months she'd been poked, prodded, scanned, and questioned. The dehumanizing madness had to stop. Her weary body couldn't take it anymore.

"You tell Dr. Clemens I'm through with his tests. If he doesn't have a treatment plan by now, clearly I need to see a more competent doctor."

Silence on the other line. The nurse cleared her throat. "Mrs. Easley, Dr. Clemens is just being thorough."

"Too thorough, if you ask me."

"Are you refusing more testing?"

"Yes. That's exactly what I'm doing."

A pause. "I'll mark that in your chart. You'll still need to meet with Dr. Clemens at your earliest convenience. He will want to talk to you."

"And I want to talk to him." This nonsense had gone on long enough. She already had a diagnosis—Parkinson's. What she didn't have was a cure.

After making her appointment, Cora clicked off her phone and laid it on the glass coffee table. She walked to the large window in her penthouse and looked at the landscape in front of her. New York. The city of her birth, the place she'd lived all her life. But everything had changed in the past few months, changes she never expected.

Her hands trembled. The shaking had worsened over the past two weeks. Dr. Clemens had said to expect it. She hated that he was right.

Parkinson's. The diagnosis terrified her. She'd briefly glanced at the literature about the disease, only to promptly dispose of the pamphlets after reading about some of the symptoms. Loss of memory. Loss of motor function. Loss of control.

Cora Easley had never been out of control. She'd dictated and orchestrated every aspect of her life except for one. And now she was facing the possibility that within the next couple of years, she wouldn't even be in control of her bodily functions. What kind of life was that? Not one she wanted to live.

"Señora?"

Cora turned to look at her maid, a faithful servant for the past several years. If it hadn't been for Manuela, her grandson, Sawyer, wouldn't have found out the truth about his parents and the reason his mother ran off with his father. Or the story behind the estranged relationship she had with her daughter, Kerry, and how Kerry had tried to mend the rift between them. Cora's stubbornness had thwarted that. And now her grandson didn't seem to want to have anything to do with her.

When he left to find Laura Stutzman two months ago,

he swore he'd return. But he hadn't. She wasn't sure he ever would.

"*Señora?*" Manuela repeated. "*Por favor.* Did you hear me?"

"Sorry. Lost in my thoughts, I suppose."

"Is everything all right?"

"Everything is fine." But it couldn't be further from the truth. She walked away from the window. "I need a glass of sparkling water."

"*Sí.* Anything else?"

"No, just the water. Bring it to my bedroom."

Manuela nodded and disappeared from the room. Cora made her way to her spacious bedroom. She sat on the edge of her bed, the silk comforter rustling from the movement. She picked up the landline phone on the mahogany end table. Dialed a familiar number. Tensed when she heard the voice mail.

"This is Sawyer. Leave a message."

She opened her mouth to speak, but words failed. She couldn't tell her grandson about her diagnosis. Not like this. She'd have to find another way. But she had no idea how.

CHAPTER 2

The next morning was a busy one at Mary Yoder's. Katherine had served four tables nonstop. It was nearly lunchtime before she got a moment to catch her breath, and then another customer showed up in her section—an Amish man. He looked to be about her age, but she didn't recognize him. She ran a hand across her brow, took her pad out of her apron pocket, and went to the table.

"*Wie gehts,*" she said. "What can I get you to drink?"

He looked up from the menu. When he met Katherine's gaze, he grinned. A small dimple dented his lower right cheek. "What do you recommend?"

"We have iced tea, lemonade, water, soda pop."

"Hmm." He kept looking at Katherine. "Iced tea sounds *gut.*"

"I'll have it right out for you."

"Thank you." He lifted an eyebrow and looked at her name tag. "Katherine."

She nodded and headed for the beverage station. Chrystal, a Yankee waitress, came up beside her. "Do you know that guy?"

Katherine glanced over her shoulder. Instead of looking at his menu, he seemed to be focused on her. Or maybe he was noticing Chrystal, with her tall, slender figure and long black hair. "No. I've never seen him before."

"Me either. But he sure seems interested in you."

Katherine shrugged, her cheeks heating at the thought. "I doubt that."

"I don't." Chrystal started to walk away. "He hasn't taken his eyes off you since he walked in."

Katherine shook her head. "You're imagining things."

She picked up the tea and took it to him. "What else can I get you?"

"I don't rightly know." He pointed to the menu but continued to look at her. "I've never been here before. I'm new in town."

"That's nice." She kept her pencil poised above her pad.

"Name's Isaac. From Walnut Creek. I'm staying with a cousin of mine, helping him with his logging business. This is my first day in Middlefield."

Katherine nodded. "Your order?"

Still he didn't answer. Instead he kept staring at her, smiling. He had kind blue eyes and sandy-blond hair. She had to admit he was handsome.

"Why don't you surprise me?" he said.

"What?"

"Surprise me," he repeated. "You decide what I'm going to have." He leaned back in the chair.

"That would be hard, considering we don't know each other."

His grin widened. "Maybe someday we can change that."

Katherine froze and stared at him, then mechanically wrote down an entrée. "Our fried chicken is *gut*."

"Fried chicken it is."

She made her way back to the kitchen. Chrystal leaned against the door frame and winked. "Told ya. Never seen someone flirt so hard in my life."

"I don't understand."

Chrystal chuckled and patted Katherine on the arm. "Sweetie, if that guy has his way, you will."

***

"Are you sure about this?" Laura asked.

Sawyer Thompson reached for her hand as they sat in well-worn rockers on Adam and Emma Otto's front porch. "Like I said before, I'm more sure of this than anything."

"Anything?" Laura smiled.

Sawyer stared at her in the dimming evening light. He could see the outlines of the thin scars on her face, damage Mark King had caused. But they didn't detract from her beauty. Now that Mark was in jail and Laura had let go of her revenge, peace enhanced her loveliness, making her more attractive to him than ever before.

But she wasn't referring to their relationship. They were discussing something far more important. "Laura, I want to join the church. And I want to marry you. But like I told everyone else, my faith is the most important thing. Becoming Amish is what I want above all."

Laura smiled wider. "As it should be." She rubbed her soft fingers against his rough ones, his skin callused from working for so many years in his adoptive father's carpentry shop. They remained silent for a few moments, enjoying the quiet of the evening and the loving security of that simple touch.

She broke the silence first. "Have you spoken to your grandmother lately?"

"Have you talked to your parents?" He wanted to bite back the words, but he'd already put them out there.

As he expected, Laura's smile dimmed. She tried to pull away, but Sawyer wouldn't let go. "Laura, I know why I'm avoiding Cora. We both do. What I don't understand is why you're avoiding your parents."

"I'm not. I've written to them."

"It's been three months since they've seen you. I'm sure they miss you."

"I'm not ready to go back yet." She looked out into the yard. "Tennessee doesn't feel like home anymore. I don't know how to explain that to them."

"You'll figure out a way."

"I hope so. I've let them down so much."

Sawyer knelt down in front of her. "No more regrets, remember? No more punishing yourself."

"I know, but I've made so many mistakes. And I still need to pay Cora back—"

He put his finger on her lips. What he wouldn't do to sneak a kiss, even a small one . . .

But he stopped himself. For one thing, he respected Emma

and Adam too much. Laura had become like a member of their family. Adam had admitted as much to him the other day. "Emma likes having her around," he'd said. "So does Leona. Laura is like the *schweschder* I never had."

More importantly, he respected the Amish way. He might not be Amish yet, but Sawyer had grown up in an Amish home during his teen years, and he understood their courting customs. The chaste attitude toward each other. No public displays of affection.

He not only respected it, he appreciated it. Outward expressions of emotion in front of others had never been his thing, even when he attended a Yankee high school, where it seemed there were couples holding hands—and trying to do more— everywhere he looked.

Some things were meant to be private.

Still, that didn't keep him from *wanting* to kiss her.

"Sawyer?" Laura said against his fingertip.

He moved his hand away. "What?"

"You're staring."

"Don't I have the right to stare at my future bride?"

She blushed and smiled at him. "I can't believe how blessed I am."

He looked at her for a few more moments, feeling equally blessed. Finally he pulled his gaze away and stood up, sighing. "It's getting late. I better get back home."

"Is that your way of not answering my question?"

"What question?"

"Have you talked to your grandmother?"

Sawyer turned away from her. "Not lately. I know she wants me to come back to New York."

The last conversation he'd had with his maternal grandmother, Cora Easley, hadn't gone well. He'd been in New York, in her huge penthouse apartment. She had tried to stop him from leaving to find Laura, who had gone to track down Mark King and exact vengeance upon him.

At the time, Sawyer had promised Cora he would return. Yet he'd done little more than answer her phone calls. Within a few months he would be baptized in the church. After that he wouldn't have access to a cell, or the ease of traveling like he did now. He'd sold his truck and was adding that money to a down payment on a house for the both of them. He had his life planned out. That didn't include his rich grandmother, who wanted to bequeath him her business interests. Business he had no interest in.

"Does she know you're getting baptized?"

"She wouldn't understand."

"Then you should explain it to her." Laura moved to stand in front of him. "You can't pretend she doesn't exist."

"But she can't be part of my life either. Not the way she wants to." He sighed. "I know. I need to see her. I made a promise."

"And you're always faithful to your word."

"Tell you what. I'll visit Cora if you'll go back to Tennessee and see your parents. You can let them know about the wedding."

"But we haven't set a date yet."

He looked around and, despite himself, kissed her cheek. "How does November sound?"

Laura smiled. "Sounds *perfekt*. All right, I'll visit them in a week or so. I promise." But her smile faded as she said the words.

He took her hand. "I'll be praying for you."

"*Danki*. I'm going to need it."

Sawyer thought about his impending visit to Cora. He would need a few prayers too.

"So?" Johnny turned to his *daed*. "What do you think?"

His father tilted back his straw hat but said nothing. His salt-and-pepper beard lifted in the slight summer breeze. He took a step forward. Still he remained silent.

"I know it needs work."

Daed nodded and walked around the property, making his way through knee-high grass. Johnny trailed after him. When they reached the backyard, *Daed* stopped. "I didn't realize you were in such a hurry to leave us."

"I'm only ten minutes down the road."

"*Ya*. But this purchase—it's sudden. Very sudden."

"I've been thinking about it for a while," Johnny said.

"Guess I thought you'd want my advice when you bought your first place."

"The opportunity came up—"

"And you took it." His father's gaze stopped on the barn, which leaned to one side and was missing more slats than it possessed. "I'm concerned about how you're going to make this work."

"Glad you have such faith in me." He couldn't keep the bite out of his tone. Normally his father wasn't so negative.

"I have faith in you, *sohn*. I just hope you're putting your faith in the right place."

Johnny frowned. What did that mean? Of course he had faith. Faith in God, in the church he joined when he was seventeen. "The land was cheap. It was as if God dropped it in my lap."

"I see." His father's gaze strayed. "Do you reckon to move in right away?"

"Tomorrow."

"So soon?" He raised an eyebrow. "Doesn't seem like a safe place to live right now."

"It will be fine."

"The door is hanging off the frame."

"I'll fix it." His fingers clenched, then released. "I already checked everything out. It's better inside than out. Wanna take a look?"

His father paused. Shook his head. "If you say it's safe, I'll take you at your word. But, *sohn*—"

"*Ya?*"

"Why don't you wait a few days. A week at least. Caleb and Micah and I can come over and help you get the place in decent shape." He glanced around again. "Or some kind of shape."

"I appreciate the offer. And I'll take you up on it, the construction part. But I'm moving in tomorrow."

His father sighed. "So eager to be out on your own?" He pressed his lips in a half smile. "I remember feeling the same way when I was *yung*."

Johnny exhaled. Finally his father understood. "Once I get the farm going, I'll be able to help you and *Mamm.*"

His dad's eyes narrowed. "We don't need any help. We do fine on our own."

"But I want to. You've spent almost twenty-one years taking care of me. I can give something back."

Daed chuckled. "Why don't you wait a little longer? Like twenty more years. Your *mamm* and I aren't useless yet."

"I didn't mean—"

"I know what you meant. And I appreciate the thought. But I feel the same way. We would have helped you buy a better place, as much as we could. You could have paid back any money you borrowed."

"Would you have let me?"

A ghost of a smile flitted across his *daed's* face. "Probably not."

"Which is why I didn't ask. I've been working for Bender since I was fourteen, saving my money, waiting for an opportunity."

"For a farm."

"For a business. It's hard to make a living farming. But raising horses?" Johnny grinned. "That's a mare of a different color."

"It will still take hard work."

"Which I'm willing to do."

"And time." His father's gaze intensified. "Are you willing to give it time?"

Johnny nodded. The tension he had been holding in his body began to release. His father was coming around. "I'll give the business as much time as it needs to become successful."

Daed clapped Johnny on the back. "Well, if sheer enthusiasm counts for anything, I'd say you're off to a *gut* start. Now show me this *haus* you're so eager to move into."

Johnny exhaled heavily as he led his father toward the small, shabby structure he had optimistically referred to as a "house."

Enthusiasm, his *daed* said.

He might present a good bluster to his father, but he was walking a razor-thin financial tightrope, and he knew it. This purchase was a bargain, but it had wiped out most of his savings.

God willing, with enough sweat and determination, he would make this work. Even if he had to live on peanut butter sandwiches for the next six months, he would force this business to thrive.

He had made the commitment and declared the desire to see it through. He couldn't turn back now.

Even after the workday was over, Katherine couldn't get out of her mind what Chrystal had said about Isaac. Had he been flirting with her? She didn't have much experience with flirting. He did give her an extra tip, but he wasn't her first generous customer. He also kept smiling every time she passed his table. Maybe he was just being friendly. Still, she couldn't stop wondering.

Katherine didn't feel like going home, so instead she turned down Mary Beth's street. Summer was just beginning, and the evening sun dappled the lush green leaves on the trees. June was a perfect month, when the days weren't too hot and the nights sometimes held a bit of chill.

She arrived at Mary Beth's and knocked on the door. No answer. Mary Beth's husband, Chris, worked for a construction company that did a lot of jobs in Cleveland, so he probably wasn't home. She was just about to knock again when she heard a scream come from the back of the small house.

She dashed into the house, the door slamming so hard behind her it bounced back on its hinges. Another wail reached her ears.

Katherine burst into the back bedroom. "Mary Beth?"

Her best friend lay on the bed, writhing in agony.

"The *boppli!*" Mary Beth gasped, sweat pouring down her face. "It's coming!"

"But it's too soon!" Katherine gripped the door frame.

Mary Beth clenched her teeth as another contraction overtook her. When it subsided, she leaned against the pillows. "I know." She started to cry. "Please. Get *Mamm.*"

CHAPTER 3

Katherine sat on the couch in Mary Beth's tiny living room, her hands clasped together, elbows resting on her knees. The house was so small she could hear every sound, and she flinched and prayed at each wail, each cry of pain coming from the bedroom.

Mary Beth was in good hands—her mother had been a midwife for the past five years. But Hannah Mullet hadn't been able to hide her concern when Katherine told her the baby was coming.

Another agonizing cry. Mary Beth had been in labor for five hours now. Katherine looked outside the picture window into the black night.

"Katherine?"

She turned at the sound of Hannah's voice. "The *boppli?*"

Hannah shook her head. "It's breech. I think I can turn it around, but it's going to be a long night. Do you mind staying?"

"Of course not. What can I do to help?"

Mary Beth cried out again.

"Pray," Hannah said. "Just keep praying."

For the next half hour Katherine paced the room, continuously praying, yet feeling helpless. Just as Mary Beth was screaming through another contraction, the door opened and Chris walked in. His tanned face paled. His tool belt hit the floor with a heavy thud.

"Katherine?"

She went to him, forcing herself to remain calm. God was in control, no matter what happened to Mary Beth or the baby. "It will be okay, Chris." She explained the situation. "Hannah is with her now."

Chris nodded. He picked up his tool belt with shaking hands and slung it over his shoulder. "Got to check on the animals."

Katherine nodded. His reaction wasn't unexpected. If he'd tried to see Mary Beth, Hannah would have told him to leave. She turned as the door clicked shut, paced again, and resumed her prayers.

Late for supper again.

Johnny sighed as he turned in the driveway. At least his parents knew why he kept coming home late. But this would be the last time they would have supper together, at least here, for a long time. He'd taken the day off work and moved his few belongings to the new house. He thought his boss, Gideon Bender, might give him a bit of a hard time about it. An exacting business owner, Bender ran his small machine repair shop with the same precision he used to make repairs. But since Johnny hadn't asked for a day off in months, Bender must have decided to cut him some slack.

As he pulled into the driveway, Johnny noticed an unfamiliar buggy parked in front of Mary Beth and Chris's house. He pulled into his parents' barn and unhitched his horse. When he went inside, he expected to smell supper cooking. Instead he saw Caleb making a sandwich for Eli.

"Where's *Mamm* and *Daed?*" Johnny hung his hat on the peg in the mudroom next to the kitchen. When he met Caleb's worried eyes, his stomach dropped to his knees. "What's going on?"

"Eat your sandwich, Eli." Caleb put the bologna sandwich in front of their younger brother.

"Yum." Eli picked up the sandwich and took a huge bite.

Caleb motioned for Johnny to follow him to the living room. When they were out of earshot of Eli, he said, "Mary Beth is in labor."

Johnny gaped. "Isn't it early?"

Caleb nodded. "That's what *Mamm* said when Katherine came to get her a few hours ago."

"Katherine's here?"

"*Ya*. She found Mary Beth." Caleb swallowed. "Chris is home by now, I'm sure. *Daed* had a school board meeting tonight, so he doesn't know what's going on. Probably best that way. Micah's at a friend's house."

"Have you talked to *Mamm?*"

"*Nee*. I've been praying, but that women's stuff—" Caleb shuddered. "It's best left to them."

"I'll *geh* find Chris." Johnny said a quick prayer as he left the house. He and his twin had always been close, but Caleb was right. His mother and Katherine were taking care of Mary Beth and the baby.

He found Chris in the barn, on his knees. A faint shrieking sound reached Johnny's ears. Was that his sister?

Johnny cleared his throat. Chris looked up. His Adam's apple worked in his neck, as if he were trying to swallow and failing at the attempt. He closed his eyes and shook his head.

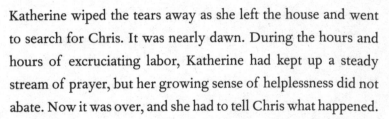

Katherine wiped the tears away as she left the house and went to search for Chris. It was nearly dawn. During the hours and hours of excruciating labor, Katherine had kept up a steady stream of prayer, but her growing sense of helplessness did not abate. Now it was over, and she had to tell Chris what happened.

In the grayish light of sunrise she could see a dim light burning in the barn. She walked toward it, breathing in the damp morning air. When she entered she saw Chris and Johnny, each of them sitting on a hay bale, their heads hung low, their lips moving in silent prayer.

Her gaze drifted to Johnny, taking in the concentration on his face as he prayed for his twin sister. The familiar sting of unrequited love reared up inside her. She shoved it down.

"Chris?"

Both men stood, but Katherine kept her gaze on Mary Beth's husband. Weariness and worry had left gray circles underneath his eyes. He moved to Katherine.

"Mary Beth? The *boppli?*"

Katherine took his hand. Tears started to flow again. "Chris, they're both fine. *Geh* meet your *dochder.*"

Johnny let out a whoop while Chris's hand went limp in Katherine's. He nodded and ran out of the barn. Katherine started to follow him, ignoring Johnny as she had vowed to do.

"Katie?"

She stopped. He had never called her that before. She turned around. He looked as tired as she felt.

"You stayed here all night?" he asked.

Katherine nodded. "She's *mei* best friend. Although I couldn't do much but pray."

"That means a lot." He glanced away. "To Mary Beth. To all of us. I mean, uh, I'm sure it will mean a lot when she finds out."

Katherine nodded. As always things were awkward between them, and it was mostly her fault. If she hadn't chased him so incessantly, hadn't been so pathetic in her yearning for him, he might not run the other way every time she was near. They might have been friends.

But he wasn't running now. He hadn't moved. Instead he continued to stare at her.

Katherine turned away. She couldn't afford to overanalyze a simple look. Still he stared at her, the way . . .

The way Isaac did.

The thought dropped into her mind unbidden: There were other men in the world. Johnny Mullet wasn't the only one.

Johnny couldn't stop staring at Katherine.

In his weariness he'd slipped and called her Katie. It was how he referred to her in his mind. There were many Katherines in Middlefield, but only one Katie Yoder.

"I better get home. I'm sure *mei* parents are worried about me," she said, turning away.

He didn't want her to go. But he wasn't ready to tell her the truth. Not yet. "Katherine?"

"*Ya?*" she asked, not facing him.

"*Danki.* For staying with *mei schweschder.*"

She nodded and hurried out of the barn. Away from him.

He leaned against the thick barn post. The horses whinnied in their stalls, signaling their hunger. "Just a minute," he said softly. He gathered his thoughts and his energy. If he was tired, he could only imagine what Mary Beth had gone through.

Actually, he'd rather not imagine it.

He said a prayer of thanks that his sister and niece were well, then turned to take care of the horses. Despite his exhaustion, he couldn't quit grinning. He was an uncle now. Hard to believe. He couldn't wait to meet his niece.

As he fed the horses and cleaned up the barn, he said another prayer of thanks. Things were going well. He had his own place, and in a few months, the start of a horse farm. His sister and her baby were fine. And Katie—each day he was closer to telling her his real feelings. To starting the future he had dreamed of the past few months.

His life couldn't get any better.

CHAPTER 4

"I'm sorry, *sohn*. I wish I didn't have to do this."

Johnny froze in disbelief as Gideon Bender spoke. Just this morning he was counting his blessings. Two hours later his boss yanked the rag rug from under his boots.

"But I thought business was picking up." He looked around the small shop, filled with broken machines in need of repair.

"It is. But other businesses aren't." Bender wiped his grease-covered hands on an old towel and flung it onto a nearby workbench. "John, Zach lost his job at Kline's buggy shop. Kline laid him off yesterday."

A knot of dread formed in Johnny's gut.

"You're like *familye* to me. I hope you know that. But *mei sohn* has a *frau* and *kinn* to take care of. He needs the work. He needs my help."

So do I.

"You understand, *ya?* Business is *gut*, but I don't have enough work to keep both of you." He glanced away, running his thumb against the dirty Formica countertop. "I can give you two more weeks."

"That's it?" The words thawed Johnny's body. He clasped his hands behind his head, not caring anymore how desperate he looked. Or sounded.

"I wish it could be different. You've been loyal to me and the job. I've always appreciated that." His expression turned grim. "You have a *gut* work ethic, more so than my *sohn* had. At least at first. But Zach's come around. He's grown into a fine *mann*." Bender's throat bobbed.

Johnny was familiar with the strife between father and son, strife that had lessened over the years, especially after Zach married Ruth Byler and became a father. But Johnny hadn't thought he'd be replaced. He knew Zach had been happy at the buggy shop. Like Johnny had been happy working here.

Bender sighed. "I don't see any other way. I can't abandon *mei* own *familye*."

Johnny nodded, swallowing the stone lodged in his throat. "I know."

"If you need a recommendation, I'll be happy to give you one." The old man's weary gaze finally met Johnny's.

A recommendation.

Johnny gritted his teeth. A recommendation wouldn't pay to fix the house or rebuild the barn. It wouldn't provide grain for his horse or food for his own table. Only a week had passed since he bought the farm, and he'd barely started work on it. Without a job, he couldn't afford to do anything.

"Here are your past two weeks' wages." Bender handed him a check.

Johnny looked at the amount, and his last shred of hope crumbled. Enough to last him two or three weeks of living on his own, taking care of his basic needs and not much more. He'd have one more check, then that would be it. Less than a month to find another job—and jobs were hard to come by. Even Caleb was struggling to find work—he hadn't had a steady job since he graduated from school three years ago.

Even in the midst of his own desperation, Johnny couldn't hold this against Bender. He could see the man was struggling with the decision. *"Danki, "* he said, folding the check and putting it in his pocket. Then he held out his hand. After a moment's hesitation, Bender shook it.

"Don't thank me. You earned every penny." He paused before touching Johnny's shoulder. "I hope you know this isn't personal. It's just business." Johnny could only nod. Bender turned away, snatched up a screwdriver from the toolbox, and began working on a generator a customer had brought in last week. The conversation ended as quickly as he'd ended Johnny's employment.

During the day Johnny tried to focus on repairing a wringer washer, but his mind kept drifting. Where would he find another job? He would start at the woodshop first. Maybe Sawyer's family was hiring. But the only job they ever seemed to hire out for was the office position, and Laura, Sawyer's girl, already had that job.

Bitterness surged inside him. His dream was slipping away before he'd had a chance to make it come true.

At five o'clock he picked up his still-full lunch cooler and left the shop. As the sun dipped behind the roof of Bender's shop, Johnny tossed the cooler into his buggy and climbed inside.

When he reached home he pulled into the driveway and parked the buggy outside the decrepit barn. It reminded him of the old barn Sawyer had hid in when he was fourteen, the year his parents died and he ran away from foster care. Mary Beth had found Sawyer there, and he and Johnny had become best of friends.

For the first time that day Johnny's mood lifted. Sawyer would get him a job at the Bylers'—even something part-time would be a start. He could trust his friend to help him out. And he would continue to look—and pray—for other work to turn up.

But he had to find something soon.

He couldn't fail. Everything hinged on this horse farm.

Everything.

Katherine sat at the kitchen table, piecing together pale green and white squares of fabric. Another baby quilt, this time for her friend Rachel, who was expecting a baby in the summer. Katherine was nineteen and Johnny had just turned twenty, but many of their friends had already married or were paired off.

She sighed and her fingers slipped. The needle plunged into the pad of her thumb.

"Ow." She brought her thumb to her mouth just as her younger sister, Bekah, came into the kitchen. Bekah grabbed a cookie from the plate on the counter.

"I think *Mamm's* taking those to the Mullets later today."

"She won't miss just one." Bekah leaned against the counter and bit into the soft cookie. "You look tired."

"I am." Fatigue wrapped around Katherine as she bent over the quilt. But the work kept her mind off Johnny.

She had dreamed about him the few hours she slept. Again. She didn't remember much of the dream, but he'd been there. During the day she could keep her mind occupied with other things, but she couldn't control him in her subconscious.

"That's great news about Mary Beth," Bekah said. "What did she name the *boppli*?"

"Johanna." Katherine slid the needle through the three layers of fabric and batting.

"That's a lovely name." She sat down across from Katherine.

"Don't get crumbs on the quilt."

"I won't." Bekah finished the cookie, brushing her hands to the side. She cupped her chin on her hand. "So . . . was Johnny there?"

"He was praying in the barn with Chris. Caleb was in the house with Eli."

"I didn't ask about Caleb."

"I figured you would eventually."

"Because he's a friend." She sighed. "Caleb Mullet is the least of my problems."

Katherine put down the needle. "What do you mean?"

"I think I figured out a way to get Melvin Miller to leave me alone."

Katherine suppressed a sigh. It pained her that Bekah, who

wasn't interested in boys at all, had a whole supply of them nipping at her heels. "I didn't realize he was bothering you," she said, focusing on her quilting, not wanting Bekah to see any trace of jealousy.

"He's not a bother. Just annoying. Like everyone else." Bekah shook her head. "I wish he'd get the point. Some people can be so hardheaded."

Katherine winced.

"Oh, I didn't mean you." Bekah held out her hands. "I know what you feel for Johnny is real. He'll come around. Eventually." But she didn't sound convinced.

"How do you know Melvin's feelings aren't real?" Before Bekah could answer, Katherine added, "Why do you want to break his heart?"

"I'm not breaking his heart." Bekah leaned back in the chair. "*Ach*, you can be so dramatic sometimes."

Katherine ducked her head down. "I don't know what you mean."

"Melvin pestering me isn't like you and Johnny."

"You mean he won't be chasing after you for the next decade?"

"You don't chase after Johnny." Bekah leaned forward. "You can't help what you feel, Katherine."

"Neither can Melvin."

Bekah didn't say anything. Katherine went back to the quilt, making tiny, perfect stitches.

"Maybe you should do something about Johnny," Bekah said.

"You know I've tried." Katherine looked up. "Since grade school I've let him know how I feel. I've dropped hints about going to singings. I tried to make him jealous, which was a stupid idea. He didn't even notice when I was sixteen and pretended to like Tom Herschberger."

Tom hadn't noticed either. She was clueless when it came to men.

Bekah grew quiet again. Finally she said, "Then maybe you should find someone else."

Katherine looked up. "Well . . . I might have."

Bekah's eyes lit up. "Really?" She leaned forward. "Do tell."

She shrugged. "I'm not sure there's anything to tell. I met someone at the restaurant yesterday."

"Who? Do I know him?"

"His name is Isaac. He's new to the area."

"What's his last name? Where's he from? What does he do?"

Katherine set down the needle. "I don't know his last name. He's from Walnut Creek." She looked down at the quilt. "Chrystal said he was flirting with me."

"And why wouldn't he? You're so *schee*. And nice. Just because Johnny is too *dumm* to realize it—"

"Bekah. He's not *dumm*. He's just not . . . interested."

"But Isaac is." Bekah grinned.

"I don't know. Maybe." Katherine smiled. Bekah's enthusiasm was infectious.

Their mother came into the kitchen. "Oh *gut*, Bekah.

You're home. Come with me to visit the Mullets. You can see the new *boppli*." She walked to the counter, picked up the plate of cookies, and scowled. "How many did you have, Bekah?"

"Only one. I promise."

As her mother turned around, Bekah mouthed the words, *How did she know?* Katherine shrugged. Very little got past their *mamm*.

Bekah stood. As she and *Mamm* left the kitchen, Katherine called out, "Say hello to Caleb for me."

Bekah turned and stuck her tongue out.

"Bekah!" *Mamm's* voice came from the living room. "That is not appropriate behavior for a young woman."

Bekah rolled her eyes and followed her mother out of the house.

"You don't have anything?"

Sawyer looked at Johnny and shook his head.

"I'd be willing to work part-time. A few hours a week, even."

The pleading in his friend's eyes surprised and confused Sawyer. He'd never seen Johnny so desperate. "Business has slowed down."

"Where have I heard that before?" Johnny muttered.

"What?"

"Things are tough all over."

Sawyer brushed sawdust from a dresser top. "I know.

There's barely enough work for me right now." He peered over the top of the dresser, a sanding block in his hand. "I wish there was something I could do."

Johnny didn't reply. His eyes darted around the workshop— a trapped animal looking for a way of escape. Sawyer had been surprised when Johnny told him about getting laid off from Bender's. He thought his friend had a future there.

"Where else have you looked?" Sawyer asked.

"I started here." Johnny started to pace.

Sawyer shook his head. "Dude. I'm sorry."

Johnny shrugged. "Not much I can do, other than look elsewhere. Maybe pray for a miracle." He turned, his expression suddenly turning from despair to a grin, but Sawyer could still see the worry behind the man's eyes. "Enough about my problems. When's the big day?"

Sawyer went back to sanding. "Which day?"

"Joining the church." Johnny smirked. "Why, is there another special day I should know about?"

Sawyer grinned. "I talk to the bishop next week. So probably after a few weeks of Bishop Esh's counseling and teaching I'll be ready to join."

"*Gut*. Looking forward to you being an official part of the community."

Sawyer put down the sanding block. "If you need a little help—you know, until you find work—"

"I'm *gut*." He waved his hand. "I'll figure something out."

"Well, if you need anything—other than a job . . ." Sawyer paused. "You know where to find me."

Johnny nodded. *"Ya."* He looked around. "I'll let you get back to work. Don't want you to lose *your* job."

When Johnny started to leave, Sawyer called out after him, "You know that other day you mentioned?"

Johnny turned around, peering at him from beneath a battered straw hat. *"Ya?"*

"November." Sawyer grinned. "Clear your calendar."

Johnny grinned. "You got it."

The door hit the frame with a soft bang. Sawyer paused and said a short, silent prayer for his friend. He wasn't sure what drove Johnny's desperation, but God knew, and he prayed for His will to be done.

CHAPTER 5

"Mrs. Easley, I urge you to reconsider your decision about the tests." Dr. Clemens looked up from his chart.

After nearly three weeks Cora had finally given in and kept her appointment. She wasn't used to being sick and hated all this poking and prodding. The only time in her life she had ever spent a night in the hospital was when she had given birth to her daughter, Kerry.

Maybe she should have hired a personal physician instead, one who would make house calls. But a personal physician wasn't the same as a specialist, and Dr. Clemens was reputed to be one of the best neurologists in Manhattan.

Still, that didn't give him the right to use her as a pincushion. She glared at him from her chair in the corner of the exam room. She had refused to sit on the examination table; she was here out of courtesy only, to make sure the doctor understood her position.

She fingered the diamond tennis bracelet dangling from her thin wrist. "I'm finished being your guinea pig."

"Mrs. Easley, these tests aren't experimental. I just want to make sure we've covered all the bases. I assumed you would want me to be as thorough as possible."

"I believe you have been, Dr. Clemens. You've already given me a diagnosis. I need to know how much time I have."

The doctor paused for a moment. "I can't tell you that. Parkinson's is different in every patient. Some, with the right medication and therapy, live for a long time. For others the time is . . . shorter." He sighed and whirled on his stool so he could face her straight on. "All the information is in the pamphlets I gave you."

"Oh yes. Scintillating reading. I can't wait for my body to shut down completely. What a glorious day that will be."

Dr. Clemens didn't say anything. He turned and wrote something down on her chart. "This can be a difficult diagnosis to accept, Mrs. Easley. We have counseling services available—"

"Are you saying I'm crazy too?"

He shook his head and stopped writing. "What I'm saying is that if you're having a difficult time emotionally, there are ways we can help you."

Cora stood. "This conversation is over."

"Mrs. Easley." The doctor also stood. "If you would prefer another physician, I can recommend a few of my colleagues. My goal is for you to receive the best care, and if you feel you need a second opinion, I will respect that."

His words stopped her from leaving. She looked up at him, stunned that this man, whom she only knew on a professional basis, cared enough to drop his ego and step aside. But she didn't want a second opinion. She didn't want any of this.

"Dr. Clemens, your care has been . . . adequate. I do not want to switch doctors."

"All right. I'll continue to monitor your progress with diagnostic observation. No more tests."

She swallowed a sigh of relief.

"But I must encourage you to keep our monthly appointments. And also reconsider counseling. Mrs. Easley, chronic disease isn't easy to live with. Or to understand. It doesn't just take a physical toll, it also affects you emotionally."

"I realize that. And I'm fine."

He sat back down, pulled his prescription pad out of the pocket of his white lab coat, and scribbled on it. "Some of my patients also find comfort through prayer, or through their church family. I've seen faith have a drastic effect on their attitude, which in turn affects the body's healing properties."

"Have any of them been cured?"

He paused. "Of Parkinson's? No." He tore off the small square sheet of paper and handed it to her. "A refill for your current medication."

She shoved the prescription into her purse. She didn't have a church family and couldn't remember the last time she'd prayed. Prayers. What good would they do now? In Cora's opinion, praying was about as effective as swallowing snake oil.

As she waited for her driver in the office lobby, she thought about Sawyer. How angry he'd been with her when he found out she'd tried to buy off Laura Stutzman. That had to be part of the reason he hadn't returned to New York. No doubt he was so caught up in his relationship with Laura, and with that backward Amish life where he'd spent his formative teen years, that he'd forgotten all about her, his only blood relative.

Or he was avoiding her on purpose.

Either way, she couldn't continue without seeing him again. She couldn't afford the luxury of waiting for him to make up his mind. Somehow she had to convince him to reconsider his decision to turn his back on the legacy she'd offered him. He needed to come back to New York to face his past and accept his future. A future that didn't include the Amish—or Laura Stutzman.

She wasn't sure how she would accomplish that task. But if there was one thing Cora Easley always got, it was her way.

Cora went outside, where her chauffeur was waiting to open the back door of her Bentley. She slid inside, pulled her phone out of her purse, and dialed a number. After a few rings, a male voice answered.

"Cora. Pleasure to hear from you, as always."

"Kenneth."

"It's been a few days since your last call." Her attorney's smooth voice wafted through her ear. "Is everything all right? Have you heard from Sawyer?"

"I need to meet with you right away," she said.

"Absolutely. I can make room for you on my calendar tomorrow—"

"We must meet today."

"I'm due in court in two hours. I'm not sure how long I'll be tied up."

Cora tapped her knee. "When you're finished, come to the house. Don't worry, I will pay your overtime fee."

"I'm not worried about that. You've always compensated me fairly."

"Better than your average client." She sniffed.

"True." He paused. "Cora, business aside, I'm concerned about you."

"There is no need."

"Then why the rush to meet? The last time you were in this much of a hurry was when you found Sawyer. Did something happen to him?"

"No."

Another pause. "Has something happened to you?"

"I'll expect you at my penthouse for supper." Cora shut off the phone and stilled her trembling hands as she leaned back in the luxurious leather seat.

Whether her grandson liked it or not, she had to get everything in order. Her affairs had to be set in stone—before it was too late.

Johnny helped Caleb lift the heavy oak spindle and set it in place between two fence posts. He took the nail out of his mouth and started hammering. The fence around his parents' small horse pasture needed fixing, and Johnny had spent the afternoon helping out Caleb while their father was working. He should have been working on his own place and looking for a new job, but Caleb had asked for his help, and Johnny wouldn't refuse his younger brother.

"Appreciate you coming out," Caleb said as Johnny took another nail out of his tool belt.

"No problem."

"Hopefully I can return the favor soon at your place. Have you gotten much done?"

"A little." He wouldn't admit that he'd spent all his spare time looking for a job. This past Wednesday was his last day at Bender's, but he hadn't told his family. The excitement of Johanna's birth had made it easy for him to keep his secret. "When I get the materials, Caleb, I'll take all the help you can give me."

Caleb stopped hammering. "Maybe when you get the farm going I could come work for you." He stared at his hammer. "The *gut* Lord knows it's hard finding a job right now."

Ain't that the truth, Johnny thought. But he didn't say so out loud. Instead he set his problems aside to focus on their task. He and Caleb worked on the fence until the sun was directly overhead, beating its rays down on their backs, then took a break and sat in the shade of a huge oak tree.

Caleb picked up a blade of grass and stuck it between his teeth. Johnny looked at him. It wasn't like his brother to be this quiet. "What's on your mind?"

"*Nix.*"

"Thou shalt not lie," Johnny said in the most serious voice he could muster. "Especially to thy older, smarter *bruder*."

"You got the older part right." Caleb pulled the grass out of his mouth. "Not sure you can help me with this."

"Why?"

Caleb glanced at him. "It has to do with a *maedel*. You're not exactly an expert."

"Ouch." Johnny put his hand over his heart. "Way to drive in the knife."

"Hey, it's your own fault."

Johnny let that comment slide. "So which *maedel* are we talking about? Bekah Yoder?"

"Bekah?" Caleb snorted. "Why would you bring her up?"

"You two have always spent a lot of time together."

"As friends. Only." He stared out into the field. A light wind blew against the grass, making it lean sideways. "It's actually her friend Miriam. She made a big deal yesterday when I asked her to Sunday's singing." He shook his head.

"So she told you *nee?*"

"She said she had to *think* about it. What's there to think about?"

"Why are you chasing after her anyway? You're seventeen. Too *yung* for courting."

Caleb shook his head. "I knew you wouldn't understand. You ruined any chance you had with Katherine Yoder."

Johnny grimaced. His little brother had sprouted in the last two years. The *bu* was not only an inch taller than him now, but he was built like a barrel and had arms twice his size. "Pretty free with the insults today, *ya?*"

"I'm not insulting you. Just stating the truth. And I'm not too *yung* for courting." He picked up another blade of grass. "Apparently God doesn't see fit to drop a *maedel* in *mei* lap. Because if He did, I wouldn't let her get away."

"If you're referring to me and Katherine, I don't want to talk about it."

"Oh, that's right. You never want to talk about her."

Johnny hopped up. He brushed the grass off his denim pants, not looking at Caleb. "Let's just work on the fence, *ya?*"

Caleb nodded, standing. "Whatever you say."

"I don't understand."

Cora peered at her attorney from across her large dining room table. She took a sip of her water. She hadn't had wine since Sawyer left a few months ago. For some reason she no longer had a taste for it. "I believe I've made my wishes clear. I want you to liquidate my assets."

Kenneth's jaw dropped as he held his fork in midair, filled with a piece of tender Alaskan poached salmon. She found that her attorney responded better when rewarded with delicious food. "Cora, that's a considerable amount of assets."

"I realize that." Cora pierced a green bean with her fork but made no move to eat it. "I'm well aware of my net worth. I've given this a lot of thought, and I want you to take care of it as soon as possible."

"I'm assuming you're referring only to personal assets." He seemed to relax a bit, taking another bite of salmon and washing it down with white wine. "Your properties in the Hamptons, Coral Gables—" He set the glass down on the polished mahogany table. "I recommend you donate your art collection to the Metropolitan."

"I've already written them a letter. You'll find it in the packet of correspondence I will give you before you leave. Then there are the company assets."

"What about them?"

"I want you to transfer them to my grandson."

This time Kenneth put the fork down. "I thought Sawyer wasn't interested in the company."

"He's not."

"Then why—"

"That's none of your concern."

Kenneth pursed his lips. "You want me to put the shares in his name?"

"Yes. *All* of them. I'm resigning from the board. The notification—"

"Is in the packet." Kenneth wiped his mouth with his napkin and frowned. "What's going on, Cora?"

"I already explained it to you."

"No, you haven't." He leaned forward. "I can't fathom why you would do this. And you do realize before this transaction is legal Mr. Thompson will have to agree to it."

"You let me handle my grandson."

"I assume he knows nothing about this."

Cora didn't reply.

"Don't you think he should? As your grandson and heir—"

"Sawyer's made his feelings about me and my money very clear." She reached for her glass. Her hands shook and she quickly put them in her lap. "But circumstances have arisen that I believe will cause him to change his mind."

"What circumstances?"

"I prefer not to divulge those at this time."

"Cora." Kenneth leaned forward. "Don't be hasty. You

need to give Sawyer time to get used to all this. And give your-self some as well. You both just found out about each other a couple months ago."

"Time won't change anything. I know what I'm doing, Kenneth." She moved to stand. "If you can't see to my wishes, I'll have to find someone else who can."

Kenneth held up his hand. "No need, Cora. Please. Sit down."

She lowered herself into her seat, watching as her attorney composed himself. He smiled, but she could tell it was forced. "Cora, you know I'll do anything you want. I will support you in any way." His smile grew tighter. "If this is what you want, then I'll make it happen. As long as I have Sawyer's cooperation."

"Which you will. I'll be in Middlefield next week. When I return I expect you to have all the paperwork in order."

"I'll have my secretary get right on it."

Relieved, Cora stood again. Suddenly she was exhausted. "See that you take care of this, Kenneth. Immediately. And now, if you'll forgive me, you'll have to show yourself out."

Kenneth rose. "Are you all right?"

"A touch of a headache. The papers are on the credenza by the front door. Peruse them and contact me in the morning with your plan. My flight leaves at nine." She looked at him. "You will be well compensated, as always." Before he replied, she left the dining room.

On shaky legs she walked into her bedroom. She closed the door and leaned against it, steadying herself. Was the trembling because of the Parkinson's or her growing doubt about the decision she'd just made? She was giving up everything she had worked for, all she'd accumulated and held important in her life. Although she would still have a vast fortune, she was willing to turn it all over to Sawyer the minute he agreed to accept it.

And if he refused?

She wouldn't allow herself to think about that. This was her last chance. She had failed in convincing him of the importance of his legacy when they first met. She couldn't afford to fail this time.

Kenneth got into the limousine, clutching the leather folder filled with Cora's personal papers. He flipped on the overhead light in the backseat and read over the documents. As he read, his frown deepened. Pulling out his cell phone, he punched in Sawyer's number. When he heard the nasal recording stating the number was no longer in service, he clicked the phone off and dialed his secretary.

"Valerie, I know it's late. No, I didn't realize you were on a date. I'm sorry, I promise I'll make it up to you. I need you to do something for me." He looked at the papers in his lap as his secretary asked him a question. "Yes, Valerie. Something is definitely wrong."

CHAPTER 6

"Let me get this straight. You want to apply for a loan, but you don't have any income?"

Johnny ran his damp palms on the thighs of homespun pants. He nodded, trying to clear the thick lump of shame lodged in his throat. He'd never had to borrow money before. Hadn't planned to, ever. But after a week of looking for work and finding absolutely nothing, he was desperate. And desperation drove him to walk through the bank's doors.

"Yes, sir, I want to get a loan. It's true I don't have a job. But I do have collateral."

The banker adjusted his glasses on his nose. He perused the loan application in front of him, set down the papers, and took off his glasses. "I'll be honest with you. There's no possible way I can give you a loan."

Desperation turned to dread in the pit of Johnny's stomach. "Why not?"

"You won't be able to make the payments."

"I'll find work soon. I just need a small loan to get me by."

The banker paused and steepled his fingers together. "You've never applied for a loan before."

Johnny shook his head.

"It's not easy, especially in these times. It could take up to a month just to process the paperwork."

"A month?" Johnny sank back in the seat.

"I've worked with the Amish before. I know you would have the best intentions of repayment. But I can't in good conscience give a loan to someone without a means of income." His sharp features seemed to soften a fraction. "I'm sorry."

Johnny composed himself. "I understand." His words were thick. He stood and extended his hand. "Thanks."

"Wait a minute." He motioned for Johnny to sit back down. "We're not finished."

Johnny frowned as he returned to his seat.

"Have you thought about procuring an investor? Someone who provides the money for you to grow your business? Of course that means sharing the profits as well."

Rubbing his chin, Johnny considered it. An investor. He'd still be beholden to someone, but it could just be a temporary arrangement until he got back on his feet.

The banker opened the top drawer of his desk. He pulled out a white card. "My cousin lives in Akron. He's always interested in new opportunities. The man has money to burn, so to speak."

"Must be nice."

For the first time, the banker smiled. "Give him a call." He paused, holding the card in midair. "Or would you rather I call him for you, since you probably don't use a phone?"

"I have access to a phone." Johnny took the card. James Wagner. No address, just a phone number and e-mail. A simple card, similar to the one Johnny would have used, if he had a business to advertise.

"Good." The banker extended his hand. "That's about all the help I can give you. Sorry it's not more."

"No, it's fine. I appreciate it." Johnny looked at him. "Thanks."

"Good luck. I hope it works out with you and James."

Johnny stood. He fingered the card before putting it in his pocket, feeling optimistic for the first time since he bought his property. "I hope so too."

Katherine's heart swelled as she held tiny Johanna in her arms. Mary Beth's daughter's delicate features mimicked her mother's, but her blond hair came straight from her father. "She's *perfekt*, Mary Beth."

Her friend smiled, a happy weariness forming at the corners of her brown eyes. She shifted in the recliner in the small living room. "*Danki*. And if I haven't told you before, thank you for being there when she was born."

"I'm just happy everything turned out okay. We were really worried about you." The image of Johnny and Chris praying in the barn came to her mind.

"*Mamm* is a *gut* midwife. *Daed* said she would be, with five *kinner* and all."

Katherine held out her pinky to Johanna. The *boppli's* tiny fingers gripped it.

"I think Johanna likes her *aenti*," Mary Beth said.

"Oh, I hope so." Katherine couldn't take her eyes off the child. But just as she leaned to give Johanna a light kiss on the forehead, the baby started to cry. Katherine held her closer, whispered a few nonsensical words in her tiny ear, and brought the soft baby blanket closer around her small body. But Johanna's cries grew louder.

Mary Beth rose. "I'll take her. She's probably tired." She took her daughter from Katherine's arms and settled back in the chair, leaning Johanna's head against her shoulder. Within a few minutes, the baby quieted.

"A *mudder's* touch." Katherine smiled, ignoring the ache in her heart. Would she ever know the special bond of having a child of her own?

"For now. But when the *boppli's* hungry, she lets you know. She's got a pair of lungs, that's for certain." Mary Beth patted her daughter's tiny back. "Now, tell me about the world, since I've been cooped up for almost a month."

Katherine paused. "There's not much to tell."

"There's always something to tell. How is work?"

"Fine." Katherine averted her gaze.

"Just fine? Then why are you blushing?"

She didn't answer right away. "I'm sure it's *nix*. It's just there's this *mann*—"

"Oh?"

"You sound surprised."

"I am. A little." Mary Beth smiled, but it seemed a little forced. Johanna started to fuss again. Mary Beth rose. "She needs changing. I'll be right back."

While Mary Beth was gone, Katherine stood and went to the front window. She looked out toward the back of the Mullets' house, where Caleb and Micah were doing some repairs on the back deck.

In the big oak tree, the tire swing still hung from a thick branch. A few feet away, almost hidden from view, was the pond.

So many memories. For a moment she let her mind drift to the past, remembering when she was a girl of twelve, sitting on the tire swing, waiting for Mary Beth to come outside.

The swing had been tied higher back then—or maybe she had just been smaller—and she could barely touch the ground with her bare toes. She had tried to gain purchase and propel the swing forward, but after a few failed attempts, she gave up.

Suddenly she felt herself moving. She turned and saw Johnny behind her. He'd been fishing at the pond.

"Thought you might need a push," he said. "Wait." He stopped her, brushed a green oak leaf off her shoulder, and pushed her again.

Then he smiled, and her heart turned into a puddle.

Her mind jolted back to the present. A puddle. How childish. How pointless it was, falling in love with a boy who had only smiled and given her a push on an old tire swing. It was just a kindness, nothing more. She had blown it all out of proportion.

For years she had held on to hope for Johnny. And now all the memories of time spent with the Mullets would be bittersweet.

Johnny's optimism started to wane as soon as he left the bank. He was in trouble, and he knew it. He would continue to look for a job, but he would also call Mr. Wagner. He couldn't afford to turn away any opportunity. He climbed into his buggy, every muscle in his body tense.

Maybe the best way to get his mind off of everything was to see his new niece.

When he pulled into Mary Beth's driveway, his palms started to sweat. Katherine's buggy stood in the driveway. He wondered if he ought to just turn around and head back home.

But before he could make up his mind, the front door opened. Katherine stepped onto the porch, while Mary Beth held Johanna and waved good-bye from the doorway. She caught a glimpse of him pulling up beside Katherine's buggy.

"Johnny!" his sister called out, louder than she needed to.

Katherine turned around and saw him, then looked away quickly, climbed up, and disappeared into her buggy.

He thought to call out to her, but what could he say? That he was broke? Desperate? On the verge of losing everything? He watched as Katherine chirruped to her horse, turned around in the long driveway, and drove away without saying a word.

His sister had already gone inside. Johnny scanned the tiny patch of property Mary Beth and Chris called home. Their parents had given them the small parcel of land as a wedding gift, but Chris had built the house himself. The crisp white paint, perfectly square front porch, and neatly manicured lawn were a stark contrast to the sad state of his own home. The front porch swing and flower boxes with buds just barely in bloom added a homey touch.

Johnny hadn't even thought about plants. Or his lawn.

He went inside the house. Mary Beth was sitting in the rocker. She looked up at him, her cheeks plump, much as they were when she was expecting. "You could have at least said good-bye to her, Johnny."

First Caleb, now her. "I don't need a lecture. I came by to see *mei* niece."

"And I thought you were here to see me," she said, finally smiling.

"Why would I do that?" Johnny winked at her.

"Here." Mary Beth put Johanna in Johnny's arms. "Hold her for a minute." She disappeared into the adjacent kitchen.

Johnny sat in the nearest chair and looked down at his niece. He didn't feel the least bit uncomfortable holding her—he'd never been put off by helping out with his younger brothers, especially when Eli was a baby. He liked kids. Someday he hoped to have a family. But that day would be far in the future—further now than he'd thought. How could he possibly think about marriage or a family if he couldn't even take care of himself?

Mary Beth came back with a dish towel and laid it across his shoulder. He shifted the baby a bit higher and patted her back. She gave a soft little burp, and both of them laughed. "She just finished eating, *ya?*" Johnny asked.

Mary Beth nodded. "She was fussy during Katherine's visit. I thought she was tired. Turned out she was hungry." She sat back down in the rocker, frowning a little. "I'm still getting used to being a *mudder*."

"You'll figure it out." Johanna snuggled against his shoulder, rubbing her little nose into the dish towel.

"You look tired," Mary Beth said.

"I'm fine." He gazed down at Johanna as she started to settle down.

"How's the farm coming along?"

"*Gut.*" He didn't look away from the baby.

"Chris and I can't wait to see it. When can we drop by?"

Johnny paused. "No hurry. You and Chris need to concentrate on your *familye*."

"That doesn't mean we can't visit other members of our *familye*." Mary Beth held Johnny's gaze. "Unless you don't want the company."

"Of course I want company. Things just aren't ready yet."

"You have two *bruders*, not to mention *Daed*, and even Chris, who would be happy to help you. Even Eli could do a little something."

"I know."

"But?"

He wasn't going to answer her, but she was his twin and knew him better than anyone. "It's hard to explain."

"I'm listening."

"Remember when we were kids and you used to sneak out to that old barn to be by yourself?"

Mary Beth nodded. "It was my special place. Until you found it."

"And Sawyer."

"But you were following me. We got into a ton of trouble, didn't we?"

"Considering we lied to *Mamm* and *Daed*, the barn burned down, and Sawyer almost got sent to foster care until he was eighteen, I thought we got off pretty easy."

"We did." She smiled. "But we had some great times growing up too."

"*Gut* memories." He nodded. "Well, I want to make some memories of my own now."

"Of course you do. But do you have to do that alone?"

Johnny shifted Johanna to his lap, tucking her into the curve of his arm. "Somehow I have the feeling you're not talking about the farm anymore."

"*Nee*. Katherine and I had a nice visit." She paused. "I know, Johnny."

He stilled. "Know what?"

"How you feel about her."

He didn't say anything for a long time. Just stared at his niece as her eyelids drifted shut.

"I've seen how you look at her."

"This conversation is getting *seltsam*." He didn't want to talk about this, especially with his sister.

"It's not the conversation that's *seltsam*. It's you. Even more than usual."

"Very funny."

"It's not meant to be. For a long time I've wondered when you'd come to your senses about her. What I don't understand is why you won't tell her your feelings have changed."

He bit the inside of his cheek. "It's not the right time."

"Johnny, look at me."

"What?" He lifted his gaze to hers.

"I don't want you to spend your life alone."

"I don't plan to."

"Then what are you waiting for?"

"Your *mammi* needs to mind her own business," he murmured to Johanna.

"I'm worried about you," Mary Beth said. "I'm allowed to be concerned about *mei bruder*."

"And I already said I'm fine." Would this happen every time he visited a member of his family? Why were they suddenly so nosy?

"I'm also concerned about Katherine. You don't expect her to wait for you forever, do you?"

"Of course not." Johnny frowned at Mary Beth.

"There's someone else interested in her. His name is Isaac."

Jealousy slammed into him. He didn't look at his sister.

"If you don't do something soon, you might lose her."

"I know what I'm doing." But did he? Envy and failure battled within him. He wondered if he knew anything anymore. He stood and handed his niece to Mary Beth. "I should head home," he said.

"So soon? You just got here. Chris will be home in an hour or so. I know he'd like to see you."

"I've got stuff to do." He hesitated. "Promise me something."

Mary Beth continued to pat Johanna's back. "What?"

"You won't say anything to Katherine." He couldn't risk her finding out how he felt.

"As long as you promise you'll tell her. Soon."

He nodded. "When the time is right, I will."

As Johnny drove home, he thought about Mary Beth's words. His sister was right. He couldn't continue like this. He wasn't being fair to Katherine. If only he hadn't been so dense and realized his feelings for her sooner.

He remembered clearly the day he'd fallen for her. It was a Saturday afternoon, and several of their friends whom they'd gone to school with gathered for a last-minute volleyball game at the Yoders'. Bekah, as outgoing as Katherine was shy, managed to convince Katherine to play.

"I can't," she'd said. She continued to protest, arguing with Bekah about it.

"Come on, you're holding up the game," he said at last.

Finally she relented, and they were on the same team. It wasn't long before he saw why she was reluctant to play. She was awful. Couldn't even serve. Finally, after her third attempt went into the net, he offered to show her how.

"Here," he said, coming up behind her. He showed her how to hold the ball in her left hand. "Then you fold your right hand into a fist."

"Mullet, just let her serve," someone from the other team shouted.

"Yeah," David Esh, the bishop's grandson, said. He laughed. "We're ready to get the ball back."

Humiliated, she handed Johnny the ball. "I shouldn't have played," she said.

He saw the hurt in her beautiful blue eyes. The same hurt he'd seen for years. Hurt he'd caused.

"Shut up," he yelled at the guys. Then he grabbed her hand. Pulled her closer to him and served the ball with her. Not only had it flown over the net, it made her smile.

Now, as he gripped the reins, the memory came back to him in a rush. On the surface it wasn't a big deal. But when he'd held her hand, felt the soft warmth of her touch, her eyes meeting his, for the first time he really saw her. Understood what his neglect had done to her. And knew he not only wanted a chance, he also had to make up for the past.

Being able to have a successful business, to show her she wouldn't have to struggle if they married—that was a start.

Johnny arrived home, his mind heavy with regret and failure. After he put up his horse and buggy, he went inside his pitiful house.

On the rough pine table lay his brand-new cell phone. Now that he owned a business, he wasn't going against the *Ordnung* by having a cell. He pulled the card out of his pocket and stared at it.

Maybe having a Yankee as an investor wouldn't be so bad. Maybe—just maybe—this would be the answer to his prayers.

He flipped open the phone, rechecked the number, and dialed.

CHAPTER 7

The following Monday Katherine was surprised to see Johnny arrive for lunch at Mary Yoder's. She glanced at him across the dining room. Fortunately he wasn't seated in her section. She struggled to ignore him but couldn't help noticing how his long fingers cupped a mug of coffee as he spoke to the Yankee man across the table.

She tried to focus her thoughts on Isaac as she went to one of her tables to take an order. He'd been in the last two Mondays, but so far she hadn't seen him. Which she considered a good thing, since Johnny was here. Her mind was confused enough without both men being in the same vicinity.

"Miss? We're ready to order."

Katherine looked down at the couple seated at the table. The bustling lunch crowd surrounded her. Glasses clinked and dishes clanked as waitresses, some Amish, some Yankee, delivered meals and bussed tables. She collected her thoughts, and with pen poised over her pad, she asked, "What can I get for you?"

"Faster service, for a start." The woman brushed back a lock of her silvery hair from her plump cheek. "I would think that after waiting in line for fifteen minutes to get a seat, we would have put in our order by now."

"I apologize, ma'am. Mondays are always busy. We usually get traffic from the flea market."

"We just came from there." Her dining partner, a gentleman with thick salt-and-pepper hair, gave Katherine a smile. "Found some great bargains—"

"Henry." The woman's gaze was sharp enough to snap twigs. "Our order?"

"Right. Fay"—he held out his hand toward the woman, who appeared to be in her midfifties—"will have the chicken and noodles. I'll have the meat loaf."

"And an unsweetened iced tea." She looked up at Katherine. "Did you get that?"

"*Ya.*" Katherine wrote the order on her pad. She smiled, forcing a friendliness she didn't feel, and picked up the menus. As she walked away, she tried not to look at Johnny, who had barely touched the plate of thick-sliced roast beef and gravy-smothered mashed potatoes. But she couldn't help it. She didn't recognize the man seated across from him. What was Johnny doing here anyway? He never ate at the restaurant. Yet here he was, leaning forward and listening to the man, seemingly hanging on to the Yankee's every word.

"Katherine."

She turned at the sound of her boss's voice, cringing with embarrassment at being caught staring at Johnny. "Yes, ma'am?"

The petite woman peered up at her through square-shaped, tortoise-framed glasses. "Is that an order in your hand?"

"*Ya*. I'll get this to the back right away." She started to leave when her boss put her small hand on Katherine's arm.

"You're distracted today. That's not like you. Is something wrong?"

Katherine shook her head. *"Nee."* She snuck one last glance at Johnny before looking at her boss again. "Everything's all right."

"Good. Now hurry, you don't want to keep your customers waiting."

She turned in her order, determined to focus on her job. But as she faced the dining room, she froze. Isaac was sitting a few feet away from Johnny.

"So you want me to invest in your horse farm, even though you only have one horse."

Johnny nodded at James Wagner. The robust, balding man had already plowed through his meat loaf platter, while Johnny had taken only a few bites, despite the growl in his stomach. Nerves kept him from the food. The future of Johnny's business rested on Wagner's decision.

He had no idea what it was like to have a partner. And for all his bluster about making the farm work on his own, he was still depending on someone else to make it happen.

But he didn't have a choice. He needed a man with deep pockets. While it was possible he could put his plans for the farm on hold and wait until he had a job, he didn't want to wait that long. And if it took a partnership with Wagner to speed the process along, Johnny didn't have a problem throwing his straw hat in with a Yankee, who, according to his cousin, had a good reputation. Later he would explain his decision to his father. He couldn't go to him right now, admit he failed, and ask for help. Not until he'd exhausted every possible solution.

"How many acres do you have?" Wagner tapped his fingers against the edge of the white-and-red checked tablecloth.

"Right now it's ten. But I hope to add on. There's an empty field next to my property that I plan to purchase." *Soon, if you'll help me out.*

"What about the barn?"

"Six horse capacity. Again, I plan to expand. I'll be happy to take you there. You can have a look at the property, check out the facilities." Johnny glanced at the roast beef growing cold on his plate. His stomach growled again. He fidgeted in the chair, hoping Wagner hadn't heard. "I have a business plan I can show you too."

"Sounds like you have a good start." Wagner shoved away from the table and grinned, expanding his jowls. "Tell you what. The wife and I will come out the day after tomorrow."

"Your wife?"

"She's my partner in everything, including business." He chuckled. "Especially business. Married a smart one, I did. What time is supper?"

Johnny opened his mouth to speak, but the words wouldn't come. No way possible his place could be ready for company in two days. Especially for female company. Then there was the fact that he couldn't cook worth a whit, except eggs and toast. The way Wagner's belly expanded in front of him, Johnny knew that would hardly satisfy the man's hearty appetite.

"Didn't you hear me, son?"

"Six thirty." Johnny swallowed air and forced a grin.

"Perfect. After we eat you can show me the facilities and that business plan of yours."

"*Gut.*" A knot formed in his stomach.

Wagner stood. "Looking forward to it. The food here is tasty, but there's nothing like a homemade Amish meal. Had a few over the years and thoroughly enjoyed them."

"Uh, *ya*. They're delicious." Toast and eggs definitely wouldn't work.

"Is the number you gave me still good? Just in case something comes up."

Johnny nodded. "*Ya*, you can reach me there between eight and five."

"Don't expect I'll have to, though. Lois and I will be looking forward to it." Wagner stuck his beefy hand in his pocket and jangled his keys. "Thanks for the lunch. We'll see you soon."

Johnny started to stand, but Wagner waved him off. He walked away, leaving Johnny with the bill and a near panic attack.

He leaned back in the chair, his ravenous appetite suddenly gone. What was he going to do? He barely had money to cover the check and possibly a few groceries.

The business plan was no problem. He'd been working on it for months, ever since he'd gotten the idea for Mullet's Horse

Farm. But what about the house? The dinner? Once again, his
dream was swirling the drain, and he was powerless to stop it.

A waitress came up to him. Yankee, with thick black hair
in a ponytail, and the typical waitress uniform—plain blouse
and a skirt that reached to midcalf. She looked at his nearly full
plate.

"Was there something wrong with your meal?"

"No." Johnny's mind still whirred.

She glanced at his plate again. "Are you sure?"

He nodded. "Can I get a box to *geh*?" He'd eat it later, if his
appetite ever came back.

"Sure. Anything else?"

"Got a miracle on the menu?"

The girl gave him a puzzled expression. "What?"

"Just the box."

He rubbed the back of his neck and tried to think. Maybe he
could get the house in decent shape by day after tomorrow. But
making a meal was an entirely different story. And it would have to
be delicious, one that would make Wagner sign on the dotted line.

He couldn't ask Mary Beth to help. Or his mother. His
parents were leaving in the morning for Pine Craft, an Amish
settlement in Sarasota, Florida, for a long overdue vacation.

Mary Yoder's delivered. He might have to be satisfied with
that—if he could figure out a way to pay for it.

He looked up, searching for his waitress to ask for a takeout menu. At least he could get an idea of the cost of the meal.
Then he saw Katherine delivering a tray of drinks to an older
couple across the room.

His heart thumped in his chest as he turned his back on her. He closed his eyes, but her face swam before him. She was so sweet. And so pretty. And one of the best cooks in Middlefield. Which would impress the Wagners.

He stilled. No. He couldn't ask her. He didn't want to encourage her, not now. Not yet.

While he was still arguing with himself, Johnny stood and headed toward her. His heart pounded in his chest. This was a stupid idea. Absolutely idiotic. But when it came to cooking and sewing and all those other girly things, no one was better than his Katie.

Katherine avoided looking in Johnny's direction as she carried the tray of drinks toward her own table. Johnny and his Yankee friend were Chrystal's customers, not hers. And even though she knew Isaac was waiting for her to get his order, she had to make sure her current table was pleased not only with the food but also the service.

"Here's your tea." She misjudged the distance and set the glass down a little harder than she intended. Droplets shot out of the glass. "Oh, I'm so sorry."

The man waved her off, but the woman glared at her. Katherine's face heated. Why couldn't she get it together? Even without looking at Johnny, she could sense his presence. Why did forgetting about Johnny Mullet have to be so hard?

"Miss?"

Katherine looked down at the table. Her hand was still on the glass. She released it.

The woman picked up her napkin and set it in her lap. "I've heard good things about this restaurant." She narrowed her gaze at Katherine. "So far I'm disappointed."

"Don't mind her," the man said, giving Katherine a friendly smile. "My wife gets cranky when she's hungry."

"I do *not*."

"Thanks for proving my point."

Katherine relaxed a little and even managed a smile. "I'm truly sorry," she said. "I promise to take *gut* care of you for the rest of your meal."

The woman's expression softened a little bit. "I appreciate the apology."

Katherine nodded and turned to walk back to the kitchen, determined to make up for the mistakes she'd made with the couple. Instead she slammed right into Isaac.

"Oh!" She closed her gaping mouth. "You surprised me."

"Sorry. Didn't mean to." He grinned. He was always smiling at her. That must be part of the flirting Chrystal was talking about.

"I was getting ready to *geh* to your table," Katherine said. "I didn't intend to make you wait."

"*Nee*, that's all right. Actually, I can't stay."

But she barely heard his words. A few steps away, Johnny Mullet was approaching. She looked at Isaac. "What?"

"I wanted to ask you something," he said.

Johnny came up beside him. He crossed his arms over his

chest, his lips tilted in a rare frown. He stared at Isaac. "Am I interrupting something?"

Katherine opened her mouth to speak, but Isaac interjected, "*Ya*. You are." His grin had changed into a straight line.

Johnny looked at Katherine. "I need to talk to you."

She couldn't speak. There she was, closer to Johnny than she had been in months, ever since that embarrassing volleyball game last year, and she couldn't breathe, much less think or say anything coherent. Both men stared at her, as if waiting for her to choose which one to talk to first.

Finally she found her voice. "Johnny," she said, then cleared the bullfrog out of her throat. "This is Isaac, uh—"

"Troyer." He held out his hand. Johnny paused, then shook it.

"I won't keep you," Isaac said, turning to Katherine. "I know you're busy today. I wondered if you would *geh* to the singing with me this Sunday evening?"

Katherine's eyes widened. So did Johnny's, right before they narrowed at Isaac.

"Uh . . ."

He smiled again. "Think about it. I'll be back tomorrow." He looked at Johnny. "She makes the best coffee in town."

"But I don't make the coffee—" The words died on Katherine's lips as Isaac walked away. Whistling.

Johnny looked at her. "You're not considering going, are you?"

His question suddenly annoyed her. "Why should you care if I did?"

He swallowed. His gaze dashed around the room, lighting on the kitchen pass-through, the clock, the door—anyplace except on her. But he didn't answer her question. Instead he said, "Um, can I talk to you for a minute? In private?"

She nodded.

He led her down the hallway toward the restrooms, away from the rest of the customers. He touched her arm, then withdrew it quickly, as if he'd made a mistake.

She didn't care. The warmth of that brief touch seeped through her skin. And for all of her rational thoughts, all of her praying that Johnny wouldn't have this effect on her, she thought she'd faint right there.

He looked down at her, his chocolate-colored eyes meeting hers. "I, um, wondered if you could come over tomorrow."

Her heart almost flipped out of her chest.

"As a favor. I mean, I have a favor to ask."

"Anything." The word burst from her mouth like the juice from a ripe tomato. She sounded too eager. Too desperate. Isaac completely forgotten, she tried to act casual, leaning against the wall, putting her hand on her waist. She missed, and her hand slid down her dress. She recovered and said, "Sure."

"What time would be *gut* for you? To come over?"

"I'm off tomorrow, so anytime." Her voice trembled. This couldn't be happening. Johnny wanted her to come over? Could he have changed his mind after all these years?

"How about morning? The earlier, the better?"

"Six?"

He grinned. "Maybe not that early. Eight will do."

"Oh *ya*. That makes more sense."

"Okay. Great." He gave her the address, then started backing away, wiping his hands against the front of his pants. "Um, I'll see you tomorrow. At eight."

"*Ya*. Eight."

The corner of his mouth lifted into a half smile. He nodded, then spun around and walked away.

"See you tomorrow!" she blurted out. He—and nearly everyone else in the restaurant—turned around.

He lifted his hand, giving her a small nod.

Katherine watched him walk away, the sounds around her dimming to nothing. Johnny needed her. She could barely comprehend it.

She came to her senses and hurried to the kitchen, leaning against the counter as she tried to catch her breath.

"Katherine?" A coworker pulled her out of her thoughts. "We need to get this food out there."

Katherine nodded and hid a smile.

Tomorrow she would see Johnny. Alone. The thought made her giddy and nervous and thrilled—more emotions than she knew what to do with.

Could it be true? Could he finally be interested in her?

After all this time, perhaps her fervent prayers were coming true.

CHAPTER 8

The next morning Katherine turned into Johnny's driveway at five minutes to eight. Never mind that she'd been up since four thirty, unable to sleep. She'd read her Bible, cleaned her room, rearranged her closet, and ended up pacing for the last hour before it was time to go downstairs and help *Mamm* with breakfast. Now she was here, in her parents' buggy and parked in Johnny's narrow dirt driveway. She put her hand on her chest, felt her heart flutter. She then checked to make sure her hair was tucked into her *kapp*.

All her determination to move on from Johnny had vanished. She was as excited as she had been all those years ago when he had pushed her on the swing, giving her that smile that never failed to capture her heart.

God had given her this chance. Whatever Johnny Mullet needed her to do, she would gladly do it.

She took a deep breath. *Don't act stupid. Calm. For once, be* normal *around him.*

A memory from sixth grade swam unbidden to the surface of her mind. Johnny had been playing baseball at recess with his friends. While he waited his turn to bat, she had brought him a bouquet of wildflowers she had spent most of her recess time picking just for him. When she finally got the nerve to hand it to him, he laughed.

"*Buwe* don't get flowers." He looked at the bouquet with childish derision. "They give flowers. I don't want those *dumm* things."

Fighting tears, she'd taken the flowers and thrown them away before going back inside the school *haus*. The rest of the afternoon she tried to hide her humiliation, from him and everyone else. She wasn't super smart, like Mary Beth and some of the other children in class. Sometimes she said dumb things, and sometimes she wasn't as quick to catch on to a joke or sarcasm as other people were.

Yet despite that horrible day, she forgave Johnny. It wasn't his fault she didn't know better.

She shook her head, releasing the memory. Now wasn't the time to dwell in the past.

As she stepped out of the buggy, the back screen door banged against the door frame. When she reached the front of the horse and grabbed his reins, she saw Johnny across the yard, dressed in dirty work pants and shirt. Had he been outside working all morning? His boots were caked with mud, dirt, and straw. From the smell as he came closer, she knew for sure he'd been in the barn.

"Here, I'll take him for you." Johnny reached and took the reins. He looped them over the wooden tie.

"Danki," she croaked. She cleared her throat and spoke louder. "Thank you."

"No problem." He turned toward her, pushing his hat back from his head. He stared for a moment before averting his gaze. Silence stretched out between them, making her ill at ease. She shifted on her feet until he finally spoke.

"I don't know how else to say this. And I don't want to ask, but I don't have a choice." Worry clouded his eyes. "I need your help."

She stepped toward him, concerned. "What's wrong?"

He took a step back, widening the space between them. "I'm having company over tomorrow. A couple from Akron. For a business meeting."

"Okay." She frowned. "I don't know much about running a business."

"I don't need help with the business. Well, not in the way you think."

"What kind of business?"

"Mullet's Horse Farm."

"You and your *daed* bought a farm?"

"Nee." He wiped his forehead with the back of his hand. "I bought a farm."

She turned and glanced at the empty land surrounding a sad-looking barn. "Where?"

He spread out his arms. "You're looking at it." He gave her a halfhearted grin.

She surveyed the place more closely, taking in the sagging barn, broken, splintering fence, and weedy yard. When she looked at the house, she saw it wasn't in much better shape. This was a horse farm?

"I know it's not much, but it will be once I get it going." He started pacing. "And this *mann*—Wagner"—Johnny pronounced the *W* with a *V* sound—"he's thinking about investing. But first he wants an authentic Amish meal. Don't ask me why, but he does." He stopped and looked at Katherine, holding his palms up in defeat. "I can't cook."

"So you want me to make the meal?" Her confidence started to grow. Cooking she could handle.

"That . . . and something else." He motioned for her to follow him toward the house. He opened the door and she stepped in.

"*Ach.*" Katherine looked around the grimy kitchen. No curtains on the windows. Motes danced in the air as sunlight streamed through filmy windows. She sneezed, sniffed, then turned to him. "Does the rest of the *haus* look like this?"

"It's worse." A sheepish look came across his handsome face. "At least I spend time in the kitchen. Not much time, but the room gets used more than the others, except my bedroom."

She almost laughed at his embarrassed expression. Even dirty from work and obviously unhappy with the state of his house, he was so cute. But he was worried too. She didn't want him to worry about anything.

"I'll be happy to help you, Johnny. I know just what to do."

He let out a long breath. "I've got a lot to do outside before the Wagners get here. That leaves me with almost no time to clean up the inside. I thought about ordering some food from the restaurant—"

"*Nee.*" That wouldn't do. "If the Wagners want a *gut* meal, I'll make the best one they've ever had." She started walking around the kitchen, mentally making a list of everything that needed to be done. When she turned, she saw him watching her. Her pulse suddenly thrummed, a different rhythm than it did when she thought about him, or the few times she'd been around him. Heat rose to her cheeks and she turned away. "Do you have cleaning supplies?" she asked, grateful her voice sounded somewhat normal.

"*Ya.* You'll have to blow the dust off them, though."

She turned to see him smile. With his grin he looked a bit more like himself. "Just kidding. They're underneath the sink. *Mamm* made sure I was well stocked after I bought the place. Although she probably thought I would have used them by now."

Katherine smiled back. "You've been busy." She moved closer to him, still taking in the kitchen, seeing its potential. "It's a sweet *haus.* How many bedrooms?"

"Three. More than enough for me."

His words made her smile inwardly. So far no mention of another woman. Their district was small enough, of course, that she probably would have known if he was seeing someone. Then again, maybe not. Johnny was nothing if not private, and perplexing at times. But if he was dating someone, surely he would ask her for help, not Katherine. Or maybe he wasn't dating anyone seriously enough for him to feel comfortable—

"Katherine?"

She focused on him, realizing she had been staring past his shoulder. He moved to the back door.

"I'll leave you to do whatever it is you're gonna do." He opened the door. "I'll be in the barn if you need anything."

"All right." She moved toward him. "I'm sure I'll be fine." She smiled. *"Danki."*

His brow lifted. "You're thanking me? Why?"

She cringed. That did sound stupid, thanking him for asking her to clean his house. She tried to think of a quick reply, but nothing came.

"I should be thanking you." He smiled again, and her knees nearly buckled. "I better get to the barn."

Katherine nodded. The door shut behind him. She clasped her hands and looked around the kitchen again. "First thing, open a window." She yanked it open. The fresh spring air filtered through, disturbing the dust motes further. Everything needed airing out.

She went through the house, taking note of what needed to be done. The dingy brown curtains were ragged and ill fitting, as if they'd been hanging there for years. Those would have to go.

She pulled open the pitiful curtains to let some light in. The furniture placement in the room needed improvement too. The couch was shoved up against a wall in front of the big window, with a saggy chair next to it. A small coffee table was placed too close to the couch and covered with horse magazines, along with feed and farming catalogs. Everything looked second-, even thirdhand.

The bathroom downstairs was surprisingly clean. Katherine then went upstairs to the bedrooms. Two of them were completely empty. A bit of sweeping the dust off the hardwood floors and she would be done. The third bedroom was Johnny's. Her hand touched the doorknob, and she paused.

How foolish. She was cleaning his house. Nothing else. Yet knowing she was going into Johnny's bedroom gave her mixed emotions. Like she was intruding. Yet her curiosity was getting the best of her.

"Katherine!" Johnny's voice sounded at the bottom of the stairs.

She released the doorknob and went to the top of the staircase. *"Ya?"*

"I meant to tell you not to worry about the upstairs." He took off his hat and brushed off some of the dust. It floated to the floor. It meant more sweeping for her, but she didn't care. He plopped his hat back on his head. "The Wagners won't be going up there, so there's no need to clean."

"I don't mind. Really. It won't take me long at all." Despite her hesitation in going into his room, now she was disappointed to be denied.

"Nah, it's fine. Don't want you to have to do any extra work."

His courtesy touched her. Again the thought entered her mind that this might just be more than a favor. Maybe it was an excuse to be with her. To break the ice that had thickened between them over the years, at least on his side.

She tried to temper those expectations, but as usual, her feelings overruled her thoughts. As she watched him walk away, for a brief instant she imagined what it would be like if the house were theirs. If they were married, and he was going to work the farm while she took care of the house and their *kinner*.

She gripped the knob on the stair rail, forcing the dreamy thought away.

Johnny walked out the back door, intending to head to the barn. Instead he turned back and looked at the house, thinking about Katie working inside. Her face had lit up when he asked her about cooking the meal, and she didn't even flinch when she saw the mess in the house. In fact, she seemed excited to clean it.

But he knew that excitement came from her kind heart. It had taken everything he had not to keep staring at her as she'd walked around his kitchen. She was so lovely, with her reddish-blond hair peeking out from beneath her starched white *kapp*. She was willowy and graceful. He couldn't believe he ever thought her awkward. Or annoying. And when he recalled how he'd treated her in the past, the guilt nearly drove him to go straight back in the house and tell her how much he cared for her.

Yet his feet wouldn't move. Apparently his body was wiser than his head, because to reveal his feelings now would be disastrous. Certainly she would accept that he didn't have money, lived in a run-down house, and owned a barn that would likely collapse in a faint breeze. She would agree to live in poverty and scrape by while he tried to make a success of the farm. She would work hard at her job and work even harder when she came home. Because that was the kind of person she was.

And he wanted to be the man she deserved.

At the end of the day, Katherine returned home to the house she shared with her parents and younger sister, Bekah. She was tired, and she hadn't seen Johnny since the morning—he'd spent all day outside working in the barn and mowing and trimming the yard until it looked perfect.

But like the inside, the outside needed a woman's touch. There were no flowers in the beds outlining the front of the house. There was a place in the backyard for a nice vegetable garden, but it was covered with grass, now neatly shorn.

There wasn't anything she could do about flowers or vegetables outside, but she could do something inside. Something that would not only surprise him but make him happy.

She hummed as she walked over to the stove, where her mother stood cooking supper. Having skipped lunch, Katherine was starving.

"Where have you been all day?" her mother asked.

"Helping out a friend." She didn't dare tell *Mamm* that the friend was Johnny. *Mamm* knew all about Katherine's crush, about the heartache she felt at Johnny's rejection. If Katherine told her *mamm*, she'd either get a lecture or "the look." Katherine wasn't in the mood for either. Nothing would spoil her mood.

"What's for supper?"

"Cabbage and noodles, that leftover baked chicken from last night, and the last of the canned peas." Her mother set down the wooden spoon she used to stir the peas. "I'm glad the garden's started. I miss the fresh vegetables."

"Me too." Katherine leaned against the kitchen counter. "I was wondering, do you still have those old kitchen and living room curtains?"

"The ones we replaced a few years ago? *Ya.* I haven't had a chance to repurpose the fabric. Why?"

"Could I have them?"

"Sure." Her *mamm* looked at her. "Does your friend need curtains?"

"Most definitely."

"Then you're welcome to the fabric." She opened the oven, looked at the chicken bubbling in a light, creamy gravy. Heat started filling the kitchen before she shut the oven door. "Almost done."

After supper, Bekah went upstairs while her parents sat outside on their back porch to enjoy the fresh evening air. Katherine found the curtains, the living room ones a pale blue color resembling a robin's egg, plus the thicker cream-colored kitchen ones. She heated up the iron on the gas stove and ironed the curtains, making sure each seam and pleat was perfectly straight. She had measured Johnny's windows before she left, and while the living room curtains would be an inch short, anything was better than the shaggy, dusty ones he had now.

It was past nine, and she was yawning by the time she finished. She folded the curtains carefully and put them in a large cloth tote bag she'd quilted from spare fabric when she was seven years old. Then she went upstairs and collapsed into bed.

A few moments later her eyes flew open. She had to work tomorrow! How could she have forgotten? She would be off by three, but she still had to shop for supper, hang the curtains, and prepare the meal, all before six. She shot out of bed, turned on the lamp, and made a list of everything she needed to do, right down to the last detail. There wouldn't be time to make her best dessert, raisin cream pie. She'd have to purchase a pie from the bakery at Mary Yoder's and bring it to Johnny's.

As she turned off the light and went back to bed, she prayed for everything to go smoothly tomorrow.

She couldn't disappoint Johnny. She was determined not to let him down.

CHAPTER 9

Cora took a deep breath and slowly extricated herself from the taxi in front of Anna and Lukas Byler's home. Four months ago, when she had first come here, she had been appalled at the simple, backward way her grandson lived with his adoptive parents.

Her daughter, Kerry, had set those wheels in motion by rejecting the handpicked fiancé Cora had chosen for her and falling in love instead with a man who was entirely unsuitable. An impassable rift had grown between Cora and Kerry, and when Kerry and her husband died, Cora knew nothing of their death—or of the teenage son they had left behind. Sawyer had ultimately been adopted by the Amish Byler couple—a fate she could have saved him from, had she only known of his existence.

But that was over and done with. Water under the bridge. She'd never been able to control her daughter, but she could— she *would*—control Sawyer's immediate future.

She had tried once and failed. This time she would succeed. Since he hadn't returned to New York, she would come to him. She would use every tool in her arsenal to convince him to take up his rightful place as her heir. Every tool, save one— her diagnosis. He would not make this decision out of pity. She wouldn't allow that.

The sharp edges of the gravel stones on the driveway drove through the thin leather of her ballet flats. She couldn't balance on heels anymore. Even with the simple shoes, she had to tread carefully, watching her step and making sure nothing threw her off balance. A cane was out of the question. She wouldn't use one until absolutely necessary.

The taxi driver had retrieved her bags and was already briskly passing her as he took her luggage to the Bylers' front porch. He set the suitcases down and turned as she reached the bottom step. "Is there anything else I can do for you, ma'am?"

"No. That will be all." She stopped walking, pulled her leather wallet out of her Hermés bag, and gave him a generous tip. As he left she walked up the front steps, making sure to navigate them carefully. She bypassed the luggage and knocked on the front door. Then knocked again.

No answer.

It never dawned on her that no one would be home. Sawyer and Lukas were most likely at work at the carpentry shop. But where was Anna? Didn't the woman have washing or baking or some other primitive chore to do that would keep her tied up at home?

Cora looked around, taking in the stark white houses unadorned with anything but natural landscaping. Despite several lines of washing hanging from various houses, no one was in sight. She stilled and listened for a moment. The quiet made her ears hurt.

She managed her way back down the stairs. Perhaps Anna was in the backyard. She thought, not for the first time, how much simpler it would be if these people had a phone. She could have announced her arrival properly. Now she had to comb the property just to find someone.

As she came around the back, the ground changed from rough gravel to rich, green grass. The backyard was large, with a crude, sturdy-looking wood fence surrounding it. Cora pulled her designer jacket around her body as the wind kicked up, carrying the unpleasant scent of animals and their waste with it. She would never get used to that smell. Give her city exhaust any day.

A long wooden swing positioned under two large oak trees caught her eye. The branches extended up and out, higher and farther than any tree she'd seen in the city. The leaves were just beginning to bud.

Weariness overcame her as the travel and the stress of figuring out what to say to Sawyer took their toll. The swing did look inviting. She'd sit for just a short while and wait for Anna to come home. It had to be soon. It wasn't like a horse and buggy could take her far.

Gingerly she sat down and found the swing to be more comfortable than she had imagined. Cora took in the property, the wide-open field beyond the fence, the tall trees dotting the land. This time when she breathed in, she smelled something different. The sweet smell of grass. The freshness of the air. It filled her lungs, calming her inside.

She closed her eyes. This time the silence wasn't as over-whelming. In fact, it seemed to be just right.

Sweat dripped from Johnny's brow as he swept up the last pile of dirt and straw from the barn. He put the broom back on the rack with his other tools and surveyed his work. It wasn't per-fect, but it would have to do. The Wagners would be here in less than three hours. He didn't have much time to do anything else. Besides that, he was worn out.

But where was Katie? He thought she would have been here by now.

When he went inside last night, the place sparkled. He hadn't realized how filthy it was until he saw it clean. For the first time, the house almost seemed like a home.

Just then Katie pulled into the driveway. He let out a breath of relief and went to take the reins from her. Her cheeks were pink, and she was a little breathless, as if she'd been rushing around. All on his account.

He would have to make this up to her somehow. In a way she would never forget.

Several paper bags lay on the seat beside her. "Need some help with those?"

"*Nee*, I'm *gut*." She got out of the buggy and hurried to the other side.

Johnny started unhitching her horse. "I'll put him in the barn. I have one extra stall. Fresh and clean. Some oats and water, and he'll be happy." He stroked the calm animal's face. "If you're okay with that."

"*Ya*. Anything you want."

Johnny bit his lip. If only she knew how hearing those words affected him . . .

She snatched up the grocery bags and her colorful quilt tote and rushed into the house. He took a deep breath and led the horse into the barn.

A short while later he entered the kitchen. The fragrant scent of onions filled the room. Two pots bubbled on the gas stove, the blue flames burning beneath them. Katherine ran her hand across her forehead as she continued cutting the onions. Suddenly she started sniffling, and tears began streaming down her cheeks.

"Mary Beth's eyes always run when she cuts onions," he said, moving closer to her. "You want some help with that? I can't cook, but I can at least use a knife."

"*Nee*," she said, smiling, her eyes filled with tears. "I've got it. You run and get your shower. Relax a little before company comes." She nodded. "I have everything under control."

He stared at her for a moment, tempted to reach out and wipe the tears away from her face with his thumb. Instead he put his hands in his pockets and left before he did something that would get him into trouble.

Johnny went upstairs to get clean clothes, then took a cold shower in the upstairs bathroom. It didn't help relieve his tension. She was right, he needed to relax. His body was on edge, not just from the work, but from nerves—and the woman in the kitchen downstairs.

Johnny didn't know how long he stood there, letting the water run over his fatigued body, praying that everything would be perfect for tonight. Finally he got out of the shower, dried off, shaved, and put on fresh pants and a light blue shirt. He finger combed his long brown hair and started to leave the bathroom. Then he saw the wet towel and his dirty clothes on the floor. Quickly he picked them up and tossed them in the cabinet under the sink.

When he exited the bathroom the most delectable smell reached him. He breathed in, closing his eyes. He identified the bread baking first, then the frying onions. She was making beefsteak and onions? His favorite.

He walked into the kitchen and saw the sizzling meat and stewing vegetables in the pan on the stove. Sure enough, beefsteak and onions. He'd died and gone to heaven.

"Oh, Johnny. Here." She motioned him over to the stove. "I need you to watch the onions for a second."

He didn't like the sound of that. "What if I burn them?"

"You won't. They're on low heat. I just need you to stir them a couple times." She handed him the wooden spoon. He was careful not to touch her as he took it from her hand.

"Where are you going?"

"It's a surprise." She smiled, her cheeks bright and red against the paleness of her skin. Freckles dotted the bridge of her nose and streaked across her forehead. Her grin revealed perfectly straight, even teeth, and her blue eyes were sparkling with excitement.

She was adorable.

He checked himself, quickly averting his gaze. *Focus on the Wagners.*

"Stir!" she ordered with a light laugh. Then she grabbed that colorful bag of hers and left the room.

He bent over, awkwardly stirring the onions while breathing in the aroma. They were nearly clear, tinged with a buttery flavor and a spice he didn't recognize. When it came to seasoning a meal, if it wasn't salt and pepper, he had no idea what else to use.

The scent comingled with the yeasty bread baking in the oven. Snapped green beans sat in the other pot on the stove, covered with water and a square pat of slowly melting butter. On the counter next to the stove was a cutting board with a block of Swiss cheese ready to be sliced, a jar of pickled beets on the other side. If the Wagners weren't impressed with this meal, there was something wrong with them.

He gave the onions another stir, terrified he'd scorch them and ruin her hard work. When she returned, she took the spoon from him, their fingers brushing and sending a tingling sensation through him. Now he understood why Sawyer was so pie-eyed every time he was around Laura.

"*Geh* into the living room and sit down. I'll take it from here."

"You sure you don't need help with anything else?"

"I'm the cook, remember?" She smiled again and shooed him away. "*Geh.* Unwind. Supper will be ready by the time company gets here."

He nodded and went into the living room. There was something different about it, but he couldn't put his finger on it—other than it was clean for once. He sat down on the couch and crossed his arms, sinking deep into the cushions. This was turning out better than he'd hoped. He and Katie made a good team. She'd taken on his request and handled it with an almost professional ease that impressed him.

He thought about all the years he'd avoided her, afraid of giving her the wrong impression, especially when they were kids. Back then if he even glanced at her, she seemed to take it as a declaration of love.

Things were different now. If only she knew how he really felt. How being around her seemed so . . . right. He smiled and closed his eyes, thinking about Katie doing her magic in the kitchen. A quick nap, and he'd ask her if she needed help again.

Just a minute or two . . .

"Johnny."

Katie's voice sounded far away. And very sweet. It had almost a lyrical quality to it, like a songbird greeting the rising sun. Sun? It couldn't be morning yet.

"Johnny."

He felt a push on his shoulder.

"Company's here. They're pulling into the driveway."

His eyelids flew open. The Wagners. He shot up from the couch, ran his hand through his hair. "Do I look all right?" He stared at her; she was gazing at him with an odd expression but wasn't saying anything. "Kati—Katherine?"

"You look *perfekt*."

"*Gut*. Have to make the right impression." He pulled back the curtains and peeked out the window. Wagner was heaving himself out of the car. He walked over to the other side, presumably to open the door for his wife.

"Everything's ready," Katie said. "Just like I promised."

"That's great," he said absently. Now that the Wagners were here, his nerves had returned. He followed her into the kitchen. "I appreciate everything you've done."

She nodded, still smiling. And not moving.

"I promise I'll pay you back."

"You don't have to pay me back anything." She grinned wider. "I was happy to do it. I'm looking forward to meeting your company."

"What?" Then he looked past her shoulder at the table. Four places were set instead of three. *Oh nee.*

He hadn't thought that she would stay. Any other time he would want her to. But not tonight. How could he explain their relationship—non-relationship—to the Wagners? He was worried enough about tripping over his own tongue when he talked to them. It would be impossible to describe her role in his life. He couldn't even explain it to himself.

He guided Katie toward the back door when he heard a knock at the front.

"Do you want me to get that?" she asked.

Without thinking, he put his hand on the back of her small waist. A knot formed in his stomach. "I'm sorry. You have to *geh*."

Her smile faded. "What?"

"This meeting is really, really important to me. I don't want to give the wrong impression."

Her blue eyes grew round. "Oh." She looked at the table. Another knock sounded at the door. "I'll just put my plate away then," she said, her voice barely above a whisper.

"Don't worry about it. I'll take care of it." Another, more impatient knock reverberated from the front door. "I just need you to *geh*."

She looked at him and straightened her back, but she couldn't hide the hurt that seeped into her eyes. She'd never been any good at hiding her feelings. He'd known that for years. But this time was different. This time he'd hurt her more deeply than he ever had before, and it stabbed at his heart. "Katherine—"

He flinched as the door slammed shut behind her. He looked out the small window and saw her head for the barn. To hitch up her own buggy. He hadn't done it for her because he'd been asleep. Relaxing, while she worked to help him. And this was how he repaid her.

"Anyone home?"

The sound of a high-pitched woman's voice reached him from the living room. Apparently the Wagners had no compunction about letting themselves into his house. He watched for a second more as Katherine disappeared into the barn. He closed his eyes, silently asking for her forgiveness, knowing it was pointless.

"Coming," he called.

He composed himself and turned around. Only then did he get a good look at the table. And only then did he notice the bouquet of bright yellow daffodils in a small vase in the center among the gleaming, plain white dishes.

Katherine blinked back tears. When would she wise up? She trudged to the barn to get her horse, her legs like lead. When she entered the barn, she saw her horse as happy as could be in the comfy stall, a small portion of oats left in the feed trough. Johnny had taken good care of the animal, as he said he would. He hadn't promised her anything else. Whatever ideas she'd had about the two of them were of her own making. As always.

The lump in her throat tightened to a stranglehold as she led her horse back to her buggy and hitched him up. She saw the fancy white car in the driveway. She didn't know a make from a model, but she could see it was expensive, the exterior polished to a gleaming shine. Now she could see why Johnny needed her help. Maybe his guests would notice the new curtains she'd hung in the living room and kitchen, and the way the wood floor, which had been coated and dull, now shone with homey warmth.

Johnny sure hadn't.

Bile rose into her throat as she headed home. This was her fault, not his. He'd asked for her to help him, not to jump to conclusions. What a fool she was. All the time she was preparing his favorite meal, she had been thinking about the evening— imagining herself eating supper with Johnny at his table with his friends, enjoying the meal and the conversation.

Then maybe after his company left, he would have asked her to stay awhile. He would have noticed the extra touches she'd made to impress his guests. Not only the curtains, but fresh flowers, new kitchen linens, a little extra polish on the table. He would have thanked her. Smiled at her. Maybe even—

Stop it! She smacked the reins on Chester's back harder than she intended. He whinnied. "Sorry," she said, upset that she took her frustration out on this gentle horse. Couldn't she do anything right?

By the time she got home and put Chester and the buggy up, supper was over and the kitchen was already clean. Her parents and Bekah weren't around, and no one had left her a covered plate, as her mother sometimes did when Katherine had to work late at the restaurant. It didn't matter. She was too tired and upset to eat. She went upstairs, hoping to avoid the rest of her family.

Johnny had been right to send her home. They weren't married. They weren't even dating. She had no business being there other than to fulfill the promise she gave him. Once she'd done that, she should have left on her own. She shouldn't have had to be dismissed.

She flopped down across the bed. Tears slipped down her cheeks, no matter how hard she tried to keep them at bay.

Today had started with such promise.

And ended, once again, with heartbreak.

CHAPTER 10

"Are you stopping by to see Laura tonight?"

Sawyer looked at his father as he drove the buggy home from the shop. Business had been slow that day, and his uncle Tobias said he would handle any orders that came in. "I planned to. She's leaving for Tennessee in the morning."

"Finally decided to talk to her parents, then?"

"She's been talking to them." Sawyer's words took on a defensive tone. "They've exchanged letters."

"I see." Lukas tapped the reins against the horse's flanks. "Like you and Cora have been talking on the phone."

"Yeah. Something like that." Sawyer turned and looked out of the buggy at the houses passing by, a mix of plain Amish and fancier Yankee homes.

"I didn't mean to make you upset."

"You didn't."

"Could have fooled me."

Sawyer crossed his arms. He felt guilty enough talking about his grandmother with Laura; he didn't need the same nudge from

Lukas. At least she had agreed to go see her parents. But his relationship with his grandmother was more complicated. He had
only known her for a short while, but he knew what she stood
for. What she wanted from him. And he wasn't interested.

But what Laura had said to him over a week ago, and what
his father now left unsaid, made Sawyer know that he couldn't
put off going to New York much longer. "I'll wait until Laura
gets back from Tennessee."

"For what?"

"To see Cora."

"When's Laura coming back?"

A car passed by them, slowly making its way around the
buggy. Now that he used a buggy for transportation, Sawyer
appreciated the courteous drivers. Not everyone was. "Not
sure. A couple of weeks, maybe. I'll find out tonight."

"And when are you talking with the bishop?"

Sawyer paused. "That's going to be a couple of weeks too.
He wanted to wait a bit." Sawyer had wanted it to be sooner, but
Bishop Esh was testing him to see if he was sincere about his
commitment. Sawyer didn't like it, but he understood the man's
reasoning.

"So you're going to squeeze in a quick trip, then."

Sawyer nodded. "That's the plan."

Lukas remained silent for a moment. "*Sohn*, you're an adult.
I won't tell you what to do."

"Good."

"Other than to make sure you're being fair to your grandmother."

Sawyer uncrossed his arms. "It's not like she's been fair to me."

"That doesn't give you the right to take your pound of flesh."

"I'm not doing that."

"Aren't you?" Lukas glanced at him, his dark eyes calm, serious. "Vengeance comes in different forms."

"I know all about revenge."

The word triggered unpleasant memories. Laura had wanted her revenge on Mark King for any number of reasons: for stealing her parents' life savings; for deceiving her and using her to attain his own greedy ends; for nearly killing her and leaving her scarred for life. In the end, God's justice—and the justice system—had prevailed. Mark was serving time in an Ohio prison. Sawyer didn't know which one. He didn't want to know.

But there was no comparison between Laura's deep, righteous pain over what Mark did to her, both physically and emotionally, and the strife between Sawyer and Cora. "I need to deal with my grandmother on my own terms."

"*Ya.* You do."

Sawyer opened his mouth to say something but closed it. His father got his message across.

They rode the rest of the way in silence. When they arrived at the house, Sawyer could see that Anna's buggy was gone. She was off helping his aunt Rachel, Tobias's wife, prepare the house for church service on Sunday.

Lukas pulled the buggy underneath the covered area next to the barn.

"I'll put the horse up," Sawyer said.

Lukas nodded. He got out of the buggy. "I'll check on the field, see how the corn is doing. I might weed a few rows before nightfall."

As Lukas left, Sawyer unhitched the horse from the buggy. He had just led the horse into his stall when Lukas came into the barn.

"Sawyer. You've got to see this."

His normally staid father had a smirk on his face. Sawyer couldn't help but smile, glad the earlier tension between them was gone. He quickly put the horse in his stall and followed Lukas outside to the backyard. His father didn't say a word. He just pointed.

Sawyer froze. There was his grandmother, her mouth ajar and her head tilted back, sound asleep on their swing.

"What's she doing here?" Sawyer asked, stunned not only to find his grandmother in Middlefield, but to see her in such an undignified position.

Lukas chuckled. "Came to see you, I'm sure."

Sawyer didn't share his mirth. "What's so funny?"

"Cora. Never seen the woman so peaceful. Or so quiet."

Sawyer tilted his head. "True." Then he frowned. "Wonder how long she's been here?"

"One way to find out." Lukas gave Sawyer a slight shove. "Geh. Wake her up, before she starts catching flies."

"I'm not waking her up."

Lukas shook his head. "Don't look at me. I've got a field to weed, remember?" He turned and started walking away. "Tell her she's welcome to stay here if she wants. Although Anna will probably want her sleeping in the *haus* instead of on the swing."

Sawyer groaned as he heard Lukas laugh again. At least someone thought Cora's visit was funny. He sure didn't. And he didn't want to wake her up. But he couldn't let her sleep there, so he slowly approached her. The breeze ruffled her short silver hair. As he neared, he heard a slight snorkeling sound.

Was she snoring? The elegant Cora Easley snored?

He touched the shoulder of her soft leather jacket. "Grandmother." When she didn't respond, he raised his voice. "Cora."

"What?" She sat straight up, her eyes flying open. "What's going on?" She looked at him, and for a moment she didn't seem to recognize him. "Sawyer?"

She suddenly straightened, adjusting her jacket and running manicured fingers through her hair. She stood, unsteadily and with no small effort, as the swing gave her a difficult time with her balance.

Sawyer reached out to help her. She ignored the gesture and didn't thank him.

"Where have you been?" She peered up at him, and he had the odd feeling that she had shrunk. Then he looked down and saw the flat shoes that replaced her customary heels. Still, she managed to make him feel like she was looking down on him.

"Work. What are you doing here?"

"I was waiting for you." She sniffed, fully in control now.

That was one thing Sawyer knew about his grandmother. She wanted to control everything, including his life. She'd tried it once before, and it didn't work that time. It wasn't going to work now either.

"My luggage is on the front porch," she said, pointing to the house. "Take it inside."

"So you are staying?"

"I didn't fly here for a day trip." She peered at him again. "We have to talk. You're through avoiding me."

"I wasn't avoiding—"

"Don't insult my intelligence, or yours. You were ignoring me, and you know it. And on some level I understand. But the time for games is over. You have decisions to make, important ones. And I'm not leaving until you make them."

Sawyer sighed. "Then you'll be here a long time."

"As long as it takes."

They stared at each other. He could be as stubborn as he needed to be. "I'll get your luggage," he said, turning from her.

"Be careful with it. It's very expensive."

"Of course it is," he muttered.

"I heard that."

Sawyer clenched his teeth and walked toward the house, expecting her to be directly behind him. But when he rounded the house and reached the front porch, he turned. She wasn't there. He waited a few moments and saw her appear from the backyard, walking as if she were treading on eggshells. He didn't remember her being so slow before. If anything, she'd been surprisingly energetic considering her age.

When she reached him, she sounded a little winded. He frowned. "Are you all right?"

"I'm fine." Her tone sliced through the air. "What are you waiting for? Get my bags inside before they gather more dust. And once you've taken them upstairs, we can have our talk."

Sawyer gripped the handles of the two bags. He lifted them, almost dropping them because he misjudged the weight. What did she have in here, cement blocks? "Not tonight," he said, glancing at her over his shoulder.

She narrowed her eyes. "What could possibly be more important than our conversation?"

"Laura. She's leaving tomorrow."

Cora expressed surprise, and Sawyer thought he saw hope gleaming in her eyes. "She's leaving you?"

"No. She's going back to Tennessee. To talk to her parents." He took a deep breath. "To invite them to our wedding."

Cora's face paled. With more pep than he had yet seen from her, she scaled the steps and stood in front of him. "No. That can't happen. You *cannot* marry her."

"This shouldn't surprise you. You know how I feel about her. Besides, you don't have the right to tell me who I can and cannot marry." He looked down at her. "I'm not my mother."

She flinched, as Sawyer expected. It was a cruel blow, but she was irritating him. He refused to bend to her wishes, which had nothing to do with what he wanted and everything to do with her demands.

Cora took a deep breath and hiked her chin, as she always did before aiming a well-placed barb. But no barb came. Instead she simply asked, "If you do, will you still move to New York?"

He set her two-ton bags back on the porch. "I never said I'd move to New York. I'm pretty sure I made it clear I wouldn't."

He had never met anyone so hardheaded. *Lord, give me the right words. And patience. Lots and lots of patience.* No matter how he might feel about Cora, she was his grandmother and did deserve respect. He softened his tone. "Laura and I are getting married here. We're going to live here. It's already been decided."

"Hmmph." Cora crossed her arms. "Maybe I should have a talk with her."

"Leave her out of this. Our discussion is between you and me. I promise we'll talk tomorrow."

"I know how you are about your promises."

He should have known she wouldn't let that go. "You have my word. We'll talk about whatever you want, but it has to be tomorrow." Laura was already waiting for him. Emma had cooked a going-away meal for her and had invited him over. He wasn't about to miss out on that, especially since it would be two weeks or more before he'd see her again.

"Very well. I'll give you your time with Laura." She sniffed. "But tomorrow you and I are going to talk."

Sawyer picked up Cora's bags again and headed for the front door. "Can't wait," he muttered.

"I heard that."

"Finest meal I've had in ages." Wagner patted his round belly. "Beefsteak and onions. Can't beat that."

Johnny forced a chuckle, just as he'd had to force himself to eat his favorite meal, which had been cooked to perfection. "Just aiming to please."

"Please you did." His wife, Lois, who was as small as Wagner was large, wiped the corner of her mouth with her napkin. Despite her size, she'd put away the food with as much gusto as her husband. "I'm surprised you're such a good cook, Mr. Mullet."

Guilt slammed into him. "I can't take the credit. A friend of mine made the meal."

"Oh? Well, I wish she were here so I could thank her." Lois looked at Johnny. "She is a *she*, correct?"

"*Ya.*" Remorse snowballed in his gut. He had dismissed Katherine as if she'd been a servant, his personal maid. Only after she left did he notice the little things she'd done to make tonight special for his guests. The flowers. New dish towels. A bread basket that Lois had called "charming." Stuff he wouldn't have thought about, yet Wagner's wife had noticed and seemed to appreciate.

But he needed to get Katherine out of his mind or he would blow this deal. "Are you ready to see the property?" he asked, giving off what he hoped was a confident, commanding demeanor.

"Sure."

Half an hour later Wagner, Lois, and Johnny went back into the house. Again Johnny was struck by how clean and tidy it now was. Sure, there was still more work to be done, but at least it was neat. The scent of supper still hung in the air.

All smiles, Wagner sat at the table. "I've seen enough. True, things are a little shabby, but the outside is as clean and well kept as the inside. Shows you're serious about making a go of it. Let's review the business plan. You all right with that, Lois?"

She nodded, scooting her chair closer to her husband.

Johnny rose and pulled a red folder out of a kitchen drawer and handed it to Wagner. "Here's a copy of my business plan."

Wagner slipped his reading glasses out of the pocket of his shirt and put them on. He and Lois read the plan together, both of them nodding at certain points almost at the same time. Johnny gripped the edge of his chair. He couldn't tell from their blank expressions what they were thinking.

Finally Wagner put the plan back in the folder and closed it. He set it on the table. "This is a decent plan. It could use some tweaking, but I can see you've been thinking about the future."

"Yes. I want to make a success of this farm, Mr. Wagner."

Wagner held out his hand. "Please. Call me James. I'm always on a first-name basis with the folks I do business with."

Johnny relaxed his grip. "Does this mean you'll invest?"

"We'll have to discuss it, of course." Lois smiled. "We'll get back to you as soon as we've made a decision."

Johnny's smile slipped a bit. He should have known they wouldn't instantly agree to something this big without giving it some thought, and hopefully some prayer. When he had bowed his head to give thanks for the meal, they had both joined him, which fortified his belief that the Wagners weren't in his life by accident.

"I understand," he said. "Take the time you need."

Just don't take too long.

After they left, Johnny went back inside to the living room, collapsing on the old couch he'd picked up at the thrift store the day after he moved in. Every bone and muscle in his body ached with fatigue and tension. He tried to relax, but the silence in the house overwhelmed him.

Odd, it had never bothered him before. But having Katherine here, just for these two days, with her smiling and her humming as she cleaned the house and prepared the meal, made him realize how lonely it was here.

The late evening sun shone through the front window, the beams penetrating the clean glass. He stared at the soft, fading light for a moment before his eyes widened. He shot up from the couch and touched the curtains. Curtains that hadn't been there before.

Curtains she had brought. And knowing Katherine as he did, probably curtains she had made with her own hands.

He ran his fingers over the fabric. What other small gestures had escaped his notice? He shut the curtains against the fading sun and tried to close his mind against his conscience. He was about to go out to the barn and settle his horse in for the night when he spied Katherine's colorful cloth bag on his only end table.

Now he had an excuse to see her. He'd return the bag, pay her for the groceries, and tell her how well the meeting went and how much he appreciated her help.

He wanted to do more. Needed to do more. But he couldn't, not now.

When he returned from the barn, he saw remains of the dinner on the table. One piece of cherry pie left—Mary Yoder's pie, bought at the restaurant. The Wagners had devoured it with delight, just as they had the rest of the meal.

He put the dishes in the sink; he'd wash them tomorrow. As he stood in the kitchen, his mind filled with the image of Katie standing at the stove smiling at him, making a delicious meal from a few simple ingredients.

She was amazing. He couldn't deny that.

He just had to deny everything else.

CHAPTER 11

Katherine took a deep breath and tried to compose herself before she walked into the house. She was bone-tired, having worked a full shift at Mary Yoder's after a sleepless night.

On the way home she thought about Johnny again, which threatened to ruin the rest of her evening. On top of that she had a horrible headache.

Still, she didn't want her parents to worry or ask questions she couldn't—wouldn't—answer. She forced a smile and opened the back door. When she entered the kitchen, she saw her mother open the oven and place a loaf of bread inside to warm it.

"*Hallo*, Katherine," her mother said, shutting the oven door. "How was your *daag?*"

"*Gut.*" Katherine walked over to the cabinet and pulled out a bottle of pain reliever. Although she didn't have an appetite, she added, "Something smells *appeditlich.*"

"Must be the ham and bean soup. I'm trying a new recipe

I saw in *The Budget*. I didn't see you at all yesterday. Did you work overtime?"

"*Nee*. I was helping a . . . friend." She couldn't lie to her mother, but she didn't have to admit all the details either. She swallowed two aspirin with a glass of water and put the glass in the sink. "Do you need help with anything?"

"You could set the table."

She nodded and fetched the plates. "Where's Bekah?"

"Helping Judith with some sewing." *Mamm* arched an eyebrow. "Although who knows how the dresses will turn out. Bekah doesn't have your gift with needle and thread."

"Sewing isn't her favorite thing." Katherine set the plates on the table.

"Definitely not. She'd rather be out with your father plowing the field, I think." *Mamm* opened the gas oven to check on the bread. "Guess we'll have to eat without her tonight. Will you *geh* outside and get your *daed*?"

Katherine nodded and went out the back door, through the small backyard. She waved at their neighbor, Mr. Harvey, who was sitting in a rocker on his front porch. After a bad start settling into the neighborhood, one that involved his son trying to steal from him and hurting Bekah in the process, the elderly man had turned out to be a nice yet quiet neighbor who liked to keep to himself.

She found her father behind the barn, cleaning caked dirt off the plow. "Supper's ready."

He rose, pushing his straw hat back from his florid face. A cool breeze flipped up the ends of his red hair, which was only just now showing signs of gray. He looked out at the small plot of land where they put in their vegetable and flower garden. The grass, green from summer rains, covered the field, except for the short stubs of cut cornstalks still poking out of the ground.

"Getting a fine start on the garden," her father said. "Next week I'll start plowing. I'm a little behind on that this year." He looked at Katherine. "Your *mamm* will be glad."

"*Ya.*" A sharpness pierced her temple. She shut her eyes against the pain.

"Katherine?" Her father approached her. "Are you all right?"

"Just a headache. I took something for it." She forced a smile. "I'm sure it will be better soon."

He nodded but still looked at her with concern. "Are you sure everything is okay?"

"It's just a headache, *Daed.*"

"That's not what I mean. You seem . . . different."

Her father could always sense when something was wrong, even when she tried to hide her feelings. His question, combined with the pain, sent her over the edge. "There's nothing wrong, okay?"

"If you say so." He frowned, his blue eyes stern. "Tell your *mamm* I'll be there in a minute."

Katherine clenched her hands into fists. Frustration welled up inside.

She was tired. Tired of loving someone who didn't love her back. Weary of her life being at a standstill. Resentful of everyone thinking she was sweet but not very smart. Not good enough. *Especially for Johnny.*

But there was nothing she could do about any of it, except what she'd always done—pretend it didn't bother her. She let go of her foul mood and gave him the brightest smile she could, adding the right touch of genuineness. "I'm sorry, *Daed*. It's been a long day. Don't worry about me. Everything is just *perfekt*."

His concerned gaze faded. He grinned. "That's my *maedel*. The eternal optimist." He set down the plow. "I'll deal with this later. Let's eat." He started for the house and she followed.

After supper, Katherine headed for her room upstairs. When she reached the top, she heard Bekah call her name.

"You have a visitor."

She turned around and went back downstairs, wondering who. Not Johnny, of course. Or Mary Beth—she was too busy with her young baby. When she reached the living room, she was surprised to see Isaac Troyer standing there.

"Hi, Katherine."

"Hello, Isaac." She turned and glared at Bekah. Couldn't she have a moment of privacy?

Her sister smiled and left the room.

"I'm sorry to bother you," Isaac said. "But this couldn't wait until tomorrow. One of your coworkers told me where you lived. I hope you don't mind."

She shook her head. "Is something wrong?"

"*Nee*. It's just that I have to *geh* back to Walnut Creek to help my father for a couple of weeks. Not just in Walnut Creek, but a few other towns in Ohio and New York, helping some farmers establish their alpaca herds."

"Alpacas?"

"*Ya*. We've raised them for years. Seems more families want to get into the business. He likes giving them advice in person, and this time he wants me to *geh* with him." He pushed his hat back from his head. "I won't be here for the singing Sunday."

The singing. She'd been so wrapped up with Johnny she'd forgotten all about Isaac's invitation. "That's all right."

"But I wondered, would you mind if I wrote to you? I don't want to lose touch while I'm gone."

Katherine paused, only to wonder why she was hesitating. She didn't have Johnny. Or any other offers. And Isaac had always been nice to her, and attentive. "*Ya*," she said. "I'd like that."

"All right." He started to back away. "I've gotta *geh*, but you'll be hearing from me soon. Bye, Katherine."

She followed him to the door and watched him leave. As he got into his buggy, he waved. She waved back.

"Who was that?" Bekah said.

"None of your business," Katherine said. She was done wearing her heart on her sleeve for everyone to see. She deserved something—someone—that belonged only to her. At least for the moment.

And hopefully, finally, with Isaac's help, she could put her feelings for Johnny to rest once and for all.

Sawyer and Laura stood by Lukas's buggy in Emma and Adam's driveway. Emma's cooking had been delicious, but the company had been subdued. Knowing Laura was leaving in the morning had put a damper on everything. Now, standing so close to her under the midnight-black sky, he could only focus on her. Two weeks seemed like an eternity. He frowned.

"What's wrong?" Laura moved closer. There was still enough space between them that if anyone driving by saw them together, they wouldn't suspect anything. But in the silvery moonlight that barely illuminated her beautiful face, Sawyer could see the love in her eyes, a love that reached his heart.

"Nothing," he said softly.

"It's not nothin'. You were quiet during supper. You didn't eat much either, which isn't normal for you."

"I wasn't very hungry." He sighed and leaned against the buggy. He took her hand, rubbing his thumb across the back of it. "You're leaving tomorrow. I can't get excited about that."

"You wanted me to *geh*."

"I know. But you want to go too. You need to go."

Laura nodded. "I'll be back. Two weeks isn't that long."

"It is to me."

"Sawyer, this isn't like you. You believe me, don't you?"

"Of course." He continued to rub her hand. "Besides, if you don't come home, I'll go to Tennessee and bring you back myself."

Laura let out a soft giggle, but her laughter faded quickly.

She released Sawyer's hand. "There's somethin' else, isn't there? Somethin' that doesn't have to do with me leavin'."

He took a deep breath and stepped away from her. "Cora's here."

Her delicate blond eyebrows arched. "When did she arrive?"

"This afternoon." He chuckled. "Lukas and I found her asleep on the porch swing in the backyard, if you can believe that."

"That must have been a sight." Laura grinned. "This is *gut* news, *ya?* You don't have to *geh* to New York now. You were dreadin' that trip."

"I'm dreading talking to her. Here or in New York, it doesn't matter."

"Sawyer, she's your grandmother—"

"And she wants to rule my life."

Laura paused. "She is a little forceful."

"A little?" Sawyer shook his head. "I know exactly what she wants. She wants me to move back to New York. To live like her."

"Then she doesn't know you decided to join the church?"

"Not yet. But it shouldn't come as a surprise." Although he figured it probably would. Cora Easley was used to snapping her fingers to make things happen. To make them go her way.

But not this time. He was following God's lead. And his heart.

He took Laura's hand again. "I don't want to talk about my grandmother." Sawyer led her to the barn. In the distance he could hear the barking of the dogs in Emma Otto's new shelter on the other side of the house. The shelter replaced her grand-father's old workshop, which had burned down in the fire Mark King had started, the fire that had almost taken Laura's life.

Since rebuilding and turning the building into a dog shelter, Emma had fostered several stray and abandoned dogs until she could find places for them to live. She and Adam had taken what Mark destroyed, and from the ashes had risen something compassionate and worthwhile.

"What are you doing?" Laura asked as he took her to the back side of the building.

"This." He cupped her face in his hands, the ribbons of her *kapp* touching his fingers. He kissed her, gently, but longer than he'd ever kissed her before. When he finally pulled away, he brushed the back of his hand against her scarred cheek, feeling the heat of her skin. He expected her to pull away, to protest halfheartedly, the way she usually did when he sneaked a kiss. Instead she sighed and leaned against him. He shuddered as he wrapped his arms around her slim body.

"That has to last two weeks?" He leaned his cheek against the top of her *kapp*.

They didn't say anything for a long time, just held on to each other. Before he was ready to let her go, she said, "It's gettin' late, Sawyer."

"I know." He held on to her.

"I have to *geh* inside. I'm catchin' the early bus in the mornin'."

"You sure you don't want me to take you?"

She shook her head. "I already arranged for a taxi. Besides,

I can't take sayin' good-bye twice." She touched his clean-shaven cheek, her fingers light, making his skin tingle. "Don't be too hard on your grandmother while I'm gone. She does love you, in her own way."

"How do you know that?"

"Because you're so lovable." She kissed the tip of his nose. She pulled out of his embrace and walked toward the house.

"Two weeks, Laura."

She nodded, giving him one last long look before disappearing from his sight.

He exhaled. This was going to be the longest two weeks of his life.

Johnny dragged himself upstairs to his bedroom. He had hoped to stop by Katherine's today and return her bag, but he spent most of the day fixing a pipe under the sink, which had suddenly burst that morning. He wasn't much of a plumber, but he managed to turn off the water, go to town and talk to a guy at the local plumbing supply shop, then come back and give the pipe a quick fix. He'd even asked for a job there, but like everywhere else he'd tried, they weren't hiring.

He went back home and repaired the pipe, but not as fast as he hoped. The whole process took up most of the day—precious time he didn't have. He'd rather be repairing the barn or stripping the old paint off the decrepit back deck than dealing with a plumbing problem. But the guy at the shop assured him the section of pipe should hold for at least a couple of weeks, until he could get around to replacing the entire line.

Enough time for the Wagners to decide to invest in his farm or not. If they did, he could afford a professional plumbing job.

If they didn't—

He shook his head and collapsed on the bed. Katherine's bag lay on top of the dresser—tempting him, mocking him. He had brought it upstairs last night, feeling responsible for keeping it safe. *As if someone would break into this shack and steal an old patchwork bag.*

The thought was ridiculous, but so was his real reason for keeping the bag in his room: it gave him a little piece of Katherine close by.

Johnny shut his eyes. Maybe his sister was right, along with everyone else. He was being *dumm*. If Katie couldn't accept him at his worst, then that wouldn't bode well for their marriage—*if* they got married. After the other day he wouldn't be surprised if she told him to take a flying leap into a swampy pond. Actually, even before the Wagners, it wouldn't have been a shock if she rejected him.

For years he hadn't been able to imagine himself with her. Yet in the past year, he couldn't stand to think about life without her. And he had assumed she'd wait for him, just like Mary Beth said.

But what if she didn't? What if she found someone else? Or what if she just plain didn't want him anymore?

He sat up in bed. Maybe that's what was holding him back. Not the farm or being independent or not being good enough for Katherine Yoder. He was afraid she'd say no. And after all this time, after everything that had—and hadn't—happened between them, she would have a right to.

Johnny shot out of bed and paced. He tried to clear his mind, tried to pray. *Are you telling me something, God? Have you been telling me that all along and I've been too knuckleheaded to hear?*

He stopped in front of his bedroom window. Looked out at the stars winking in the night sky. God didn't need to tell him anything. Johnny had always known the truth. When it came to Katherine, he was a coward. And it was time he did something about it.

He moved away from the window. Yanked off his shirt and tossed it on the floor. Walked over to his dresser and touched her bag.

He'd give this back to her tomorrow.

And he would give her something else too. The truth.

Which she had deserved all along.

CHAPTER 12

Katherine rubbed the back of her neck and stared down at the book on her lap. Pain shot through her skull, and she couldn't concentrate on the words. Today the aspirin hadn't touched it.

She'd had headaches before, but not one that lasted this long, or was this painful. The thought occurred to her that perhaps she should go to the doctor, but she didn't want to waste a trip for a simple headache. Still, she might have to if the headache didn't go away.

She lifted her book, studying the quilt patterns on the page. She had picked it up from the library and was fascinated not only by the bright, vibrant colors but by the intricate stitching. There were some Amish quilts featured, but other quilts and patterns from around the world were included as well. She was particularly intrigued with the Hawaiian quilts—rich, bold patterns appliquéd on a large piece of fabric, with the quilting stitches following the contour of the design. She would never make one of these herself, but she did admire the artistry and skill of the quilters.

She lifted her head as she heard Bekah come in. "Where have you been?" she asked.

"Out with some friends. If I'd known you were home, I would have invited you to come along."

"I had to work late." A sharp pain pierced her temple. She winced.

Bekah didn't seem to notice. "How about if you *geh* to the singing with us this Sunday? It's at Judith Miller's."

The same singing Isaac had invited her to. "Sure you'll be able to avoid Melvin?"

"I'm not worried about him." She plopped down on the couch. "I'm not going to let a *bu* ruin fun with *mei* friends." She looked at Katherine. "So? Will you come?"

Katherine shook her head and looked down at the book. "I don't think so."

"You haven't been to a singing in years."

"I'm not interested." She didn't mention Isaac's invitation. "There's no rule that says I have to *geh* to those things."

Bekah sighed. "Are you afraid you'll run into Johnny? Because that won't be a problem. He never goes either."

Katherine glanced up. She knew why she didn't go—she couldn't bear to see him talking to the other girls. But Johnny was more social than she was, and she knew he had attended singings when he was younger. Why had he stopped?

"Maybe that *schee mann* who visited yesterday will be there."

"He won't."

"How can you be sure?"

"Because he already left town." She touched her temple again.

"Still have your headache?" Bekah leaned forward, the ribbons of her *kapp* swinging against the front of her lavender dress.

"Ya." Katherine forced a smile. "But it should *geh* away soon."

"You took something for it?"

She nodded but didn't say how many aspirin she'd taken over the past twenty-four hours trying to rid herself of the pain assaulting her head. "I'm sure it will start working soon."

"I hope so." Bekah yawned. "I'm heading upstairs. *Guten nacht.* Hope you feel better."

"Danki."

As Bekah went upstairs, Katherine started to open the book again. But she set it aside instead. She wished she could be like Bekah. She wanted to go to a singing, enjoy time with her friends, and be cavalier. Maybe she would attend the next one. Or she would wait for Isaac to return—if he kept his promise to write to her.

She headed upstairs, turned on the battery-powered lamp, and took off her *kapp*. As she undressed, the pain in her head started to lessen. She brushed out her hair and put it in a ponytail, pinning a kerchief over it. She turned off the light and lay down.

But she couldn't sleep. The headache was almost gone, but her thoughts still whirred. She tossed and turned for a short while, then gave up in frustration and went downstairs. Maybe a snack would help her sleep.

As she approached the kitchen, she saw the lamp was still

lit. Bekah obviously had the same idea. But when she walked into the room, she saw her mother cutting a piece of chocolate cake left from supper.

Katherine frowned. Her mother was always early to sleep and early to rise. *"Mamm?"*

Her mother jumped, and the cake knife clattered to the floor. She turned to Katherine, her hand on her chest. "Goodness, you surprised me."

"I can see that." Katherine picked up the knife off the floor and rinsed it in the sink. "Is there any cake left?"

"I only took a small piece." Her mother picked up her plate and walked to the table. She put her finger to her lips. "Don't tell your *daed.*"

"He won't care if you have a snack, *Mamm.*" Her mother was still as thin as she was when she married. Katherine's father had said as much when her mother had complained about one of her dresses being a little tight. But in Katherine's eyes, and obviously her father's, her mother's figure was perfect.

"I don't mean that." *Mamm* sat down. "If he knows there's cake left, he'll want some. That *mann* needs to watch his waistline."

Katherine smiled. Unlike her mother, her father had plumped up a little over the years.

"Don't get me wrong. I love him as he is. I just want him to be healthy." She looked at the cake in front of her. Then she pushed it away. "I should probably set an example, then."

Katherine pushed the plate back in front of her mom. "A small slice won't hurt. Let me get a piece, and I'll join you."

Moments later they were both eating cake and drinking milk.

The gas lamp in the kitchen hissed, casting the room in a low, yellowish glow. "We haven't done this in years," *Mamm* said.

"What?"

"Have milk and cake together. Or milk and cookies. Or milk—"

"And whoopee pies."

Mamm smiled. "You did love whoopee pies."

"I still do." She took a sip of milk. "I just don't eat them very often."

"It's nice to see you eating now." Her smile faded. "I've been a little worried about you lately, Katherine. The headaches, and you haven't had much of an appetite. And you've been very secretive. You never did tell me about the friend you helped a couple days ago." She set down her fork. "Is there anything you want to talk about?"

"There's *nix* to talk about."

It was a small lie. All right, a big one. There was plenty she could talk about, but not with her mother. Lately she hadn't even talked with God. Why should she, when He never answered her prayers about Johnny? Or maybe His silence had been her answer, and she hadn't been able to accept it. Until Isaac showed up.

"Does this have anything to do with Johnny Mullet?"

Heat crept up Katherine's neck. She couldn't outright lie to her mother. Yet embarrassment kept her from saying anything. "There's nothing going on, *Mamm*. I just helped a friend. That's it." Katherine ran her finger against the edge of the table, not looking at her mother.

Mamm sighed. "I suppose it's none of my business. You're

a grown woman now. You have a right to your own life. To your own secrets."

"That's not what I meant—"

"I'm not upset, Katherine. Every woman has a right to keep a few things to herself. I just hope that whatever you've been doing doesn't have anything to do with Johnny. Because that's one person in your life you've never been secretive about." She picked up her fork again. "I know you care about Johnny. But he's only managed to make you miserable."

"That's not true."

"Isn't it? What has he done lately to make you happy?"

Katherine couldn't reply. If anything, Johnny made her feel worse about herself. Like a fool. She looked away.

"You've wasted enough time and energy on that *mann*, Katherine. Please tell me you've finally come to the point of letting him *geh*."

"I—"

She tried, but the words wouldn't come. Inside, she'd given up on Johnny. To say it out loud, however, would make it *real*. But wasn't that what she was trying to do? As difficult as it was, she needed to admit that Johnny was out of her life. For good.

Her mother let out a long breath and leaned back against her chair. "You don't know how long I've been praying for you." She smiled. "To move on with your life. Find a *mann* who deserves you. One who appreciates you for the special woman you are."

Katherine's eyes burned as the full realization of Johnny's rejection went through her. He didn't care. He didn't appreciate her. He never had.

"*Ya,* " she said, swallowing the tears that threatened to fall. "You're right."

Excitement sparkled in *Mamm's* eyes. "I was talking with Sarah Detweiler the other day. She said that her sister's *gross-sohn* just turned twenty. He lives in another district, but she was telling me about him. He's a nice *yung mann.* Has his own business."

"*Mamm*—"

"I'm sure Sarah would be happy to introduce you."

Katherine looked at her slice of cake. She'd only taken one bite. The ache in her neck returned. Should she tell *Mamm* about Isaac? Even if she wanted to, she couldn't bring herself to mention his name.

"You don't have to meet him right now." Her mother stood up and took her empty plate to the sink. "How about next week?" She turned and smiled. "But I don't want to put any pressure on you."

Right. No pressure. "I'll think about it."

Mamm walked over to her and kissed the top of her head. "*Gut.* Your *daed* and I just want you to be happy, *dochder.* When you put Johnny behind you, I believe you will be."

Her mother left, but Katherine didn't move. She just sat there, staring at the cake in front of her.

She'd wasted years believing Johnny was the man for her, that they would be happy together. Praying, hoping, longing, imagining. Now she knew that wasn't going to happen. And her heart was in more turmoil than ever.

CHAPTER 13

After saying good-bye to Laura, Sawyer had made his way slowly home, his heart heavy. Not just with missing Laura, but also knowing his grandmother was at home, waiting for him. It was late, well past sundown. Perhaps she'd decided to go to bed. Even better, maybe she'd decided to go back to New York.

Wishful thinking.

He pushed back his yellow hat and scratched his head. He had no idea what he was going to do about her. She had shown up in his life four months ago, making demands, telling him he had to abandon the life he had lived the past several years in Middlefield—even the life he'd lived with his parents before their deaths—and accept her values, and especially her money. She'd been genuinely shocked that he'd refused.

If she had bothered to find out anything about him, instead of expecting him to jump at her command, she would have known that he wouldn't have been tempted by her money and her power, or by the opportunity to take over her company and settle in New York City.

And yet here she was again, with her expensive clothes and snooty attitude, looking down with contempt on the adoptive parents who had loved him as if he were their own.

He gripped the reins until his hands ached. Where did she get the nerve, when she'd never done anything for him?

He released the reins, trying to push the anger and resentment from his heart. If he was going to join the church, he needed to be clear of these negative emotions he held against Cora. Even though he'd claimed he'd forgiven her, he knew he had a lot more work to do in that department.

He wished she would just stay in New York and leave him alone. Forgiveness was a whole lot easier long distance.

He reached the house and put up the horse, giving him a little extra hay. He was beat, and it didn't help to be thinking about Laura, how much he'd miss her. It amazed him how deeply he'd fallen in love with her in such a short time. The sooner they were together, the better.

"How nice of you to keep me waiting."

Sawyer halted halfway to the stairs. He peered into the living room and made out Cora's slim shape. She was still wearing the white leather jacket she had on earlier, and she glowed like a ghost in the darkness.

"What are you doing sitting here in the dark?"

A pause. "I couldn't find the lights. There are no switches in this house, in case you haven't noticed."

He went to the end table and lit the gas lamp. "You could have asked my parents."

He saw her bristle at the word *parents*, but he didn't care.

That's what Anna and Lukas Byler were to him—parents, and much more of a family to him than Cora would ever be.

"I didn't want to bother them."

She glanced away as she spoke, and Sawyer realized her lie.

She was too proud to ask his parents where the lights were. A simple question, yet one that would make a woman like Cora Easley feel like a fool. Maybe he understood his grandmother better than he thought.

He eased down onto the couch opposite her. "You didn't have to wait up for me."

"You didn't give me much choice."

"Why didn't you go to bed? We could have talked in the morning."

"Oh no." She wagged her finger in his face. "I know the insane time you people get up. You would have been long gone to work. I know from experience that I couldn't talk to you there. And you would have found another reason to avoid me after you finished working." She leaned back and crossed her thin arms. "I'm no fool, Sawyer."

"As you've said many times." He leaned back against the cushions of the couch. "Okay. I'm here. You have my attention. What do you want to talk about?"

"As if you don't know." She sniffed, peering at him. "I suppose the first thing I should find out is if you really plan to marry her."

"Straight to the point, as usual." Sawyer crossed one foot over the opposite knee. "Yes. I'm going to marry her. I already told you that."

She frowned. "When?"

"After I join the church."

"Join what church?"

"The Amish church."

"I don't understand. Why do you have to join a church to get married?"

"It's the Amish way." He wasn't ready to explain everything to her. Or rather, he didn't want to. She didn't respect the Amish way of life; how could he expect her to appreciate their faith? How could she possibly understand that the church wasn't a building, but an all-encompassing lifestyle?

"The Amish way." She waved her hand. "I suppose a New York wedding is out of the question."

She uncrossed her arms and put her hands in her lap. Sawyer thought he saw her hands tremble, but she quickly clasped them together.

"We're getting married here. In the Amish church. During an Amish ceremony."

"Can I at least plan a reception at my penthouse? It will be small. Your . . . *family* . . . will be invited, of course."

"This isn't a typical wedding. After the ceremony there will be a community meal. That's it. Nothing fancy or expensive. Definitely nothing involving the penthouse."

"So you would deny me the chance to celebrate my only grandson's nuptials?" Her thin eyebrows angled downward.

"I never said that. You're welcome to attend the wedding. It will be at Adam and Emma Otto's house."

"But you won't come to New York. That's hardly fair."

"That's how it has to be."

"I don't see why you're being so stubborn. About everything."

He could see the hurt in her eyes and realized he owed her an explanation. "When I join the church, I'm making a promise. Not just to serve God, but to live by the *Ordnung*."

"The Ord what?"

"The *Ordnung* is a set of rules we—the Amish—abide by. I've been following some of them since the Bylers adopted me, but they never forced me to go all in with their lifestyle. They let me make the decision."

"So the rules forbid your grandmother to have a wedding reception?"

"Yes. The district will hold the reception." He leaned forward. "I don't know why you don't understand this. Can you imagine introducing me and Laura to your friends?"

"I would explain the situation."

"How would you possibly explain it, when half of what I'm saying doesn't make sense to you?"

"Then wait." Cora's voice sharpened. "Postpone the ceremony. Let me get to know you and Laura better."

"So you can convince us to do things your way?" He shook his head. "No thanks."

"That's not what I mean." Her face suddenly sagged. "Did it ever occur to you that I came here without an agenda?"

"To be honest, no."

As he spoke the words, guilt pinched at him. Maybe he shouldn't have presumed. Then he shook his head. This was Cora. When did his grandmother *not* have an agenda?

"I want to get to know my grandson. Why is it so hard for you to believe that?"

Sawyer paused and looked at her. She seemed sincere. More sincere than he'd ever seen her. But he still couldn't trust her. Not completely. "You know you can stay here with the Bylers as long as you want. I won't be joining the church for a little while. We can get to know each other in the meantime. But I need you to know—I'm not changing my mind. Not about the church, or about Laura. I've prayed about this. Joining the church is what I want to do. It's what I need to do."

"If you don't join the church, can you still marry Laura?"

He shook his head. *"Nee."*

Cora eyed him. "So this decision—it has everything to do with God and nothing to do with Laura?"

Sawyer stood. "I knew you wouldn't understand."

She held up her hand. "I'm trying. You're not giving me a chance."

"Look, even if I didn't marry Laura, I would still join the church. Visiting you in New York helped me make up my mind."

"That wasn't exactly what I intended."

"I know. You wanted me to stay." He shoved his hands in his pockets. "But Middlefield is where I belong. This is my family. That doesn't mean I can't come visit you, and you're always welcome to visit us, when we're settled down."

"So you intend to be a carpenter for the rest of your life?" Cora lifted her chin. "You're going to waste your intelligence by making tables and chairs?"

"It was good enough for Jesus."

"What are you talking about?"

"Jesus was a carpenter . . . never mind."

"I don't see what Jesus has to do with this conversation."

Of course she wouldn't. They were further apart than he'd imagined. "My point is that being a carpenter is a good job. It requires skill. People need tables and chairs, you know."

"I need you to run my company!"

He scowled. "It's still all about you, isn't it? What you want, what you need."

She rose from the chair—slowly, with measured movements. Yet she spoke as she moved. "Sawyer, listen to me—"

"I think I've listened enough." All this talk about wanting to get to know him and Laura was a bluff. He saw that now. And once again he felt betrayed by it. He wasn't a grandson to her. He was just DNA, someone to make sure her precious company stayed in the family.

"I know you don't think you can run a company, but I can show you."

"No. That's not what you want to hear. I get that. But it's my decision."

She looked up at him. "You've made that very clear."

"Then why are you still hounding me about this?"

He noticed a sudden weariness in her eyes, and he realized how late it was. When he'd been in New York, she'd complained of headaches and had gone to bed early at times. He thought it was a ruse, something she did to put off all his questioning and keep him with her longer. But maybe it was something else.

"Sawyer, please. Listen to me. You know what I can offer you."

"Money, power, prestige. I'm not interested in those things."

"Those aren't the only things." She stood and leaned her hands on the chair. "I'm offering you my legacy."

Her words stopped him. He hadn't thought of it that way. And for the first time he understood exactly how much she wanted to give him. It just wasn't anything he wanted.

"It's not God's will for me to live in New York. Or run your company."

"God's will?" Cora's voice grew indignant. "What does God have to do with any of this? He didn't create the company or make it what it is today. I did."

Sawyer shook his head. "You might not have acknowledged it, but God was with you all that time."

"I suppose He was with Kerry when she died too?" She stepped toward him, anger replacing the weariness in her eyes. "If He was, He would have saved her."

"We don't always understand God's ways."

"And I don't understand you. All this God talk. What does that have to do with anything?"

"God has everything to do with it. He's in control of my life, He guides my decisions." Pity made him start to reach for her hand. But he stopped. Anger radiated from her. Suddenly their fight about money and companies wasn't important anymore. "I know you miss her. I do too."

Cora looked away.

"For a long time I didn't understand why my parents died.

Why I had to live in a foster home. Even when I first lived with the Bylers, I was confused. But over time, I saw how God worked in other people's lives. In my life. He took me from the foster home to a loving family. Brought me to a community where I fit in, where I can make a permanent home. He brought Laura to me. Without Him, none of it would have happened."

"Coincidence. Circumstances. There's a rational explanation for everything."

"Along with a spiritual one."

They stared at each other. Sawyer could see this conversation wasn't going to end here. She didn't understand. He wasn't sure she ever would.

A few minutes ago all he wanted was for her to leave him alone. Now he realized something else: she was lost, in so many ways. She might have enough money to buy a small country, but she didn't have peace. Over the past few months he'd come to understand peace, how it only came from developing a closer relationship with the Lord. He wished the same for his grandmother.

How could he turn his back on her? If he did, he couldn't live with himself.

He touched her shoulder. She seemed to flinch at the gesture, and he realized he'd never even hugged her before. "Why don't you go upstairs and get some sleep? You look exhausted."

"I'm fine."

"Well, I'm exhausted. We can finish talking tomorrow. I promise. After work."

She turned from him, her shoulders slumping. Normally

she had perfect posture. "I suppose it's impossible for you to take a day off."

"How many days off have you had?"

Cora paused. "Touché."

"Grandmother, listen to me. We're not finished talking. Tomorrow when I get home from work—"

"I may not be here."

"I hope you will." A moment ago he'd wanted her to leave. Now he needed her to stay.

"Do you mean that?" She looked puzzled.

"Yes. I do. Good night, Cora."

He went upstairs. Shut his door. Leaned against it. And even after seeing how transparent she was, how single-minded and selfish she was being, he still knew that what he needed to do now was pray for her.

Cora stood, watching her grandson ascend the staircase. She held on to the edge of the chair, trying to keep her balance and her wits. Weariness washed over her, a heaviness that was more than physical. Her grandson had changed, even in the short time since she first met him. There was something about him—confidence, surety, calmness—she wasn't sure. Maybe it was all three. Of one thing she was certain: talking wouldn't convince him to change his course, even if they continued their conversation for the next five years.

Time she didn't have.

She dropped heavily into the chair. Even with all her money and prestige, she couldn't compete with these simple people. With the God who ruled their lives. It was as if her grandson had been brainwashed. He would join the church, get married, and she'd never see him again, despite any promises he might make to the contrary.

That filled her with more sadness than the idea of someone else running her company.

She couldn't let that happen. Yet how could she stop him?

Cora looked at her trembling hands. She had one weapon left in her arsenal. One she hadn't wanted to use. The last thing she wanted from anyone was pity. But this one time, perhaps she could use it to her advantage.

CHAPTER 14

Johnny woke up before dawn the next morning. He quickly did his chores and went back to the house. He showered, shaved, and put on a shirt and homespun pants, the ones that were the least wrinkled in his closet. He went back to the bathroom and combed his hair. The brush slipped out of his hand. He snatched it off the floor and tried to collect himself.

He had spent last night rehearsing what he would say to Katherine today when he dropped off her bag. He didn't know if she had to work, so he hoped to catch her at home. If he had to, he'd go to Mary Yoder's and wait for her to finish her shift. He was determined not to be a coward anymore.

But determination didn't settle his nerves—or eradicate the fear that she wouldn't see him, much less talk to him. He couldn't imagine sweet Katie sending him away. Yet he wouldn't blame her if she did.

He got himself in presentable shape and was just about to leave when his cell phone rang. It was a small, cheap phone, the kind you could buy off a rack at a discount store. And even though he had permission as a business owner, he felt guilty using it.

All thought of guilt vanished when he saw the name on the ID: *Wagner*. He clicked on the phone. "Hello?"

"John! How are you this fine morning?"

"Good." He looked at Katherine's bag lying on the table. He started pacing the length of his kitchen. "Yourself?"

"Doing fine. Wanted to let you know, Lois and I made a decision about investing in your venture." His boisterous voice paused.

"And?" Johnny gripped the phone. Held his breath. Prayed for the right answer.

"We'd like to talk about it with you further. We have some ideas we'd like to run past you before we make a large financial commitment."

"Ideas?"

"Yes. Lois came up with some terrific ways to make your little farm a huge success. But I don't believe in talking business over the phone. How about if we come out tonight? Have another one of those tasty meals you served last time?"

Johnny hesitated. No way he'd ask Katherine for her help again. Not until he'd smoothed things over with her. Even then, he wouldn't treat her like his personal caterer. He was done taking advantage of her.

"Tonight is fine. But I'll be honest, I'll have to order out."

"Your friend isn't available to cook?"

Johnny thought Wagner seemed overly fixated on food,

but who was he to judge? "No. She's not," he said firmly. "But takeout from Mary Yoder's is just as good."

Almost. It was a meal he could ill afford—it would take up most of what was left from his last paycheck. But what choice did he have?

"All right, that will be fine. About six o'clock?"

"Sure."

"We'll see you then—wait." Wagner's voice sounded far away. "What's that, hon? You want to meet earlier?" A pause, then Wagner's voice came through the phone receiver at full strength. "Lois said tonight isn't any good. Bridge club. She can't miss that."

"Ah." A muscle jerked in Johnny's jaw.

"How about lunch? We can be there in an hour."

Johnny looked at the clock on the wall. He'd have to put off seeing Katherine until tonight. But hopefully by then he'd have good news—an investor in his horse farm and a secure future to offer her. He relaxed and smiled. "I'll see you in an hour."

"Great. You're gonna be excited about what we have planned, John."

Johnny grinned wider. "I already am."

⌘

Laura sat on the small back deck of her parents' house in Ethridge, Tennessee. It was after eight, and a waning quarter moon bathed the scene in blue-white light. She'd arrived less than an hour ago, and she had barely set down her suitcase before her mother had put a cup of strong coffee in one hand and a donut stick in the other.

She sipped the coffee and breathed in the fragrance of blooming flowers. Azaleas, gardenias, even a whiff of night-blooming jasmine.

Everything here was the same as it had been when she left. Familiar. Comforting. Why had she waited so long to return?

But she knew the answer. Sawyer. She hadn't wanted to leave him. Even though she was sure of his love, a small part of her feared that her relationship with him was too good to be true. She had trusted Mark King too. Had thought she loved him. And that had brought her nothing but pain.

She gripped the coffee cup. Sawyer wasn't Mark, she reminded herself. And her love for him didn't compare to the infatuation she'd felt for Mark. Sawyer would be there for her when she returned. She was sure of it.

"I can't tell you how happy your *daed* and I are that you're home." Her mother bustled onto the deck and sat down next to her, also holding a cup of coffee and a plate of donut sticks. Her plump cheeks filled out further when she smiled. "We thought we might have to come after you."

"I didn't mean to worry you." She smiled, feeling at peace. "I'm glad Sawyer convinced me to come home."

"Sawyer. He's the *yung mann* you wrote to me about?" Laura's mother deposited the plate on the small table between them and cradled her cup in her hands.

Laura nodded. "He is."

"From your letters he sounds like a special *bu*."

"Very special." She grew serious. "He's nothing like Mark. I promise."

"*Lieb*, I'm sure he isn't. And you weren't the only one taken in by him." Her mother sighed.

"What?"

"I just wish you'd come home sooner. We missed you so much." Her mother blinked back tears. "I can't tell you how many times your *daed* and I thought about making the trip to Ohio. But after what happened with Mark, we didn't want to force you back. We knew you needed time. And your letters did give us some comfort. At least we knew you were all right."

Remorse filled her. "I'm sorry. I didn't mean to cause you both so much pain. Again." Laura stared at her lap. "I made so many bad choices."

"You're being too hard on yourself. We never blamed you for what happened."

"But it was all my fault."

"Not just yours. We trusted Mark too, remember? He worked for us in the bakery. We thought he was who he said he was." She touched Laura's arm. "He had us all fooled."

"He took your money because of me."

"He stole our money for himself. Although I appreciate you repaying it, we never expected you to." She looked at Laura. "How did you make so much money so fast? You mentioned an office job with a carpenter. I didn't realize they paid so much in Middlefield."

This was the moment Laura had dreaded. In her letters, her mother had never asked how she came up with the money. But it was only fair that she knew the truth. "Sawyer's grandmother gave me a check."

Her mother frowned. "She paid off your debt? To people she doesn't even know?"

"It's more complicated than that." She faced her mother and swallowed. "She paid me to leave Sawyer. I took the money and used it to find Mark." Shame filled her. "Then I gave the rest to you and *Daed*."

"Laura." Her mother shook her head.

"Mark would never have returned the money he stole."

"We would have managed without it. God always provides. Often in ways we don't expect."

Like Sawyer. God had provided a man who healed her heart, even when she thought she'd never love again.

"I wish you hadn't left us," her mother continued. "I wish you'd stayed here and let it all be. Then maybe . . ." She looked away.

"I wouldn't have the scars?"

Her mother nodded. With her fingertip she wiped underneath her eyes. "I wish you hadn't gone through it alone."

"I didn't. I had the Lord. He was always with me. And I had Sawyer." She angled her body toward her mother. "If I hadn't gone to Middlefield, I wouldn't have let *geh* of my resentment toward Mark. It would have grown inside of me until it would have taken me over completely. I realize that now. I would have never learned to trust God. To let Him deliver justice, not me. Mark's in prison for what he's done, but he'll also have to face the Lord."

"Very true." Strain showed on her mother's face. "But how can you love a man whose *familye* would pay to be rid of you?" Laura let out an involuntary gasp. "I don't mean to hurt you, *kinn*," her mother continued, "but you told me as much just now."

Laura gripped her coffee cup. "That was Sawyer's *grossmudder*. She doesn't understand."

"Maybe she understands more than you think. Don't you think you're rushing into things with Sawyer? Much as you rushed into a bad relationship with Mark?"

"I'm in love, *Mamm*. Truly in love."

Even in the moonlight, Laura could see the hard look her mother gave her. "You thought you were in love with Mark."

"This is different." She set her cup down on the deck. The peace she felt a moment ago vanished. "I should have stayed in Middlefield."

Her mother stood. "*Nee*. You did the right thing. You came back. And you need to stay here, and not just for a couple of weeks. Put some separation between you and Sawyer. Pray about what you're doing—"

"How can you judge someone you haven't met?"

"I'm not judging."

"Sounds like it to me. And you sound just like his *grossmudder*, dismissing him before you get to know him."

"Has he joined the church yet?"

She shook her head. "He plans to in a few weeks. He's meeting with the bishop. And he's lived with his adoptive *familye* since he was fourteen. They let him make his own decision to join the church. Like you let me."

"And is he joining the church for the right reasons?"

Laura didn't hesitate with her answer. "Absolutely."

Her mother sat down. She didn't say anything for a long time. Dread filled Laura. She had wanted her parents, especially her mother, to be happy for her. Instead, *Mamm* seemed anything but. "We plan to marry in November," she said.

"So soon?"

"That's nearly six months away."

"When is he coming to Ethridge?"

"We're getting married in Middlefield."

A heavy sigh escaped her mother. "Why would you do that?"

She looked at her mother, her gaze intent. "Middlefield is home to me now. I love you and *Daed*, but I have to be where *mei* husband is. His business is in Middlefield. His *familye*." She didn't mention Cora.

"But what about your friends here? Your *familye*?" Her mother bit her lip. "Does this mean you'll never come back home?"

"Of course I'll visit as often as I can," Laura said. "And I hope you will come and see us."

Her mother looked away. "You're determined, then."

"*Ya*. I am."

Suddenly her mother jumped up from her chair. "I can't believe this, Laura. First you want me to accept that you're marrying someone who's not Amish—"

"He will be—"

"Who we don't know, whose *familye* tried to get rid of you—"

"I already explained that."

"It doesn't make sense. And now you want to get married

not only in another district but another state. All this after we haven't seen you for months?" She crossed her arms over her chest. "You're being selfish, Laura. Flat-out selfish."

Tears welled in her eyes. "*Mamm*, please—"

But her mother spun around and went inside the house.

Laura flinched as the door slammed shut.

Johnny showed up at Mary Yoder's right before noon. He'd called in his order half an hour earlier and had a taxi bring him so the food wouldn't get cold on the way home. He went inside to the counter and gave the girl behind the register his name.

"Your order will be right up." The Yankee girl smiled and gestured for him to move to the side. Another couple behind him was ready to cash out.

Before he stepped away, he asked, "Is Katherine Yoder working today?"

The girl paused. "I don't think so. I haven't seen her."

"Okay, thanks."

He shoved his hands in his pockets and looked at a few of the items in the gift shop—Amish novels and cookbooks on the rack, Amish-themed gifts, candles, and baked goods. He knew this stuff appealed to tourists and that the tourist trade was important to lots of Amish families in the area. He wouldn't begrudge them making an honest living. But he had no desire to cater to the Yankees in that way.

The hypocrisy of his thought struck him. He was willing to have Yankee partners, but not have a tourist business?

But the two things were completely different. He would be running a farm, not a visitor center.

Johnny rocked back on the heels of his boots, waiting for his order to arrive. He felt a tap on his shoulder. He turned around and saw the girl who had waited on him behind the counter.

"Do you want me to check and see if Katherine's in the kitchen?" she asked.

"*Ya*. That would be great, thanks."

The young woman nodded and left him in the gift shop area. Plenty of people surrounded him, murmuring about this or that item. Within a few moments she was back, shaking her head as she walked toward him.

"She was scheduled to work, but she called off sick."

Johnny frowned. Katie was sick? She'd seemed fine the other day. "Do you know what's wrong?"

"She didn't say. Katherine rarely calls off, so I'm sure whatever it is, she isn't feeling well. The cook also told me to let you know someone will bring your food right up."

He nodded as she walked away. Now he was worried and wanted to see her more than ever. But it would have to wait until after his meeting with the Wagners. He started to pace. Where was that food?

Finally an Amish girl brought out two bags. Johnny took them from her, quickly paid, and went to the taxi waiting outside. He tried to mentally prepare for his meeting with the Wagners, but that took a backseat to his concern for Katherine. As soon as they left, he would go and check on her. Right now all he could do was say a silent prayer that she would be better soon.

CHAPTER 15

Katherine lay on the couch in the living room, her eyes shut against the dim light coming through the front window. Her mother had drawn the curtains, but it hadn't helped much.

She put her arm over her forehead and prayed for the pain to go away. She was rarely sick, and never this sick. It had aggravated her to call off work, but she couldn't do her job properly with such excruciating pain radiating through her head and down into her neck.

"Katherine?"

She turned and barely opened her eyes as her mother came into the living room carrying a tray with a mug and a plate of saltine crackers. She wasn't hungry or thirsty, but she tried to sit up anyway.

"Feeling any better?"

"A little." It wasn't true, but the words slightly alleviated her mother's worried expression.

"*Gut.* I brought you some tea. I put a cinnamon stick in the water as I brewed it. This should help with the headache." She set the tray on the end table next to the couch.

Katherine sat up and took the mug. The strong cinnamon scent made her stomach lurch, as did the sight of the crackers. But if the tea would get rid of the pain, she'd drink it. She took a small sip, the hot tea burning as it slid down her throat. *"Danki,"* she said.

Her mother perched at the edge of the chair, frowning. "If you're not better by tomorrow, I'm taking you to the doctor."

Katherine shook her head. "I'm sure I'll be fine. It's a simple headache."

"A simple headache doesn't last two days. And it doesn't put you on the couch."

"Then maybe it's a migraine." She took another sip of tea and forced a smile. "See? Better already."

"It doesn't work that fast." She stood. "Try to eat a couple of the crackers too." Her worried expression returned. "And don't try to do any quilting. Or crocheting. Or knitting. Or—"

"Ya. I understand." Her mother knew her too well. Despite the pain, she was bored, and irritated because she could be doing something productive instead of lying on the couch. The tea had cooled off a bit, and she took a longer drink, praying it would relieve her headache. Even if it went away enough so she could work on Rachel's quilt, she'd be satisfied.

But after she finished the tea, she lay back down, still in pain. Her mother said it would take time. Until then she'd try to get some sleep.

Johnny sat in silence as Wagner and his wife, Lois, chowed down on the meal he'd brought from Mary Yoder's. He'd guessed right about the fried chicken, as well as the mashed potatoes, green beans, coleslaw, and pecan pie for dessert. They'd barely said anything while they finished their meal. He tapped his fingers against his kneecaps, waiting.

Finally Wagner wiped his mouth with a paper napkin. "Good stuff. And speaking of stuffed, that's what I am."

"Me too." Lois took one last bite of her pie. "Thank you for lunch, Johnny." She eyed his plate. "You didn't eat much."

He thought about making an excuse, but if he was going to be partners with them, he should be honest up front. "I'm worried about a friend. She's not feeling well. I'm hoping to check on her after our meeting."

"I'm sorry to hear that. I hope she gets well soon."

"Me too."

Wagner shoved his plate aside. "We should get to the point, Lois. We can't take up this young man's day. Not when he has a *friend* he's concerned about." Wagner winked at Johnny.

"Yes. You're right." Lois set her plate to one side. Then she picked up her enormous lime green handbag and pulled out a folded sheet of paper. When she spread it out on the table, it looked like a sketch of his property, but with buildings, paths, and small stick drawings of people scattered all over it.

He leaned forward and examined the paper. "What is this?"

"This," Wagner said, beaming, "is our future."

"Huh?"

"I just want you to know that I could get behind your original idea of a horse farm. Thought it was a great one, actually." He paused to pick at his teeth, then continued, "But Lois and I were talking the other day, and she came up with something I think is even better." He looked at his wife. "That's my Lois. She's a smart one."

Lois grinned. "Thank you, dear."

Johnny looked up from the drawing. "I don't understand. You're not going to invest in the farm?"

"Oh, we're going to invest, all right."

Johnny released a sigh of relief. "That's good to hear."

"But it won't just be a horse farm." He turned to his wife. "Lois, tell him your brilliant idea."

A knot of dread twisted in Johnny's stomach even before Lois said a single word. He looked at the drawing again, this time more carefully. As he leaned closer, he could see words written on the square-shaped buildings, printed in neat, uniform script. His eye caught the shape that represented the barn where it currently stood. But instead of barn, the words *candy shoppe* were visible.

"I believe this place has so much more potential than being a simple horse farm," Lois said.

"But I *want* it to be a simple horse farm."

She looked at him with a mix of sympathy and pity. "John, John," she said. "You have to take into consideration the bigger picture. You want your business to be a success, right?"

"*Ya.*"

"And we want to make money," Wagner interjected. "We want a large return on our investment. And frankly, we couldn't make the numbers work, even though the idea was appealing."

"So I did a little research about the area." Lois folded her slender hands on the table. "We live near Holmes County. Do you know how many people visit that area in a year?"

Johnny shook his head, the knot growing tighter inside him. "I have no idea."

"Thousands. And they all bring money with them. Money they're happy to spend. You could have that kind of money right here on your property. All you'd need are the attractions."

He frowned. "Attractions?"

"Let me show you." Lois pointed to the candy shoppe. "We can tear down the barn and put a smaller building here. This would be Mullet's Candies and Gifts. We'd sell everything from chocolates and pies to knickknacks and small furniture. Of course, everything would be Amish made."

"Or would have an Amish name." Wagner grinned. "The word *Amish* is golden, son."

Johnny held up his hand. "But—"

"And then behind the house we would have a petting zoo." Lois tapped at a large rectangle on the sketch.

"A zoo?"

"Kids love a zoo. With all those cute little goats and pot-bellied pigs and lambs and sheep. And if we can bring in kids, we can bring in their parents." She grinned. "But that's not the best part."

"It isn't?" Johnny said weakly.

"The best part is the bed-and-breakfast."

His heart sank. He wasn't even sure what a bed-and-breakfast was. He'd seen a couple around town but never paid much attention. "Where would that go?"

"Right where we're sitting." She spread out her arms. "We'd have to gut the house, of course. And add on. But we could turn this into a charming bed-and-breakfast. A place where people can escape their hectic worlds and enjoy the simple life the Amish so quaintly live."

Johnny clenched his jaw. He didn't appreciate Lois talking about his community as if it existed to serve and entertain Yankees. And they still hadn't told him what he really needed to hear. "Where would the horses go?"

Lois pointed to the petting zoo. "Not to worry. We'll have ponies here too—"

"Not ponies. Horses. The ones I plan to breed and sell." He scanned the drawing. "I don't see a horse barn here. Or a pasture." He did see the words *guided tours* scribbled on the paper, as if the idea had been an afterthought, but an enthusiastic one considering the three exclamation points after the words.

"The barn is right here." She pointed to a smaller rectangle a short distance from the petting zoo. "An authentic Amish barn, complete with old-fashioned equipment."

"Like a plow," Wagner said.

"And a thresher," Lois added.

Wagner nodded. "Don't forget the buggy."

"Of course. But it will be for show only." Lois snapped her

fingers. "Honey, what do you think about putting a spinning wheel in there?"

"I think it's a fine idea." He put his arm around his wife. "Won't the tourists just love that?"

Johnny looked at both of them. Were they serious? "We don't use spinning wheels."

"Oh, like that matters." Lois waved him off. "No one will know the difference, and people will find it adorable."

"Okay." Johnny could feel the irritation rise inside of him. "Maybe I wasn't clear at our first meeting. This is a horse farm. Not a tourist stop."

"Son," Wagner said, dropping his arm from Lois's shoulder. He looked directly at Johnny. "This place is a dump right now. It's nothing. And without our money, it will stay nothing for a very long time."

Johnny sucked in a breath. He couldn't say anything, because they were right. At least about the place being a dump.

"Lois has a gift for seeing potential. She has a good head for business, and she's smart." Wagner looked at his wife. "It's why I married her. And I fully support her plan."

Lois patted Johnny's hand. "I understand your resistance, John."

"I'm not so sure you do," he said.

"But sometimes you have to let go of a dream and build a new one." She smiled. "A better and more lucrative one."

"So this is all about money for you."

Wagner shook his head. "It's also about success. Why do you think we have enough money to sink into something like this? It's because we don't invest in anything that could fail."

"My horse farm won't fail."

"How much do you know about breeding horses?"

Johnny's eyes narrowed. "I know a *lot* about horses. I've bred them. I've raised them. I've trained them."

Wagner leaned back. Crossed his hands over his expansive stomach. "Then how much do you know about running a business? Have you ever started one? Have you nurtured it to fruition? Have you expanded it and made it better than your initial idea ever was?"

Johnny paused. "No."

"Then you should listen to people who have. We know what we're talking about here."

"John." Lois gave him a sympathetic smile. "If you want to have a little horse breeding operation on the side, you can do that. We'll purchase the land next door and you can build your own barn. You mentioned that in your cute little business plan, if I remember. You can raise two or three horses, if that makes you happy."

Suddenly Johnny realized the full extent of what the Wagners were saying. The farm wouldn't be his. His house wouldn't be his. The Wagners would own everything. They would run everything. They hadn't invested a dime, and Lois was already coddling him, giving him permission to play at horse farming, as if he were a child.

"I can't do this," he said quietly.

"What did you say?" Wagner asked.

Johnny took a deep breath, collecting his thoughts. "Don't get me wrong. I don't have anything against businesses that attract Yankees. But that's not the type of business I want to be in. And you're right, I don't know how to run a business. But I also don't know how to run a bed-and-breakfast or a petting zoo or a candy shop."

"Oh, you won't have to do any of that," Lois said. "We'll hire locals to work those jobs."

"Then what would I do?"

Wagner smiled. "Sit back and count your money."

Johnny shook his head. "That's not what I want."

Lois's kind expression hardened. "I think you need to take a long, hard look, not at what you want, but what you need. Right now you have nothing. We're giving you the opportunity to have something. Something great."

Again Johnny wiped his sweaty palms against his pants. As much as he didn't want to admit it, the Wagners were right, at least in part. He didn't have anything. That was part of the reason he hadn't told Katherine how he felt about her. He'd wanted a secure future. A successful business. The Wagners were offering him that opportunity.

But what would Katherine think? And his family? He'd made such a big deal about being successful as a horse farmer. Even though he wasn't seriously considering signing the Wagners' offer, he also couldn't bring himself to say no. But if he partnered with them, the business wouldn't be his.

And yet if he agreed to their terms, he wouldn't have to worry about the future. He wouldn't have to scour Middlefield looking for a job, like he and his father and Caleb were doing. Last week he'd gotten his last check and worked his last day for Bender. He wouldn't live hand-to-mouth, which was the life he was facing right now. He could provide a comfortable life for him and Katherine—if she still cared about him.

"You need some time," Lois said, her cheerful demeanor returning. "I'll leave this with you." She patted the sketch. "You take a look at it. Then let us know in a couple of days what you decide." She stood, grabbing her handbag from the floor.

"Just don't take too long." Wagner also rose, standing close to his wife. "We've driven around Middlefield. There are plenty of properties for sale around here, properties that would be just right for this type of business." He grinned at Johnny. "But since you came to us, we feel it's only fair to offer you the opportunity first."

Johnny nodded. "I'll give it some thought." Even saying the words out loud made him ill. But maybe Lois was right. Maybe he'd have to give up one dream to pursue a better one.

He just wished he didn't feel so apprehensive about it.

Cora sat outside the Bylers' home, in the swing where she'd fallen asleep the day she first arrived. During the day while Sawyer was at work, she'd been spending more time outside. The longer she stayed here, the more her body seemed to crave the fresh air. The warmth of the sun. She seemed to get cold more easily lately. She would wrap her scarf closer to her neck, put on her cashmere sweater, and swing, trying to keep her mind more focused on the present than the past. Too many bitter memories there.

Yet there were times when she didn't think about anything. Her mind, her heart, became quiet. Almost still.

She chalked it up to boredom. Or at least tried to.

The cell phone in her pocket rang. She retrieved it and looked at the screen. Her attorney. She pressed the green answer button. "Kenneth."

"Hello, Cora. Just checking in."

"Nothing to report. I've only been here a few days."

"Are you at least trying to enjoy yourself? I hear Amish country is lovely this time of year."

Cora scowled. "What do you know of Amish country? You were born and raised in Manhattan."

"I did a bit of reading about the area. May have to visit there myself. If I ever get a vacation."

"Is that a dig, Kenneth?"

"Of course not." He chuckled. "A joke, Cora. You had a sense of humor once upon a time."

Years ago. "What do you need, Kenneth?"

"I was wondering if you had a return date in mind. I've done all I can with your assets, but there are still a few documents that need your signature. And . . ." He hesitated. "I want you to be certain you want to do this."

"I'm certain. As for when I'm coming home, I'm still not sure." She looked up to see Anna coming out of the house, carrying two glasses. "I have to go, Kenneth. I'll be in touch."

"Cora—"

She clicked off the phone. Anna smiled as she approached.

"Mind if I join you?" Anna asked. "I brought us some lemonade."

Cora gestured to the empty seat beside her. She accepted the glass Anna offered but didn't say anything.

The two women sat in silence for a few moments, surrounded by the soft sounds of chirping birds. Cora looked down at her lemonade. No ice. Pieces of pulp floating around. Fresh squeezed, no doubt by Anna herself. She turned to the woman who called herself Sawyer's mother. "How do you stand it?"

Anna frowned, her blue eyes squinting in the bright sunlight. "What do you mean?"

"This." She held up the glass. "Squeezing your own juice. Milking your own cows. Dusting your own tables." At Anna's incredulous look, she added, "How do you manage to live like a drudge?"

To Cora's surprise, Anna laughed. "I never thought I was a drudge. I'm just living my life. Like you live yours."

"But your life is so . . . difficult." Cora looked at her manicured nails, comparing them to Anna's stubby ones. "And, dare I say, dull? Housework day in and day out, baking, sewing clothes." She shook her head. "Don't you think you're destined for more?"

"Like the business world?"

"Perhaps. Or at least a job outside the house. Why do you choose to be tethered like the horse that pulls your buggy?"

Anna stared out at the green lawn in front of them. "I used

to own a business. Me and *mei mamm*. It's what brought us to Middlefield."

Cora's mouth dropped. "You did?"

"*Ya*. A gift shop. I met Lukas when he came into the store before we opened. He helped us fix up the building, which is near the flea market. We sold all kinds of Amish goods, including small toys and crafts Lukas and his *bruders* made in their shop."

Stunned, Cora angled toward her. "What happened to the business?"

"A short while after Lukas and I married, I sold it. *Mei mamm* and her *schwoger* moved back to Maryland, where I'm originally from."

"Do you miss it?"

"Maryland? *Ya*, sometimes."

Cora shook her head. "Owning a business. Having something you can call your own, that you can be successful at."

Anna waved a hand at her surroundings. "This is mine. Well, not completely. It's a gift from God." She smiled. "This is *mei* job, to take care of *mei familye*. And I don't consider it drudgery. It's a privilege." She took a drink of her lemonade and stood. "Speaking of work, I have bread in the oven I need to check on."

Cora watched Anna walk back to the house. She had answered Cora's questions honestly and with kindness. For a fleeting moment, she thought about Kerry. Her daughter would approve of Anna Byler.

They might even have been friends.

CHAPTER 16

Later that afternoon Katherine still hadn't left the couch. Bekah was sitting with her, reading a book. Katherine's headache hadn't lessened. If anything, it was getting worse. But she wasn't about to admit it. Instead she closed her eyes and pretended she was asleep.

A knock sounded at the door. Katherine's eyes flew open. Bekah had already jumped out of her seat. "I'll get it."

Katherine slowly sat up, the throbbing in her head intensifying. She'd tried aspirin. *Mamm's* tea. Neither had worked, and she didn't know what to do. Maybe she'd have to go to the dreaded doctor after all.

Bekah's voice came from the doorway. "Oh. Hi, Johnny."

Katherine jerked her head toward the doorway, which didn't help her neck or head pain. Johnny? What was he doing here?

Bekah turned and mouthed those exact words to Katherine. Katherine shrugged, and Bekah stepped aside to let him in.

Johnny came in looking spit-shined and polished, not dirty and dusty from working outside, as he had the other day. He had obviously taken special care with his appearance.

Despite the raging headache, Katherine couldn't help noticing how handsome he was. She pushed the unwelcome thought aside. Whatever reason Johnny had for coming here, or why he'd spiffed up in the middle of the day, it had nothing to do with her.

Then his gaze met hers. His chocolate-brown eyes grew soft. "How are you feeling?"

She frowned. "How did you know I was sick?"

"I stopped by Mary Yoder's, and they said you'd called off work."

Despite her resolve to give up on Johnny Mullet forever, Katherine felt her heart flip. What had he been doing at her workplace? Then she saw the bag in his hands. Her quilted bag, the one she'd brought to his house when she'd fixed supper for him and his friends.

He was here to return her bag, that was all. Not because he cared about her, not because he wanted to see her. Not any of the things she had wished for—

"I wondered if I could talk to you," he said, shifting from one foot to the other He glanced at the floor, then at Bekah. When Bekah didn't move, he added, "Privately." He looked at Katherine. "If you're up to it, that is."

Bekah turned to Katherine, giving her a questioning lift of her brow. Katherine nodded. "It's okay."

"I'll *geh* help *Mamm* in the kitchen."

Katherine hoped her sister had enough sense not to tell their mother that Johnny was here. If she did, her mother would probably come storming out and demand that Johnny leave. Katherine didn't want that. She needed to know what he wanted to talk about.

Johnny stood there for a moment, as if unsure what to do. Then he walked over to her, holding out her bag. "You forgot this the other *daag.*"

"*Danki.*" She took the bag from him and set it on the floor beside her feet. When he didn't move, she gestured to the chair across from her. "You can sit down, if you want."

"Oh. *Ya.*" He gave her a half smile and took the chair. He swiped his hands over his knees as she waited for him to speak. But now he didn't seem in any hurry to talk.

The silence echoed in her aching head. Finally she couldn't stand it anymore. "You said you wanted to talk to me?"

"I—um . . ." He looked away again, color reddening his cheeks. She'd never seen him act shy around her like this before. Even when she was at his house, after a few short, awkward moments they had settled into being comfortable with each other. Now he looked ready to leap out of his skin.

A sharp pain rattled her head. She touched her fingertips to her temples and closed her eyes.

"Katherine?"

She opened her eyes at his tender tone. He was leaning forward, almost to the point where he was slipping off the chair.

"Are you all right?"

"I'm fine." But the pain intensified.

"You don't look fine." He searched her face, concern furrowing his brow. Then he got up and sat next to her. "How long have you felt like this?"

"Long enough." Her head and neck hurt so fiercely that she didn't have the energy to figure out why he was sitting so close to her. Worse, she couldn't even enjoy it. Her stomach twisted like a baked pretzel.

"You're pale," he said.

"I'll be all right." She looked at him. Under normal circumstances she'd be ecstatic that he was here, showing her such concern. But her headache, combined with her determination to move on with her life, pushed her over the edge. "What did you want to talk about?"

"Maybe I should wait until you feel better."

"Maybe you should let me decide that." The words came out sharp as a knife, but she couldn't help it. She'd spent her whole life not being in control, especially where Johnny was concerned. She'd had enough. "Is there something else you want from me? Clean your *haus* or mend your clothes or cook your supper?" Sarcasm dripped from her words, but she didn't care. "Then you can kick me out when I'm done."

His jaw dropped open. "*Nix*, that's not it at all. I came to thank you. You know, for the other day. And to apologize for rushing you out of there. I'm sorry I hurt your feelings." He looked at her intently. "I'm sorry for all the times I've hurt you."

A dizzy sensation overcame her as she looked at him, digesting his words. She gripped the edge of the sofa. He was so close she could see the black stubble of his beard, which he'd shave off in the morning as a sign of not being married. His long, dark lashes brushed against the top of his cheeks. Her own blond lashes were practically invisible.

She shook her head, trying to focus. He had just apologized, something she'd hoped to hear for years. Why was she thinking about eyelashes at a time like this?

Johnny put his hat on the table. "I acted like a jerk. I've been acting like a jerk."

She squinted at him. Vaguely, in the back of her mind, she realized that this was something new. She ought to be impressed. Ought to respond.

He kept talking. "The Wagners really liked supper. They thought the house was cozy. Or quaint, I can't remember the exact word. But that was all due to you." He looked down at her again, and she felt her cheeks grow hot. "I noticed the curtains."

"You did?"

"They're very nice. You didn't have to do that."

"I know. But the living room needed something."

"A *maedel's* touch." He glanced at her hands, which were settled in her lap.

Now her stomach was twisting like a tire swing in the wind. A wave of nausea crashed over her, just as another throb of pain radiated down her neck.

He was still rattling on. "So, anyway, I came to thank you for those—the curtains, I mean—and everything else you did." He stared at her straight on with his deep, dark brown eyes, longer than he'd ever looked at her before. "I appreciate it. I just wanted you to know that."

The sudden softness in his voice barely registered. Even though the living room was warm, she hugged her arms, her body shuddering with a sudden chill. The stiffness in her neck increased, as if she'd just woken up from sleeping at an odd angle. She rubbed at it, trying to ease the pain.

"Katie?"

She looked up at him. He seemed a long way away. "What did you just call me?"

He cleared his throat. "Are you sure you're okay?"

Another wave of nausea came over her. She stood up, ready to run to the bathroom. "I—I don't know." Then the dizziness hit full force. She reached out, grabbing his forearm with her hand.

Instead of removing her hand, he covered it with his own. "I should get your *mamm*."

"*Nee!*" Her mother would just throw him out. There was something Katherine needed to know first. Her mind, hazy, guided by pain and a sudden need for the truth, forced her to speak the words that had been on her heart for years.

"Johnny, why are you really here?"

"I told you, to say thank you—"

"You already thanked me."

"I had to bring you your bag."

She closed her eyes and rubbed the back of her neck. "You could have waited until Sunday." Her gaze narrowed as she looked up at him. "Why do you treat me like this? The other day you couldn't wait to get rid of me, and today you're at *mei haus*."

He gripped her hand but averted his gaze. Guilt flashed in

his eyes before he looked away. "I know. Just let me explain. I came to tell you something else—"

Katherine pulled out of his grasp and gripped her head in her hands. The pain was almost unbearable. "You know how I feel about you." She tried to turn her neck to look up at him, but she could barely move. "You've always known. And you've never done anything about it."

"Katie, I—"

"Why can't you be honest with me?"

"I've never lied to you."

"Don't play dumb, Johnny. You're lying right now."

Suddenly the room heaved and shifted, as if she were on an out-of-control merry-go-round. She bent at the waist, trying to steady herself, and breathed in deeply. She should sit down. Call for her *mamm*. Or do both. But she couldn't let this go. Not until she finally got a straight answer from Johnny.

"We're too old to be playing games."

Johnny put his arm around her shoulders. "I'm not playing games. Not anymore. I care about you. A lot. I should have told you a long time ago."

But she didn't respond. Instead, she looked at the floor, then closed her eyes.

"Katherine, I think there's something seriously wrong. This isn't like you."

"I'm tired of being like me. Tired of getting my feelings hurt, tired of people feeling sorry for me." She gripped her temples. Was somebody pounding nails through them? "I'm tired . . . so tired."

"Katie?"

He sounded far away. And why did he keep calling her Katie? Black dots swam before her eyes. Her ears pounded and her head roared.

Then the blackness closed in like a suffocating blanket, and there was nothing more.

Fear clawed at Johnny as he held an unconscious Katherine in his arms. Her skin, normally fair, was now stark white, her lips colorless. He rubbed her cheek with the palm of his hand, as if the gesture would wake her up. She didn't respond.

"Katie? Katie!" Johnny picked her up and laid her on the couch. He knelt beside her, holding her hand.

"Katherine?" Her mother dashed into the room. She glared at Johnny. "What are you doing here?"

"I just wanted to talk to her—"

"What did you do?" She edged her way between him and Katie, forcing him to drop her hand. "Why did you upset her?"

"I didn't!" But she had been upset, right before she passed out. She'd also been acting very weird. Her beautiful face, normally so bright and placid, had been contorted with pain. "She was complaining about her head hurting."

"And you didn't come get me? Bekah!"

Katherine's sister appeared behind them, her frightened expression mirroring her mother's.

"*Geh* to the call box and dial 911." Her mother didn't

turn around. She gripped Katie's hand. "Katherine? Can you hear me?"

Johnny yanked his cell phone out of his pocket. "I'll call the ambulance." He quickly dialed emergency services. When he hung up, Katherine was still unconscious. Helpless, he asked, "Is there anything else I can do?"

"You can leave." *Frau* Yoder's tone sliced through him.

Johnny looked at Bekah, who nodded. Without a word he stood, picked up his hat, and went outside. He'd leave the house, but not the property, not until the paramedics arrived. He paced the front porch a couple of times. Then the front door opened and Bekah stepped outside.

"Is she awake?" he asked, fisting his hands.

Bekah nodded. "She's coming to. But, Johnny, you have to leave. *Mamm* is really upset right now, and if she sees you here—"

In the distance he could hear the wail of a siren. "I'm not going anywhere. Not until I know she's all right."

Bekah frowned for a moment, then took Johnny away from the front door. "What's your phone number? I'll make sure to let you know what happens at the hospital."

"But you don't have a phone."

"I'll find one!" She pulled a pen out of the pocket of her apron and opened her palm. "What's your number?"

He told her and she scribbled it down before closing her fist. "Now *geh*. I promise, I'll be in touch with you." She turned and ran back in the house.

Johnny remained on the porch as the siren grew closer.

Panic gripped him, and he closed his eyes, his own problems fading away as he focused on Katherine. *Lord, please help her. Make sure she's all right. And I promise, when this is over, I'll never leave her side.*

Cora sat on the edge of the plain, uncomfortable single bed at the Bylers' house. She missed her king-size down mattress, where she had plenty of room to stretch out and get comfortable. Lately, despite her fatigue, she'd had trouble sleeping at night. Since she'd stopped drinking wine, she feared she'd have to resort to sleeping pills.

More medication. Just what she didn't want.

Despite her conversation with Anna that morning, Cora had refused her lunch invitation. She had little appetite, and having had more time to ponder Anna's words, Cora realized she'd accomplished nothing other than discovering how deeply entrenched Sawyer was in this Amish foolishness. She wouldn't be able to get him back to New York. Not anytime soon.

She sighed. Why couldn't his adoptive family be cretins? Or money hungry? Anything that would allow her to buy her grandson's freedom. Yet they were neither, and they were happy with their lot. That even seemed to include Cora's presence. Neither Anna nor Lukas had made her feel like an imposition.

She wouldn't be able to say the same if the situation were reversed.

She needed to regroup, to figure out another way to get

Sawyer away from these people and with his true family. Yet she rejected every idea she'd come up with. She'd even thought to draw on his compassion, which he seemed to have in spades. After all, he'd fallen in love with a permanently scarred young woman. But the only way she could draw on his pity was to admit her weakness—Parkinson's. And she just couldn't bring herself to do that. Not yet.

The phone beeped, indicating the battery was almost dead. She didn't have an outlet to plug it into, or even a car to charge it. Fine, let the phone die.

A knock sounded at the door. Cora sighed and stood. She was a little wobbly, but quickly regained her balance and walked to the door. When she opened it, she saw Anna standing there. "Yes?"

"I wondered if you'd like some tea. I just made a fresh pot." She twisted the end of one of the white ribbons dangling from the headgear she wore. What an unflattering hat. Cora thought that if the women in this community had to wear something on their heads, at least it could be fashionable. Yet these were the least fashion-conscious people she'd seen in her life.

"I'm fine," Cora said, not inviting Anna in. Instead she started to close the door.

Anna slipped inside. "You've been up here all afternoon. I know you're waiting for Sawyer to come home. He should be here in an hour or so. I thought we could visit a little more downstairs until he and Lukas came home."

Cora lifted her chin. "I think we both understand each other's perspectives."

Anna's smile slipped slightly. "That's not what I meant. We haven't had much of a chance to get to know each other. I thought you could tell me about Sawyer's mother."

Cora turned away. "I'd rather not talk about my daughter."

"Okay." Anna's voice held a small tremble. "Then maybe you could tell me about New York? I've never been there before."

A tiny sliver of ice thawed around Cora's thickly encased heart. Anna knew why Cora was here—to take Sawyer away. Still, she made an effort not only to be hospitable and friendly but to make Cora feel at home. She would never understand these people. "I'll just wait here until Sawyer returns."

Anna nodded, taking a few steps backward. "I'll send him up when he gets here."

"Thank you." Cora followed her, almost pushing her out the door. When Anna left, Cora closed the door and sat back on the bed. She folded her hands in her lap, keeping her back straight.

The phone beeped two more times. Cora watched as the screen turned black. Her last contact with the outside world.

She didn't care about that now. All she wanted was to talk with Sawyer. To make one last effort to convince him where his true destiny lay—not here with these people, but with his blood family.

This was his last chance. She was done begging. And if he refused her—then he would never see her again.

CHAPTER 17

Sawyer was just finishing cleaning up the shop when Adam Otto walked in. "Always nice to see you, Adam. But in case you didn't notice, we're closed." He grinned.

"I noticed. That's why I came by. Emma would like you to come over for supper."

Sawyer ran the broom over the sawdust-covered floor. "That's nice of you, but I was just there. Anna does feed me, you know."

Adam nodded. "I'm sure she does." His expression grew serious. "Actually, it wasn't Emma's idea. It was Leona's."

"Oh?"

"She wants you to bring your grandmother."

Sawyer stopped sweeping. "Why?"

Adam shrugged. "I don't know. Leona didn't explain—just told me and Emma that she wanted both of you to come."

"When?"

"Before Laura gets back. How about tomorrow night?"

Sawyer leaned the broom against the wall. "I'm not sure."

"Not sure you want to come over?"

"Not sure *she'll* come." He put his hands on his hips. "Still, it might be a good idea. I've been trying to explain to Cora why I'm joining the church. She doesn't understand it."

"I take it she doesn't have faith."

"I'm positive she doesn't."

"Well, I know from experience that no one can force you to accept God's role in your life. I ran away from that for so long. Good thing God didn't give up on me." He grinned. "Or Emma either, for that matter."

Sawyer nodded. "I have to admit, I get where Cora's coming from. When I first came here, I didn't understand anything about this way of life. But she's a tougher nut to crack."

"Maybe talking to Leona would do her some *gut*."

"If I can convince her to come."

Adam slapped him on the shoulder. "I'm sure you'll think of something. We'll see you both at six." He started to leave.

"Hey, Adam," Sawyer said.

Adam turned around. *"Ya?"*

"You and your *daed* wouldn't happen to have any extra work on your farm? Johnny came by a few weeks ago. I know he's looking to pick up a few jobs here and there."

Adam shook his head. "Not right now. Come harvest we will. Tell him to talk to me in a couple of months."

"Thanks."

Just as Adam left, Lukas came out of the office in the back of the shop. "I'll be glad when Laura gets back," he said. "I really don't like doing that paperwork."

"Have Tobias help you out."

"You know better than that." He scratched his chin. "Did I hear you right? Johnny's still looking for work?"

"I think so. Have things changed around here?"

Lukas shook his head. "*Nee*. Tobias left at lunch today because there wasn't much to do."

"Are you worried?"

"This has happened before. God will provide. He'll give us what we need while we're slow, and when it's His timing, business will pick up again."

"You really believe that?"

Lukas's dark eyes met his. "Don't you?"

Sawyer stopped sweeping. "Yes. But I wish there was something we could do for Johnny."

"As soon as we have more work than we can handle, I'll hire him on."

"Thanks. But I hope he finds work before then."

"I heard he bought some property awhile back." Lukas wiped sawdust off one of the tables. "I was talking to his father at church the other *daag*. A horse farm, apparently."

Sawyer frowned. Johnny hadn't mentioned the farm to him. "I didn't know he wanted to raise horses."

"Neither did his *vadder*. Seems like Johnny might be in over his head financially with this one."

Sawyer nodded. Now his friend's desperation made sense, and it made Sawyer more eager to help him. But he didn't have much money to spare, and what he did have he was saving for a house for him and Laura. Besides, he knew Johnny wouldn't take a handout.

Still, there had to be a way to help him.

"You ready to *geh* home?" Lukas turned off the gas lamps in the shop.

"Yeah. Cora's waiting for me."

Sawyer had pondered all day what he would say to her. After their conversation last night, he was more concerned with her soul than with getting it through her head that he wasn't leaving Middlefield.

But Sawyer had no experience talking to anyone about God. He didn't know how to go about convincing his grandmother that it was important not only to have faith but to walk in faith. Lukas had taught him that by example, as had many other Amish friends in his district. He'd also learned a lot by attending church services. But he couldn't quite imagine Cora sitting through a three-hour service in a barn.

However, a conversation with Leona—now, that was different. Maybe God was providing a way through Emma's grandmother. All Sawyer had to do was convince Cora to go to supper tomorrow night.

A task easier said than done.

⁂

Katherine opened her eyes and squinted at the bright fluorescent light on the ceiling. Where was she? Her head pounded; she reached up and touched it. Where was her *kapp*?

She looked down. She was lying in a bed, wearing a strange-looking nightgown. Through the fuzzy mess of her thoughts, she tried to remember what happened. But a thick fog sealed her mind.

"Katherine?"

She turned her head to see her *mamm* sitting in a chair beside her bed. Her mother took Katherine's hand.

"Thank God, you're awake." *Mamm* closed her eyes briefly, her lips moving in a silent prayer.

Katherine tried to sit up, but her arms felt like jelly. "What am I doing here?"

Her mother opened her eyes. "You passed out."

"What?"

"At home, in the living room. You don't remember?"

Katherine shook her head.

"You scared Bekah and me nearly to death. We had to call an ambulance, and they brought you here. You have meningitis, Katherine." Her mother sighed. "I should have insisted you go to the doctor days ago. Those headaches weren't normal. And you didn't say a word about your neck hurting. Ah, *lieb*, I should have paid more attention."

Katherine tried to follow her mother's line of conversation. Sure, she had a bit of a headache now, but her neck felt fine. Yet her mother said she had neck pain. Why couldn't she remember that? "What are you talking about?"

Mamm brushed her hand across Katherine's forehead. "The doctor thinks it's viral meningitis, so they didn't give you any medicine. Just an IV for fluids. You were a little dehydrated from not drinking and eating enough." Tears filled her eyes. "We were so frightened, Katherine. When you first passed out, it took you awhile to wake up. But now you seem to be doing better. Your *daed* will be so happy."

"*Daed?* He's here too?" She looked around the hospital room but only saw her mother.

"He was here earlier. He and Bekah went home to take care of the animals. But he'll be back tomorrow."

Katherine leaned back against the pillow. She would have to stay here overnight? She searched her mind, trying to remember what happened. But nothing was clear.

"And don't you worry about anything. I talked to your boss at work. She said to take off as much time as you need."

Katherine nodded, despite barely hearing her mother's words. Had she hit her head when she fainted? She looked around the room. She'd never been in a hospital before. "Where are my clothes?"

"We have them. When they release you, you'll put on your dress and *kapp*. The doctor says you'll need plenty of rest in order to heal." She smiled. "I'll make sure you take it easy, *dochder*. You do have a tendency to overwork yourself." She squeezed Katherine's hand. "I'll let the nurse know you're awake. You must be hungry. It's past lunchtime."

"How long was I asleep?"

"Since yesterday afternoon." *Mamm* looked at her, tenderness shining in her eyes. Then she turned and walked out the door.

She'd been here an entire day? Katherine tried to sit up again. Her gown slipped, exposing her shoulder, but she didn't care. When she finally reached a sitting position, her body felt weak all over, as if she'd run the length of Bundysburg Road as fast as she could. She brushed a stray lock of hair off her forehead just as she heard a knock on the door. "*Ya?*"

The door opened slowly. The first thing she saw coming through the crack was a bouquet of flowers, followed by . . .

Johnny? His eyes were round, soft, filled with concern, his thick brows forming a V above them. What was he doing here?

He moved a few steps into the room, holding the flowers at an awkward angle. They were pretty—a couple of small sunflowers mixed with yellow and orange carnations. "Is it all right if I come in?"

"You're already in, aren't you?"

He grinned, but she didn't think she'd said anything funny. Nothing about this situation was humorous. Just confusing. Hopefully the doctor would have more answers.

"Brought you these." He thrust the flowers toward her.

She took them and held them in her lap. *"Danki."*

He nodded, shifting his weight first on one foot and then the other. His long hair was molded against his head from wearing his hat. "They had a lot of flowers down in that gift shop. Then I remembered you liked orange and yellow."

She looked down at the flowers. Then it hit her. He remembered her favorite colors? Since when did Johnny pay any attention to what she liked and disliked?

"That was . . . thoughtful of you."

"It's the least I could do. You know. After what happened."

Katherine's gaze shot up and met his. "What happened?"

"You don't remember?" His eyes drifted to her bare shoulder, where the hospital gown had slid down. She yanked it back onto her shoulder and shifted in the bed, pulling the hospital blanket closer to her body. The flowers slipped to the floor.

"Remember what? I have no idea what you're talking about."

CHAPTER 18

Johnny watched Katherine's expression change from irritation to confusion to something resembling terror. She turned her head away from him, revealing a thick, silken braid of reddish-blond hair. His fingers longed to touch it. Instead, he maintained his distance. He picked up the flowers off the floor and set them on the tray table near her bed.

"How is your headache?"

"Not bad."

"Still dizzy?"

"*Nee.*"

She averted her eyes and gripped the edge of the white blanket.

More than anything he wanted to put his arms around her, to tell her everything would be all right. That he would make it all right. But he stood his ground, at least until he knew how she felt about him.

Her eyebrows lifted and her clear blue eyes filled with confusion. "What are you doing here, Johnny?"

"I came to check on you."

"Why?"

"Because—" He looked down at her, his heart lurching. He couldn't stand seeing her lying in the hospital bed, pale as paste, the IV tube stuck in her arm. When she passed out, he'd never been so afraid in his life. "Because I needed to see if you were okay."

"*Mamm* says I fainted."

"You don't remember?"

She shook her head.

He pulled the chair closer and sat down. "What's the last thing you recall?"

She frowned, looking toward the hospital window as if the answer were outside. Or just beyond her reach. "I . . . I don't know."

"You don't remember me coming over yesterday?"

"You did? Why did you come over?"

"To bring you your bag."

"What bag?"

"The one you left at my *haus*."

"Your *haus*? When did you buy a *haus*?"

"Almost three weeks ago." He looked at her, confused. "You don't remember that either?"

She dropped the edge of the blanket, shaking her head. "Johnny," she whispered, "what's wrong with me?"

If she didn't remember what happened at his house, he wondered if she remembered Isaac asking her to the singing when they were all at Mary Yoder's. But before he could ask, her mother burst into the room. She shot Johnny a scathing look. "Katherine needs her rest."

"Right." He stood and looked down at Katherine. "We can talk about it later, once you're feeling better."

"Johnny, I want to talk to you," *Frau* Yoder said. "Out in the hall."

It was a command, not a request. He nodded and felt himself withering under her gaze. He'd suspected she was upset with him yesterday. Now he was certain of it.

A nurse entered the room carrying a folder, which she laid on the table next to the scattered flowers. She moved to the opposite side of Katherine's bed. "Nice to see you awake," she said. "How do you feel?"

Johnny didn't move. Neither did Katherine's mother.

"I have a bit of a headache."

"You might have one on and off until you're well again. Probably for a couple more days." She checked the clear IV bag hanging from the hook beside Katherine's bed. "Viral meningitis can be harsh. Do you still have neck pain?"

"No." She glanced at Johnny, still looking puzzled.

"Then that's a good sign." She smiled as she placed her stethoscope against Katherine's chest. "The doctor will be in this afternoon to talk to you."

"When can she go home?" Katherine's mother asked.

The nurse hung the stethoscope around her neck. She lifted Katherine's wrist, pressed her thumb and finger to it, and looked at her watch. After a few seconds she let go, patting Katherine's hand. "I'm not sure, but she seems to be doing well. Hopefully she'll be discharged sometime tomorrow."

"That's great news, isn't it, Katherine?" Her mother smiled.

"*Ya.* Great," she said. She seemed distant, as if she were barely registering what everyone was saying.

The nurse moved to the end of the bed. "Do you have any pain anywhere else?"

"*Nee.* Just my head."

Johnny frowned. Why wasn't she telling the nurse about her memory loss?

"On a scale of one to ten, what is the severity of the pain?"

"Four."

"What was it before you passed out?"

Katie paused. "I—I don't remember."

The nurse paused to write something on Katherine's chart. "I'll let the doctor know. Are you hungry?"

"A little bit."

"I'll order a tray." She glanced over her shoulder at Johnny and Katherine's mother, then looked back at Katherine. "Do you want me to order something for your mom and your boyfriend?"

"Oh, he's not my boyfriend." She said the words so fast they came out in a blur. Johnny glanced at her mother. The woman's lips were pressed into a thin line.

"I'm sorry," the nurse said. She held up her hands. "I shouldn't have assumed." She looked at him and Katherine's mom. "Would you like anything to eat? Or something to drink?"

Johnny started to shake his head when her mother said, "Nothing for me, and he is just leaving. Aren't you?"

He felt pinned to the wall by *Frau* Yoder's sharp gaze. "Yep. That's me. Leaving now."

"You can both stay," the nurse said. "Visiting hours aren't over yet."

Katie's mother narrowed her gaze at him before turning to the nurse. "Katherine should be resting, *ya?*"

"Rest is best."

"Then she doesn't need any extra distractions." Katherine's *mamm* glanced at Johnny.

The nurse nodded. "I'll check back with you in a little while." She looked at Katherine's mother. "Like I said, you all are welcome to stay as long as you want. Don't feel like you have to rush out of here."

Frau Yoder nodded but didn't say anything else. When the nurse left, she looked at Johnny. "You're leaving."

He nodded and looked at Katherine. "I hope you feel better."

"Danki." She still seemed dazed. He didn't know anything about meningitis, but it had to be serious, and he shouldn't be surprised that she seemed a little out of it. Still, the memory loss worried him. While he knew it was best for him to leave, especially since her mother was shooting visual daggers at him, he really wanted to stay. He'd spend the whole night by her bedside if he could.

Instead, he walked out the door, *Frau* Yoder close behind him. When they were both in the hallway, she shut the door. "Why are you here?"

"I came to check on Kati—Katherine. I'm worried about her."

"Oh, so now you're starting to worry? After all these years of breaking her heart, you've suddenly decided you care?"

Johnny flinched. He deserved those words.

"Katherine is very ill. She doesn't need you confusing her. You've caused her enough trouble."

Guilt nearly crushed him. He couldn't dispute *Frau* Yoder and had little to say in his own defense. "I've made some mistakes in the past. Big ones."

Frau Yoder leaned forward, her eyes sparking with anger. "Yes, you have. Katherine is moving on."

"I want to make things up to her—"

"It's too late for that." She stepped away. "She doesn't need you. At one time she thought she did. Not anymore."

A lump lodged in his throat. He nodded. "Okay." His voice sounded as thick as syrup, the single word clogging his throat. He'd leave for now. But he wouldn't give up. He respected *Frau* Yoder, yet he wanted to hear Katherine's side. Only then would he accept that his indecision and stupidity had cost him everything.

But one more thing needed to be said. "Katherine doesn't remember."

Her mother paused at the door of the room. "Remember what?"

"What happened before she fainted."

Frau Yoder spun around. "Did she hit her head when she fell?"

Johnny shook his head. "Not that I could see. I'm sure the doctor's checked for a concussion, though."

"What else did she say?"

"Not much." He paused. "We didn't get much of a chance to talk."

"Keep it that way." She turned around and walked back into Katherine's room. Johnny winced as the door clicked shut.

⁂

"I'm glad you could join us for supper."

Cora looked at the older woman across the table from her. "Thank you for the invitation." But she didn't say it with much enthusiasm. She had only accepted because Sawyer insisted that they go. They had talked again, arriving—as usual—at an impasse. At least inviting her to supper with some of his friends was a little progress.

But she didn't feel well tonight. Fatigue consumed her, and the unsteadiness was the worst it had been. She walked slower to compensate, ignoring Sawyer's quizzical looks as he helped her in and out of the buggy. The ride had jolted her bones, and with each car that whizzed past the buggy, her apprehension grew. She was a bundle of nerves by the time they arrived at the Ottos'.

Now she wished she were back at the Bylers'. Or preferably home, in her own penthouse surrounded by her own comforts, with her grandson at her side.

But apparently that was too much to ask.

She looked around the table, where serving dishes were piled high with enough food to feed an army. None of it appealed. All she wanted was tea and toast. Possibly just the tea. Yet it would be rude to refuse the food, and she wouldn't toss etiquette to the side. She did take the smallest of portions, however.

Emma placed the last plate of food, some kind of messy

casserole-looking thing, on the table. Cora glanced at Sawyer, who looked at the food appreciatively. "Looks delicious, Emma."

"*Danki*, Sawyer. I enjoyed making the meal."

Cora frowned. From the size of the woman's plump hips, Cora could see that she enjoyed eating it too.

Her gaze traveled to Emma's husband, Adam. He was handsome, but not as winsome as her grandson, of course. Part of it had to do with the ridiculous bowl-shaped haircut he wore, plus the beard with no mustache. What a strange sense of style these people had!

But his appearance wasn't what she noticed the most. She saw how his gaze followed his wife as she moved around the kitchen, preparing and serving the food. His eyes were filled with love.

It was the same kind of expression she'd seen in Sawyer's eyes when he looked at Laura.

She held in a sigh. It wasn't enough that Sawyer was bent on joining the church, whatever that meant. He was also determined to settle down, marry a country girl, and have a passel of kids. And at such a young age. What a waste of potential.

Emma finally sat down at the opposite end of the table from her husband. Sawyer sat across from an empty chair, which she assumed had been Laura's, while Cora sat on the left side of Sawyer and across from Leona. It all seemed so quaint, so Norman Rockwell.

She despised quaintness and had always thought Rockwell was a hack.

Everyone bowed their heads. Cora followed suit. The silent prayer. Praying to a silent God. Or a nonexistent one.

Her own parents were never religious, and she had gone to church only a handful of times in her life, mostly for weddings and the occasional Christmas service. She had gotten along just fine without God. Her business had thrived without any spiritual help.

She couldn't say the same for the rest of her life. But that didn't mean she needed God.

"Cora?"

She looked up at the sound of Leona's voice. She hadn't even noticed the prayer was over. Adam was already passing around bowls of food. When a big bowl of purple beet salad was presented to Cora, she almost blanched.

"Would you like some tea?" Leona took the bowl of beets from her. "I have a special blend I think you'll enjoy."

Tea sounded wonderful, but Cora was wary. Who knew what these people put into their beverages? "I can't imagine what would make it so special."

"Grandmother—" Sawyer gave her a warning look.

"It's all right, Sawyer." Leona smiled. "Nothing wrong with being curious. It's just a mix of black tea with chamomile, rosemary, and lemongrass."

Nothing she hadn't heard of before. "A cup of tea would be lovely, thank you." She glanced at Sawyer, who seemed relieved by her conciliatory tone.

"I'll get it for you." Emma jumped up from the table and went to the cabinet nearest the sink. The girl never seemed to sit still.

While Emma prepared the tea, Leona looked at Cora. "How long do you plan to stay in Middlefield?"

"As long as it takes," she muttered.

"Pardon me?"

"My plans are open." Cora looked around the table for something that appeared appetizing, but saw very little. She decided on a piece of bread, even though it was white. Didn't these people know how bad white flour was? As she watched Adam smother his thick slice of meat loaf with gravy, she couldn't figure out how he stayed so thin. Being married to Emma would probably change that.

"Here you *geh*," Emma said as she set the steaming hot tea in front of her.

"Thank you."

"You're welcome." She smiled, and Cora was struck by how pretty her face was, despite the chubby cheeks and makeup-free complexion. Her countenance almost made up for her pear-shaped body.

She took a sip of the tea. It was surprisingly good. But her hands started shaking as she held the teacup, and she quickly set it down with a loud thump.

"Is there something wrong with the tea?" Emma frowned, looking worried.

"Just a little hot." She picked up her slice of bread and took a bite. Everyone else continued to eat, except for Leona.

Cora met the older woman's gaze. She had noticed the shaking.

Leona noticed everything, Cora suspected. Paid attention,

without drawing attention to herself. Not much got past this woman.

Those were traits Cora could respect.

Emma turned to Sawyer. "When is Laura returning?"

"Week after next. I got a letter in the mail today." He grinned.

"That's wonderful." Emma cut into a large slice of meat loaf.

"Hopefully her parents will come with her. You don't mind putting them up?"

"Of course not," Adam said. "We have the room, and Laura is *familye*. I'll be glad to meet them."

"So will I." Sawyer grinned again. "Hopefully I'll get the stamp of approval from my future in-laws."

A knot twisted in Cora's stomach. Apparently her grandson cared more about two people he had never met and wasn't related to than about his own grandmother. She tightened her grip on the bread.

The conversation turned to boring topics such as gardening and the dog kennel outside. She barely listened and picked at her food while everyone else finished the meal. She took a few more sips of the tea. It really was delicious and did have a bit of a calming effect on her nerves. But she was eager to get back to the Bylers' and lie down.

"Everyone ready for dessert?" Emma grinned. "Apple pie and ice cream!"

Of course. A nice sorbet or even fresh fruit was out of the question. She resisted the urge to roll her eyes.

After dessert, which Cora declined, Emma started on the

dishes while Sawyer and Adam went outside. "Why don't we *geh* into the living room?" Leona suggested. "It's more comfortable in there."

Cora looked around for Sawyer just as the door shut behind him.

He seemed to have forgotten she was there.

CHAPTER 19

"I'll just go find Sawyer," Cora said. "Surely he's ready to go home."

Leona rested her gnarled hand on her cane. "He'll come in when it's time." She stood leaning on the wooden cane. Her shoulders were hunched, as if she couldn't stand up straight. Yet there was a strength to her presence, one that belied her physical weakness.

Cora couldn't help but stare at the cane. Simple, made of glossy wood, its curved handle worn in places where Leona had touched it over the years. It wouldn't be long before she herself would have to use one. Would she look as dignified as Leona?

Reluctantly she followed Leona into the living room, which like everything else in the house was modest, plain, and—well, boring. Leona gestured to the ancient-looking sofa.

With weary steps Cora made her way across the room and sat down on the sofa. It was surprisingly comfortable. Leona lowered herself into the wooden rocking chair across from her.

She clutched her cane, but not for support. It was as if the piece of wood was an old friend, a companion instead of a crutch. She smiled, her eyes shining bright in the yellow light of the gas lamp. "I hope you had a *gut* time tonight, Cora."

Cora nodded. The word *passable* came to mind, but she maintained her silence. She had done what was necessary to placate her grandson, but that was all. Feeling a little chilled, she started to cross her arms, noticed her shaking hands, and folded them tightly in her lap.

Leona's gaze dropped to Cora's hands. "How was the tea?"

"Soothing," Cora admitted.

"You seem tired."

"Perhaps." Cora lifted her chin and straightened her shoulders. "It is getting late, after all."

"*Ya*. Seven thirty is pretty late."

Was that all? Cora tried to stifle a sigh. She used to be a night owl, staying up until the wee hours of the morning. New York never slept, and when she was younger, neither did she.

"This must be hard on you." Leona shifted in her chair. Her plain, wire-rimmed glasses slid an inch down her nose, but she didn't move them. "And strange at the same time."

"Definitely strange." Cora looked at Leona. "I'm sorry, I didn't mean to sound rude."

"You didn't. You sound honest." She leaned forward. "I appreciate honesty."

Guilt forced Cora to look away. She hadn't been completely honest with Sawyer. She still wasn't.

"Is there something wrong?"

Cora returned her gaze to Leona. Was she that transparent?

Already losing her ability to hide her emotions? "Everything is fine."

Leona tapped her cane on the floor. "So much for honesty."

"I beg your pardon?" Cora moved to stand up. Leona held up her hand, stopping her.

"You're carrying a heavy burden, Cora. I suspect it's not just about Sawyer."

What was this woman, psychic? Then she noticed Leona's gaze on Cora's hands.

"My mother taught me the recipe for the tea." Leona finally pushed up her glasses. "She had all sorts of recipes for all sorts of ailments. I grew up watching her share her knowledge with others. She had a healing touch, not just with herbs, but with her presence. She was constantly in prayer, always asking God for help before she went to see someone who was ill."

"This is fascinating, really." Cora moved to stand up again. But as she reached her feet, she started to sway. And Leona didn't miss a move.

She didn't try to stop Cora either. As she left the room, Leona said, "I will be praying for you, Cora."

Cora wanted to tell the woman to keep her prayers to herself, that she didn't need them. But she did need Sawyer. She went into the kitchen where Emma was tidying up the last of the dishes.

"Where is my grandson?"

"He's still outside with Adam."

Fatigue and discomfort forced her to dispense with the pleasantries. "Please get him for me. Inform him I'm ready to leave."

"Okay."

Cora could see the normal sparkle in Emma's brown eyes

dim. She'd hurt the young woman's feelings. But she didn't really care. When Emma left to go outside, Cora sank into the nearest chair. She rested her head in her hands. Things would be so much easier if she felt better. Instead, everything was a battle—and she wasn't sure she would win this time.

Laura finished washing the last of the cookie sheets and dried them with a damp towel. She and her mother and father had worked late tonight filling a special order of monster cookies for an English church social. It was nearly eight, and she was weary. But more than that, she was tired of the strife between her and her *mamm*.

Since that first night on the back deck, her mother had said little to her. For the past few days she helped out in the bakery, hoping they could talk the way they used to when they baked high-rising loaves of bread, tender, creamy whoopee pies, and flaky pies with whatever local fruit was in season. But her mother had erected a wall of bitterness around herself, and Laura didn't know how to scale it. She had only a few more days before she returned to Middlefield. She didn't want to leave things like this between them.

When she put the last cookie sheet away, her father turned to them. "That's enough for the night," he said, his hands on his lower back, stretching. Gray threaded through his beard and thick brown hair, and a light dusting of flour coated his glasses.

"*Ya,*" Laura said, looking at her mother. "I think it's enough."

Her father stilled. He glanced from Laura to *Mamm* and

shook his head. "Don't you think it's time you two set things to rights?"

"I don't know what you mean," *Mamm* said.

"*Ya*, you do, Ella." He walked over to Laura. "Our *dochder* is home, and you've been silent toward her almost from the moment she got here. Come to think of it, you've been quiet all around." He peered at her. "Normally you're a chatterbox."

Laura's lips twitched into a smile, which disappeared at her mother's harsh look. "Matthew, if you knew what Laura was wantin' to do, you'd be upset too."

"Then why don't you tell me?" When neither of them spoke, he said, "You're gonna make me guess?"

Laura and her mother both spoke at once.

"She's making another mistake, Matthew—"

"I love him, *Daed*. *Mamm's* not giving him a chance—"

"Is it too much to ask that she take a little time to think about what she's doing?"

"He loves me. And he's not like Mark!"

Laura's mother grew silent. Both parents looked at Laura. "*Mamm*, I know you're worried. But if you would come back to Middlefield with me, you'll see I'm not making a mistake."

Her mother shook her head. "Absolutely not. Who will run the bakery?"

"I'm standing right here, Ella," her father said. "It's not like I haven't run the bakery by myself before. Plus, I can call on *mei bruder* Edward if I need an extra pair of hands."

"I can't leave you with all that work."

"Can't?" He took a step toward her. "Or won't?"

Laura watched as her parents gazed at each other, engaging in a silent communication born of thirty years of marriage. Her mother's shoulders drooped. "You're right," she said to *Daed*. "You can handle things here."

"Laura is right too. Give the *bu* a chance." He lowered his voice. "And give Laura a chance as well."

Laura's throat tightened. She'd been so wrapped up in her disappointment that her mother hadn't accepted her marriage plans that she failed to see her *Mamm's* point of view. "I know it's hard to trust me."

Her mother stepped away from her father. "Laura, *lieb*. It's not that we don't trust you." She went to Laura and touched her face, pausing as her fingertips pressed lightly against her thin scars. "We don't want you hurt again."

"Sawyer would never hurt me."

"You believe that, but—"

"Now it's time for you to find out for yourself, Ella." *Daed* moved to stand next to them. "Then you can report back to me. In never-ending detail. Like you always do."

Her mother batted him on the arm. Laura grinned.

Finally they were acting like the *familye* she remembered.

"Katherine, I've gone over your chart and the tests we ran on your brain." The doctor flipped her chart shut and stood at the end of her bed, peering down at her. "I think I know the reason for your memory loss."

She gripped her mother's hand. It was early the next

morning, the day after Johnny's visit. She still had trouble believing he'd stopped by, and when he told her he hoped she'd feel better, he seemed to really mean it. That made almost as much sense to her as the memory loss.

"In some patients with meningitis, there is a disruption in the blood flow across the blood-brain barrier."

Her mother drew a sharp breath. "That sounds dangerous."

"It can be, if the disruption is severe. In Katherine's case, we feel it wasn't. But that disruption caused a bit of short-term memory loss."

"Which is why I can't remember anything from the past few weeks," Katherine said.

"Exactly."

"Will she get her memory back?"

The doctor hugged the folder to his chest. "Possibly. But there's no guarantee." He looked at Katherine. "Since the loss is short-term, it won't affect you too much."

Katherine glanced away. Maybe the doctor could be so casual about her losing her memory, but she couldn't. Still, she hid her dismay from her mother. She didn't want to give her anything else to worry about.

"Other than that, you're doing well. I'll have the nurse come in with the discharge papers, and you'll be free to leave. Do you have any other questions?"

Katherine shook her head, still trying to process what the doctor had said. But she was glad to be going home.

Once he left, her mother went to the small closet in the room and pulled out Katherine's dress and *kapp*. "You can get dressed while we wait for the nurse. Do you need any help?"

"Nee." She got up from the bed, feeling nothing worse than a little weakness in her legs.

She took the dress and *kapp* from her mother and went into the bathroom to change. Under the fluorescent lighting she looked at herself in the mirror. Dark circles ringed her eyes, and her complexion was paler than normal. Johnny had seen her like this?

She shook her head and slipped out of the gown. She'd asked her mother a couple of times why Johnny had visited, but *Mamm* always changed the subject. Maybe when she got home, surrounded by familiar things, she would remember what happened. She hoped.

After the hospital released her, Katherine and her mother took a taxi home.

When she walked in the door, Bekah greeted her. "You got a letter from Isaac," she said, holding it up in the air. "It came yesterday. He sure didn't wait long to write."

Katherine frowned. Isaac?

"Don't you want the letter?" Bekah held it out to her.

"Who's Isaac?" her father asked.

"Ya," her *mamm* said, taking off her shawl. "Is there something we should know about?"

Katherine took the letter from Bekah. She looked at the unfamiliar handwriting. The return address was Walnut Creek.

"You don't remember him?" Bekah asked.

She shook her head. "I have no idea who you're talking about."

Daed frowned. "Bekah, what's going on?"

"Katherine has a beau."

Both Katherine and her mother gasped. "What?" *Mamm* looked at Katherine. "Why didn't you say anything about him before?"

"Well, he's not exactly a beau," Bekah said, plopping on the couch. Suddenly she looked concerned. "None of this rings a bell, Katherine?"

Weary, she sat down and put the letter in her lap. *"Nee."*

"You seem to know all about him, though." *Daed* looked at Bekah, his expression stern.

"All I know is that he stopped by a couple days ago, wanting to talk to Katherine." She grinned. "I think he's kind of *schee.*"

"And that's all you know?"

"Ya."

"Gut. Then *geh* to your room. Your *mudder* and I need to talk to Katherine. Alone."

Bekah looked genuinely shocked. "I'm seventeen. Don't you think I'm a little old to be sent to my room?" At their father's warning look, she said, "I'm going. But, Katherine, you and I are going to talk later."

Katherine sighed as her sister clambered up the stairs. Her parents waited for a moment.

Her father moved to stand at the bottom of the stairs. "Shut the door, Rebekah."

"Fine."

He sighed and turned back to Katherine. Katherine glanced at her mom, not missing the twitch of her lips. But Katherine didn't find this funny at all.

Her father sat on the couch, removed his hat, and rubbed his forehead. "Why haven't we heard about Isaac before?"

"I don't know."

"But you've been writing to him?" He leaned forward.

Katherine shrugged. "I don't remember. I guess I have."

Her mother sat next to her. "I think it's wonderful you've met someone."

Her father rubbed his chin. "I suppose. It would be nice to know who that someone is, though."

"Thomas, Katherine doesn't need us peppering her with questions. *Geh* upstairs and I'll bring you some tea." *Mamm* stood. "Oh, and don't forget your letter." She smiled.

Katherine looked at the white envelope in her lap. Why wasn't she more curious about its contents? Instead, she was still wondering why Johnny had visited her in the hospital. "I don't want any tea, just some sleep. I'll be down later to help with supper."

"Absolutely not. You just got out of the hospital. Bekah and I can take care of supper. We'll let you know when it's ready." She kissed Katherine's cheek. "Now, *geh* rest."

Katherine went upstairs. She shut the door to her room and sat on the bed. Stared at the letter again. Had she been writing to this Isaac? There was only one way to find out. She opened the letter and started to read.

Dear Katherine,

I hope this letter finds you well. I'm glad you said it was okay to write to you while I'm on the road with Daed. We're heading for southern Ohio tomorrow. He said we should be done with our visits to the alpaca farms in a couple of weeks. The time can't go fast enough for me.

I don't mean to be pushy, but I really like you. I got the feeling you liked me too, seeing that you were always so kind to me at Mary Yoder's. Then again, you know I had my eye on you from the start. You can write me back if you want; I'll pick up the letters when I return from our trip.

Best, Isaac

Frowning, Katherine looked at the address Isaac wrote on the bottom of the letter. The same as the return address. Walnut Creek.

She returned the letter to its envelope, disappointed. The letter was short and gave little insight into who Isaac was. All she knew was that he was with his dad and doing something with alpacas.

And . . . he liked her.

But for how long? She clenched the letter. Why couldn't she remember? A knock sounded on the door, startling her. "What?" The word shot out of her mouth.

"It's me." Bekah's voice sounded tentative.

Katherine tossed the letter on her bed. "Come in."

Bekah walked into the room. "Are you all right?"

"I'm fine."

"You always say that. Even when you're not." Bekah walked into the room. "Goodness, you look like you're about to throw up." She frowned. "You aren't, are you? You know I don't do well with that kind of thing."

"*Nee*. I'm just tired."

Bekah plopped down on Katherine's bed next to the letter. She pointed at it. "Did this help you figure things out?"

She shook her head. Curiosity filled Bekah's eyes. "*Geh* ahead," Katherine said. "Read it."

Bekah eagerly pulled out the letter. Her smile disappeared as she read. "That was kind of—"

"Vague?"

"Boring. Except for the part about liking you." She returned the letter to Katherine. "Are you going to write him back?"

"I don't know. What would I say? Other than 'I don't remember you'? The past three weeks are a complete blank."

"*Gut* point." Bekah touched Katherine's arm. "I'm sorry you have to *geh* through this."

"It's frustrating. But the doctor said I might get my memory back." *Someday*.

"So in the meantime, what are you going to do about Isaac?"

"Wait for him to come back, I suppose."

"And Johnny? *Mamm* was pretty mad about him showing up at the hospital." She turned to Katherine. "He was worried about you, Katherine. Really worried. *Mamm* says it's because he feels guilty about the way he's treated you all these years."

"She's probably right." Knowing the truth didn't lessen the pain, however.

"I don't think so. I'm fairly sure he likes you."

Katherine's heart leapt at the thought. Then she came back down to reality. "Johnny doesn't care for me."

"Maybe he's changed his mind."

"Not likely." Katherine got up and looked out the window.

"You never know—"

"Bekah, stop." She faced her sister. "Just stop it."

"I didn't mean to upset you." She stood. "I should *geh* downstairs and help *Mamm* with supper."

"You should."

But before she left, she put her hand on Katherine's shoulder. "I'm glad you're home. Glad you're all right."

Katherine nodded but didn't say anything. She wasn't angry at Bekah. Or even at Johnny. She was just frustrated with herself—and tired of feeling that way.

CHAPTER 20

Sawyer woke up the next morning not knowing what to do about Cora. She had ridden home from dinner in silence. He thought surely she would nag him again about returning to New York. But she hadn't said a word.

Maybe he should go back with her, just to show he did care, even though he had no intention of changing his mind about the church or Laura. He disliked the city and wanted to spend as little time there as possible. Still, he needed to give Cora a place in his life. He had to make her understand that although he wouldn't abandon her, once he joined the church, everything would change.

He dressed in Amish clothes, brushed his hair, and headed downstairs toward the scent of frying bacon and eggs. He smiled at Anna on his way through the kitchen.

"I'll go help Lukas with the horses," Sawyer said, heading out the door.

Anna stopped him cold. "I'm sure he can feed them by

himself this morning." She motioned toward the table. "Sit down. I haven't seen much of you lately."

"I know. Between work and meeting with the bishop—"

"And seeing Laura." Anna pulled a strip of bacon out of the frying pan and placed it on a paper towel–covered plate. "Then there's Cora."

"Yes. Cora." He looked down at the table for a moment. "Thank you for taking care of her while she's been here. I'm sure it hasn't been easy."

"Actually, she's been a *gut* guest this time. Although . . ."

"Although what?"

Anna looked at Sawyer. "She seems tired."

"I know."

"Is there something wrong?" Anna asked.

"Other than her wanting me to leave, no. At least she hasn't said anything." He snatched a piece of bacon from the plate— hot and crispy, just the way he liked it. "I was thinking about going to New York. Just for a short visit. It will be easier to do now than after I join the church."

Anna nodded. "Makes sense."

"So you don't mind?"

Anna removed the eggs from the stove and brought both plates of food to the table. "It's really not my place to say, Sawyer."

"But I want your opinion."

She sat down next to him, her expression suddenly sober. "The truth is, I feel a little guilty. It seems like all my prayers have been answered, all the things I've wanted for you. To find a *gut maedel*, to stay here in Middlefield."

"To join the church."

"I didn't dare hope for that." She smiled, her blue eyes bright. "But I have to admit I'm happy you've made that decision. I know it was hard for your grandmother to hear about."

"It was, but eventually she'll come to accept it."

"I hope so. In the meantime, be gentle with her."

Sawyer frowned. "She wasn't exactly the nicest person to you when you first met."

"*Nee*, but the circumstances weren't ideal either. Like I said, she's been a gracious guest. I almost—"

"Like her?"

Before Anna could respond, a thudding noise sounded from above them. Sawyer shot up from the chair and ran upstairs, Anna trailing him. When he arrived at Cora's bedroom door, he found his grandmother on the floor.

He knelt beside her and helped her sit up. Her face, devoid of makeup, revealed her age. The circles under her eyes supported what Anna had told him. Cora looked exhausted. And in pain.

"What happened?"

"I slipped." She attempted to sit up straight, lifting her chin in that haughty way of hers. But she couldn't do it, and when she tried to stand, she winced.

"Cora?" Anna came into the room, breathless from running up the stairs.

"I'm all right," she said through gritted teeth.

"No, you're not." Sawyer glanced at her right leg. It was twisted at an odd angle, and her normally slim ankle was already swelling. "You need to see a doctor."

"I need to stand up." Cora's voice sounded weak, but there was force behind it.

"Help her back to bed," Anna instructed.

Sawyer started to help Cora to her feet, but ended up lifting her small frame and laying her gently on the bed. Anna, at the foot of the bed, arranged a pillow underneath Cora's injured ankle.

"Ow!" Cora tried to sit up but couldn't.

"Sawyer," Anna instructed, "run to the cooler in the basement and see if we have any leftover ice. Even if it's just cold water, dip a cloth in it and wring it out."

He nodded and hurried to get the cloth. He found a few ice cubes, wrapped them in an old kitchen towel, and rushed back to Cora's side. The ankle had already swollen to twice its size. He handed the crude ice pack to Anna, who placed it on Cora's ankle.

"Stop. Please!" Cora leaned back against the pillow. Her skin had taken on a grayish color.

"It hurts that much?" Sawyer asked.

She opened her eyes and looked at him. Instead of answering, she nodded.

Anna set the ice to the side. "It might be broken."

"Then I'll take her to the emergency room."

"No!" Somehow Cora managed to sit up. "No hospitals."

"But, Grandmother—"

"Sawyer, I said no." She tried to move, only to cry out in pain again.

He turned and started to leave.

"Where are you going?" Anna asked.

"Phone box. To call a taxi." He looked at Cora. "You're going to the hospital, Grandmother. No more arguments."

Cora opened her mouth, then shut it again and sank down in the bed, nodding weakly.

Cora sat in the ER exam room, waiting for the results of her X-rays. She didn't need X-rays to tell her that her ankle was broken. The pain searing through her foot and leg told her that.

She looked across the room at her grandson, who sat in the corner with his right ankle crossed over his left knee. He shook his foot nervously, continuously. They'd been here for two hours already, but he had never left her side.

Although this was the last place she wanted to be, his presence comforted her. And made her realize just how alone she was. What if she'd fallen at home? Who would have stayed with her in the hospital? Kenneth? Manuela? Whoever it was, she'd be expected to pay overtime.

A simple slip, losing her balance after she'd gotten out of bed to get ready for the day, ended in a broken bone—and a stark reminder of her loneliness and weakness.

Sawyer had said little to her since they'd arrived at the hospital. For the first time, she felt a pang of guilt. He was supposed to be at work. She was keeping him from his job, so he could babysit her in the emergency room. "I can get a taxi back to the Bylers'," she said. "Once the doctor returns."

"I'm not leaving you here." Sawyer stood and paced across the small cubicle. "You heard what the doctor said. It's probably broken, which means a cast and crutches. You'll need help."

"I can manage."

"I'm sure you could. But you don't have to. Not while I'm here."

Cora met Sawyer's gaze, and a lump caught in her throat. His eyes, so much like Kerry's, brought back memories of her daughter when she was young. She remembered being with Kerry when she was ill with the flu, sleeping on the floor next to her bed so she could check her fever every four hours. Kerry's father had wanted Cora to let the nanny do it. But Cora couldn't leave her three-year-old daughter, not when she was so ill. Not when she needed her mother the most.

Now the roles were reversed.

She looked away, her eyes burning with unshed tears.

"Hurts pretty bad, huh?"

Cora nodded. "Yes, it does."

"I broke my arm once. When I was in sixth grade. Playing on the jungle gym at school. Tried to hang upside down like a monkey at the zoo. Instead I slipped and fell. Landed on my elbow."

"That must have been painful."

"Yep, I was in a cast for six weeks."

The door opened and the doctor came in, holding X-rays. He flipped on the light box affixed to the wall and clipped up the X-rays. "I have good news and bad news." He pointed to her ankle on the X-ray. "The good news? No break. Just a bad sprain." He flipped off the light box. "The bad? Unfortunately you'll need an air cast and will be on crutches for a few weeks."

Cora hid her despair. How could she handle crutches when she was already so unsteady on her own two feet?

Her hands started to shake. She held them together tightly.

"Mrs. Easley, other than your ankle, are you feeling all right?"

She nodded, tightening the grip on her hands.

The doctor looked at her intently. "Do you have someone to drive you home?"

"We'll be getting a taxi," Sawyer said.

"Good. And do you have someone to help you at home?"

Cora didn't respond. She wasn't at home. But she couldn't go to her real home, not like this.

"She has plenty of people to take care of her." Sawyer looked at her and smiled. "Don't worry."

Easy for him to say. It wasn't his ankle that was screaming with pain. "Are you sure it's not broken?"

The young doctor pushed up his glasses. "Sprains can hurt worse than a break. You're lucky, Mrs. Easley. A broken ankle might have required surgery. Are you in pain?"

She could deny it, but both Sawyer and the doctor would know it was a lie. "Yes."

"I'll prescribe some pain medication. What drugs are you currently taking?"

Cora froze.

"Mrs. Easley? I need to know your current medications. I don't want to prescribe anything that might interact with them."

She couldn't speak. Once she said her medication out loud, the doctor would know. She glanced at Sawyer, taking in his confused expression. "Grandmother?"

She looked away. "L-dopa."

The doctor frowned. "You have Parkinson's?"

She swallowed and looked at Sawyer. His mouth had dropped open. She glanced back at the doctor and lifted her chin. "Yes," she said, her voice trembling nearly as much as her hands. "I have Parkinson's."

Almost two hours later Sawyer and Cora were in a taxi headed back to Middlefield. He looked at his grandmother, who was facing the passenger window, her back almost to him. He clenched his jaw. Parkinson's. Why hadn't she told him?

He hadn't said anything to her in the emergency room. He knew better than to embarrass her publicly like that. And they weren't going to discuss it in the taxi either, even though he was itching to find out why she had kept her illness a secret. But he was determined: when they returned home, she was going to tell him everything.

He followed her cue and watched the landscape pass by as the taxi zoomed down the road. He didn't know a lot about Parkinson's, but he knew it was debilitating and that there wasn't a cure. It explained her fatigue, her slower movements . . . and her desperation.

He closed his eyes, his heart aching. In the short time he'd known her, she had been so strong. An iron lady. But now . . . how would they deal with this?

When they arrived back home, he helped her out of the car, paid the taxi driver, and watched as she struggled with her crutches. When he offered to carry her, she balked.

"Please. I'm not an invalid."

"I know that. But you're not used to crutches either."

She gripped the crutches and tried to balance herself on the gravel driveway. She nearly slipped as she took her first step.

"Could you put your pride away for five minutes and let me help you?"

Then she looked at him. It wasn't pride he saw in her eyes. It was fear. He went to her and held out his arm.

"At least lean on me."

She looked at his crooked arm, then handed him the crutch. She slipped her thin arm through his, and they slowly made their way toward the house. When they reached the porch steps, he picked her up. She didn't complain.

Anna opened the front door. "Is it broken?"

"Sprained." He took Cora to the couch and set her down. She weighed next to nothing.

"Thank you." She didn't look at him as she spoke.

"I fixed up the small storage room in the back of the *haus*," Anna said. "You won't have to worry about the stairs."

"A storage room?" Cora closed her eyes. "Seriously?"

"Grandmother." Sawyer sat down next to her. "It's the best we can do. I'm sure it's very nice."

"I need to make a phone call." Cora opened her eyes. "My cell is upstairs, but it's dead."

"There's the call box outside," Sawyer said. "Who do you need to call? I can make it for you."

"My travel agent." She turned her steely gaze on him. "I'm going home."

"No, you're not. Not with your ankle. And not with—"

"Parkinson's. You can say it out loud, you know."

"Apparently you can't."

Cora sneered. "How dare you judge me about how I handle *my* illness? I should sue that doctor for breach of privacy."

She was right; he had no place judging her. "Why didn't you tell me?" Sawyer asked, gentling his tone.

"I was going to. I was even going to use it, if I had to coerce you into coming back with me." She paused and looked away. "But I couldn't do it. I didn't want your pity."

"I don't pity you." Sawyer moved closer. "I want to help."

She looked back at him. "Then, please, return with me to New York. I don't know how much longer I have. My—*our*—company needs you."

He swallowed. "I—I can't."

But the words were harder to say this time. Before, he had refused because he was protecting his freedom to live the life he wanted. Now he just sounded selfish.

He looked up at Anna, who had wisely kept quiet during the conversation. But he didn't miss the shock in her eyes.

Cora leaned against the cushions. "I see."

The two simple words pierced him.

"Is Parkinson's cancerous?" Anna asked.

Cora looked at her like she was a fool. "No. It's not cancer. But it's incurable. And over time—"

"Over time, that's the key," Sawyer said. Somehow he had to fix this. Make it work for both of them. "Cora, you don't have to go back to New York. We can take care of you here."

"You can't. I saw your hospital. Primitive, to say the least."

"Now, that's not right, or fair." Sawyer scratched his forehead. "The Cleveland Clinic is an hour from here. It's one of the best hospitals in the world. We can get you the treatment you need there."

"You're asking me to stay here? With you?"

He looked at Anna. She nodded and sat on the opposite side of Cora. "You're welcome to stay as long as you need. Or want." She took Cora's hand. "You're *familye*."

Cora didn't say anything. Her bottom lip trembled. Finally she spoke. "What I need is to go home."

CHAPTER 21

"Smells *appeditlich*," Katherine said as she walked into the kitchen.

"Sounds like you got your appetite back." *Mamm* placed a pot of soup on the table. "You've been surviving on toast and tea for the past two days." She went to Katherine, scanning her face. She smiled. "You have some color to your cheeks too."

"I am feeling better." She sat at the table as Bekah brought over a plate of sliced bread. "Maybe I'll *geh* back to work tomorrow."

"Don't rush it."

Daed came in from the barn and washed up at the kitchen sink. "Rush what?"

"Work. There's plenty of time for that."

"Right." *Daed* rubbed his hands together. "I'm starving, and this all looks *gut*."

They bowed their heads for silent prayer. When they finished, her father passed around the plate of warm bread slices.

Katherine took one, slathered a thick layer of butter on it, and wolfed it down.

After supper Katherine helped Bekah and *Mamm* clean the kitchen. She had just hung the dishtowel up to dry when someone knocked on the front door. "I'll get it," Bekah said.

"Are you expecting anyone?" Katherine asked her mother.

Mamm wiped the last of the crumbs off the table but didn't look up. *"Nee."*

Bekah walked into the kitchen, her light brow furrowed. "It's for Katherine. You won't believe who it is."

"Johnny?" The name slipped out. She glanced at her mother.

"I certainly hope not."

"David Esh," Bekah said.

Mamm stepped forward, suddenly smiling. "The bishop's *gross-sohn?"*

"Ya."

"What does he want?" Katherine asked.

"Why don't you find out?" Her mother gave her a small shove toward the door. "Don't keep him waiting."

Katherine entered the living room to see David standing by the door, holding a brown paper bag in his hand. "Hi," he said, his normally booming voice sounding restrained.

"Hi, David." She peered at him, remembering how disappointed and impatient he had been with her at the volleyball game last year. "What are you doing here?"

"I heard you weren't feeling well." He held out the bag. "Ice cream. Thought you might like some."

"Danki." She took the bag from him and peeked inside. "Vanilla."

"I was gonna get chocolate, since *maed* seem to like chocolate. A lot." He gave her a small smile. They stood there for a
moment. "We should probably eat it," he said. "Before it melts."

We? Was this something else she didn't remember? Surely
she didn't have two guys interested in her.

"You probably think it's *seltsam* that I'm here. But when I
heard you weren't hung up on Johnny anymore—"

"What?"

He took a step forward. "I figured you wouldn't mind me
dropping by."

"I, uh . . ."

"I always thought you were pretty, Katherine." David took
another step closer. His breath smelled like mint, as if he'd just
chewed a piece of gum. He leaned forward, his smile turning
from shy to borderline lecherous. "After the ice cream we can
geh for a walk. Just you and me."

"David," Bekah said, coming into the living room. "Nice
to see you."

"Bekah." Annoyance entered his tone. He looked at
Katherine. "So. How about it?"

"Katherine's still not feeling all that great. I'm sure whatever you planned can wait." Bekah smoothly angled him
toward the door. "We're not supposed to let her get too tired."

"Eating ice cream's not gonna wear her out."

"You brought ice cream? That's so sweet of you." She
opened the door and practically shoved him outside. "We'll see
you later, when Katherine's feeling better."

"But—"

"Bye!" Bekah shut the door and leaned against it for a

second. Then she took the bag from Katherine. "What kind did he bring you?"

"That was rude."

"A little. But you're glad I got rid of him, *ya*?"

She nodded. "I'm not sure why he was here in the first place."

"Well . . ." *Mamm* came into the living room, twisting the dishrag in her hands. "I might have told a couple of *mei* friends that you were . . . available."

"*Mamm!*"

"I didn't think it would cause any harm. And you *are* available. I didn't even know David Esh was interested in you."

"David Esh is interested in everyone," Bekah said. "He has a bit of a reputation."

"He does?" *Mamm* gasped. "I don't believe it."

"Trust me. I just saved Katherine a whole world of pain and suffering. Now, how about we dig into that ice cream?"

"Help yourself," Katherine said, collapsing on the couch. "You earned it."

Bekah left the room. *Mamm* sat down next to Katherine. "I'm sorry about David coming by here unannounced. But I'm not sorry I said something to *mei* friends. I know you have this *bu* Isaac now—"

"*Mamm*. Please. I don't even remember him."

"But you can't put your eggs in one basket. You've wasted enough time doing that."

Bekah came back in the room, ice cream piled high in a huge bowl. "Found this in the stack of mail in the kitchen." She handed Katherine an envelope.

"Another letter from Isaac?" *Mamm* asked.

Katherine nodded.

"It's only been two days since the last one," *Mamm* said. She rose and smiled. "He must be writing you every day. See what happens, Katherine, when you give other people a chance?"

Katherine didn't respond. Anything she said would fall on deaf ears. *Mamm* didn't seem to care who wanted to court her, as long as it wasn't Johnny Mullet.

Bekah took her ice cream outside while Katherine went upstairs. She looked at the letter for a long time, unsure about opening it. Shouldn't she be eager to read the contents? Finally she opened it to find another letter almost identical to the last one, except for a little more detail about the alpaca farm he and his father were working. Once again he invited her to write him back.

Instead she put the letter back in the envelope and went downstairs.

Her father had come back inside and was seated in his chair in the corner of the room. An open newspaper lay on his stomach, which slowly lifted up and down with his soft breathing. She tiptoed past him.

"Katherine?"

"Sorry. I didn't mean to wake you up."

He sat up in the chair and folded the paper. "I'd just drifted off. Who was here earlier?"

"David Esh."

His father frowned. "There's something off with that *bu*."

"What makes you say that?"

"I've got a fifth sense about it."

Katherine chuckled. "I think you mean sixth."

"There's the Katherine I'm used to." Her father grinned. "Hon, you don't need to be worrying about dating right now." He became serious. "Have you remembered anything?"

She shook her head.

"Maybe you're not meant to."

Katherine frowned. "Did something happen? In the past month, I mean? Something bad?"

"Not that I know of. I'm not talking about forgetting anything bad. Just that maybe there are some memories that are okay to let go of."

"What do you mean?"

"Maybe instead of worrying about what you missed, you should focus on the future."

"What kind of future is that? To work at Mary Yoder's for the rest of my life? To live with you and *Mamm* forever?" *Or alone?*

"That's not for me to say. Only God knows the future, Katherine. We just have to keep putting one foot in front of the other."

Through the front screen, the sound of a buggy pulling into the driveway caught their attention. *Now what?* She went to the window and looked outside.

"Who is it?" her father asked.

"Johnny." She let the curtain fall. *What could he possibly want?*

"Well. That's interesting timing."

Johnny halted his horse, bringing the buggy to a stop. But he didn't get out right away. He knew he wasn't wanted here, at least by Katherine's mother. But what if Katherine didn't want him either? He suddenly remembered the guy at Mary Yoder's who had asked her out. Isaac something, he couldn't recall. What if things between her and Isaac were serious?

She doesn't owe you an explanation.

He thought about what Mary Beth said a couple weeks ago. About being too late with Katherine. While that always had been in the back of his mind, he never thought he'd really have any competition for her affection. Or that he could possibly lose her to someone else.

Hochmut. Nothing but pride.

What a fool he was.

How could he make up for the pain he caused her? For the first time he understood how she really felt. How much it had to hurt to know someone you loved was out of reach, possibly forever. He had never tried to put himself in her place before. Now he'd been forced there, and the guilt and regret overwhelmed him.

Somehow he would fix what was broken between them. He'd find a way not to lose her. Panic overtook him, the same panic he'd experienced when she fainted, the helplessness that consumed him when he saw her lying in the hospital bed, vulnerable and confused, unable to remember certain things. She'd been through enough. He had to put her first in his life.

Something he should have been doing all along.

He got out of the buggy and turned toward the house.

Right now. Right here. This was the first step, the moment when everything changed.

Katherine followed her father to the front porch. Johnny stepped up to meet them.

"John." He held out his hand. "What brings you by?"

"I came to check on Katherine." He shook her dad's hand and looked at her. "How are you doing?"

"Okay."

"Mary Beth sends her best. She said if you need anything, just let her know."

"*Danki.*" So he came to deliver a message from his sister. Still, that was more than he'd done in the past. "Tell her I appreciate it, but I know she's busy getting ready for the *boppli.*"

"Katherine, she already had the *boppli.* You were there when she was born."

She looked at her father, who gave her a sympathetic look. Then she faced Johnny. "What's her name?"

"Johanna. And she's beautiful."

Just hearing Johnny talk about his niece, his voice filled with love, made her melt inside. Illness might have taken her memory, but it hadn't altered her feelings for him. "I can't wait to see her again."

"We might be able to arrange that."

We? The word triggered a little thrill inside her. But it was just one word. One syllable. She couldn't afford to read anything significant into it. She'd done that before too often.

"Once burned, twice shy," her *grossmammi* used to say. And Katherine had been burned far more than once. She pressed her lips together. "*Danki* for the message."

"That's not the only reason I'm here."

Katherine's *vadder* interrupted. "Well, I've got work to do. John, tell your folks hello for me." He smiled at Katherine and went back to the barn.

When he was gone, she turned to Johnny. "Why are you really here?"

He took a deep breath. "I want to help you. I want you to get your memory back."

CHAPTER 22

Johnny looked at Katie sitting next to him in the buggy. How right it felt having her near. He kicked himself for waiting so long, and for keeping her waiting even longer. "*Danki* for coming with me."

"Where are we going?"

"Back to *mei* place. I thought it might shake something loose in your memory."

"I don't know." She sighed. "Nothing else has worked."

"That's because everything else is so familiar. I went to the library and did some reading about short-term memory loss."

"And it said to take me to your *haus*?"

He grinned. "No, smarty-pants. It said that sometimes exposure to the familiar will trigger a memory."

"But I don't remember your *haus*. And I've already been exposed to everything familiar and it hasn't worked."

"I thought I'd try something different. Something unfamiliar but recent. It couldn't hurt, and it might help."

"What are the chances of that happening?"

He let out a breath. "Slim to none."

"But you're willing to try anyway."

"Absolutely. And after we can *geh* visit Johanna."

She shook her head, the ribbons of her *kapp* flailing with the movement.

"You don't want to?"

"It isn't that." She looked at him with those huge blue eyes of hers. "I don't understand why you're doing this."

He didn't say anything for a long moment. "I already told you why."

"Tell me again."

"I want to see if you remember."

A short while later they pulled up in front of a run-down-looking place. Katherine was about to say something when Johnny held up his hand.

"Don't. My poor *haus* can't take any more insults."

"I wasn't going to insult it. Just comment that it's . . . interesting."

"Actually, it looks better than it once did, thanks to you."

"What did I do?"

"You'll see." He jumped out of the buggy and rounded it. He held out his hand. "Come on."

She slipped her hand into his. It was warm and rough and strong. As soon as her feet touched the ground she pulled out of his grasp. What was he doing? She hoped his house triggered her memory, despite her doubts. It was the only thing that kept her following him without asking any more questions.

They walked into the kitchen. "Excuse the dishes," he said.

She glanced at the tall pile in the sink.

"I didn't have a chance to wash them." He held out his arms. "Take a look around. See anything you recognize?"

She took in her surroundings, but nothing clicked. Then she noticed the curtains over the sink. "Those look familiar."

"They should. You brought them."

"I did? Why?"

"Because." He moved closer to her. "That's the kind of person you are. The kind who thinks about others. Who cares."

She averted her gaze, her heart warming at his kind words.

"Do you remember them?"

She walked toward the window and touched the fabric. "*Ya.* I do."

He grinned and stood next to her. "Really?"

"We had the same kind of curtains at home. We replaced them a couple months ago."

"Oh."

"We should forget this. Just take me home."

"Not yet. Not until you've seen everything." He took her to the living room, pointing out she'd brought those curtains too. They went upstairs, then out to the barn, which was clean but in bad shape. After giving her the tour, they went back into the kitchen. She sank down into a chair, frustrated again. "I don't remember any of this." She looked up at him. "Why was I here in the first place?"

"Because I asked you to be."

"Why?"

He didn't answer right away. "Maybe we should *geh*. I'm sure you'd rather see Johanna than stay here."

She couldn't help but notice the defeat in his eyes. Everything confused her. She started to leave, then noticed a drawing on the counter near the back door. The words *candy shoppe* caught her eye. She picked up the drawing. "What's this?"

He frowned. "My future." He took the drawing from her, looked at it for a moment, and then tossed it aside. "Let's *geh*."

When they reached Mary Beth's house, Katherine stood at the edge of the porch while Johnny knocked on the door. A few seconds later Mary Beth answered it. Her eyes widened as she looked at Johnny, then Katherine. "This is a nice surprise."

"Mind if we come in?"

She opened the door wider. Katherine looked at the sweet baby Mary Beth cradled in her arms as she stood in the doorway. But as with everything else Johnny had showed her this afternoon, the infant didn't jog her memory.

Johnny held out his arms. "Let me see *mei* niece."

Mary Beth handed her to him, and the three of them walked into the living room. Katherine marveled at how gentle Johnny was with the baby, then he put her in Katherine's arms.

"Meet Johanna."

"For the second time," Mary Beth added.

Katherine sat down with little Johanna, entranced. Johnny was right—she was beautiful.

"Is Chris outside?" Johnny asked.

Mary Beth nodded. "He's plowing the field, preparing to plant the feed corn."

"I'll *geh* out and see if he needs some help."

When he grew silent, Katherine looked up. He and Mary Beth exchanged a private look. She'd seen them do this before. As twins they shared a special bond.

He turned to Katherine. "I'll be back in a bit. Then I'll take you home."

When Johnny left, Mary Beth said, "I'm so glad you're all right. Johnny told me about your illness. He also mentioned your memory problems." She paused. "I'm so sorry."

"It's okay."

"We can *geh* into the kitchen and talk."

Within a few minutes the thick aroma of fresh-brewed coffee surrounded them.

Katherine shifted Johanna in her arms and waited for Mary Beth to sit down. "What's gotten into Johnny?" she asked.

"I was about to ask you the same thing. I don't mind a visit from *mei bruder* or *mei* best friend. I just didn't expect you both here at the same time."

"Me either."

"Not that I'm complaining."

Katherine hugged Johanna close. The baby closed her eyes. "He's trying to help me."

Mary Beth nodded. "That's really . . . nice of him."

"Which is why I'm confused."

Mary Beth nodded. "He's been doing a lot of confusing

things lately. Buying that property without saying anything to the family, for one thing." She shrugged. "I think *mei bruder* is finally ready to put down roots." Then she smiled. "You might have something to do with that."

"I doubt it." She touched Johanna's head, gently so as not to waken her. "Did I ever mention Isaac to you?"

"Who?"

"I guess not." She filled Mary Beth in on the letters she'd received from Isaac.

"And you don't recall him at all?"

"*Nee*. He mentioned in his first letter that he was at Mary Yoder's. I'll ask the *maed* about him tomorrow when I *geh* to work."

"You're ready to *geh* back?"

"*Ya*. I feel a lot better, and *Mamm's* been driving me crazy, not wanting me to do too much. I'm getting bored."

The coffee finished percolating. Mary Beth stood. "So what do you think about Isaac? From his letters, I mean."

"He seems . . . nice."

She filled two mugs with the steaming coffee. "Just nice?"

"I guess. It's hard to tell much from just two letters."

"Have you answered him?" Mary Beth put a mug in front of Katherine.

"Not yet."

"What's holding you back?"

With Johanna asleep, Katherine looked at Mary Beth. "I don't feel like it."

"You're not in the mood to write?"

"I don't care to write him. I can't explain it. Maybe because he's a stranger to me."

"Or maybe you aren't ready to move on from Johnny?"

Johanna snuggled against Katherine. "I don't know that either. He's changed. He's attentive. It's like he—"

"Cares?"

She shrugged.

"If he didn't care, he wouldn't be trying to help you get your memory back."

"Unless he feels sorry for me." Or guilty, like her mother thought.

Mary Beth groaned. "You two drive me *ab im kopp*, you know that?"

Katherine frowned. "I don't understand."

"And it's not my place to explain it to you. Although I wish I could. You two have to work it out."

"Work what—"

"I'm glad you're feeling well enough to get out." Mary Beth took a sip of the black coffee. "From what Bekah said, you were really sick."

"*Ya.*" If Mary Beth didn't want to talk about Johnny, Katherine couldn't force her to. But now her curiosity was more than a little piqued.

After spending an hour at his sister's, Johnny took Katherine home. It was nearly supper time, and she looked tired. He shouldn't have kept her out so late. He'd hear it from *Frau* Yoder for sure.

He glanced at Katherine. Her eyes were drifting shut even as the buggy bounced along the pavement. He was disappointed that she hadn't remembered anything. And when she'd asked him to tell her, he couldn't bring himself to.

She shifted in her seat, opening her eyes and yawning. She looked at him with sleepy eyes. "How long was I asleep?"

"Not long. A few minutes."

"Oh. I'm sorry. Guess I'm more tired than I thought."

"Understandable after everything you've gone through." He gripped the reins. Now was as good a time as any to ask her about Isaac. "So. About that guy from Walnut Creek."

"I really don't want to talk about him."

"Okay. Won't bring him up again." He paused. "Don't feel you have to stay awake on my account."

"We're almost home." She looked down at her lap. "I appreciate you trying to help me, Johnny."

"I wasn't much help."

"It's the thought that counts."

He glanced at her again. This time she was looking at him, her eyes questioning. "Why are you helping me?" she asked. "I asked you before. I want an answer this time."

He saw her driveway a few yards ahead. He didn't say anything until he pulled into it and stopped next to her house. "Katherine—"

His mouth suddenly went dry. Would she believe him if he told her? Would she send him away?

"What, Johnny?" She faced him now. They were close enough that if he reached out he could take her hand. Instead, he held on to the reins.

"I—I care about you."

Her eyes widened. "You what?"

He swallowed. "I like you, Katie. A lot." He looked down at the reins in his hand. "That's why I'm helping you."

She twisted in her seat, facing the front, slack-jawed. "Why are you telling me this now?"

"Because—" He bit his tongue. Every reason flying through his mind sounded lame. He released the reins and held out his hands. "I just am."

"I—I can't do this." She got out of the buggy.

He scrambled out of his side and hurried after her. He touched her shoulder, which stopped her in place. She turned around, tears in her eyes.

"Haven't I been through enough?"

"Please. I can explain all of it. You have been through enough. But I want to end that. Right now."

"Katherine?"

Johnny winced as he heard *Frau* Yoder's voice. He looked past Katherine's shoulder and saw her mother descending the stairs of their front porch. She stood next to Katherine and glared at Johnny. "You've been gone all *daag*," she said, still looking at him.

"I'm sorry." She turned to her mother.

"Supper's ready."

She started to say something, then turned around and walked inside.

He nodded to *Frau* Yoder and moved to leave. He'd have to talk to Katherine later.

"Johnny."

He squared his shoulders before turning around. *"Ya?"*

She glared at him. "I thought we had an understanding. I asked you to leave *mei dochder* alone."

He approached her. "I don't blame you for not trusting me. I haven't been exactly open with Katherine in the past. I never intended—"

"Your intentions don't matter, Johnny." Her tone softened. "It's too late. You need to let Katherine *geh*. If you care about her, let her find someone who can make her happy."

His throat constricted. "I can make her happy."

She paused, tilting her head to the side. Her hardened gaze eased, and for a second he wondered if she might change her mind.

Then she shook her head and turned away.

CHAPTER 23

Cora lay on the narrow single bed in the now-empty storage room, her throbbing ankle propped on several pillows. Sawyer had brought down a few of her things—hairbrush, toothbrush, other essentials—and Anna had made her a tray with tea and several types of cookies on a small plate. She sipped the tea but was too tired to even look at the cookies.

She had to admit her grandson and his adoptive mother were taking good care of her. The accommodations were rudimentary—there wasn't even a window in the small room. But she was comfortable, as much as she could be with a sprained ankle and an incurable disease.

She tapped her fingers on the edge of the bed. She needed to go back to New York. She didn't feel right staying here. But she couldn't very well make it to the call box by herself, and Sawyer hadn't offered to contact her travel agent. If anything, he seemed determined to keep her there.

Ironic, how the tables had turned. She had done the same thing to him when he visited her in New York.

A knock sounded on the door, and Anna poked her head in. "You have a visitor."

Cora frowned. "I do?"

"*Ya*, you do." Leona hobbled inside, past Anna, not waiting for an invitation from Cora. Rather rude of the woman. Yet deep inside, Cora was glad for the company.

"I'll get you a chair," Anna said. "Sorry there's not much room."

"It's fine, Anna." Leona smiled. "Plenty of room for the two of us."

Cora crossed her arms as Leona stood by the door. "What are you doing here?"

"A surprise visit. Ah, Anna, *danki*."

Anna placed the kitchen chair next to Cora's bed, then left.

Leona slowly lowered herself into the seat. She looked at Cora's foot. "Goodness, what did you do?"

"Slipped. You could have at least let me know in advance you were coming over."

Leona waved her off. "You would have refused to see me. This way you have no choice." She smiled again. "We need to finish our talk."

"Finish?"

"From the other night. You left rather abruptly."

"It was late, and I was ready to go home," Cora said. She uncrossed her arms. She'd never suspected this unassuming woman would be so nervy. Or nosy. Rather reminded her of herself. Cora frowned.

"See, there's something on your mind."

"My ankle hurts."

"Other than that ankle. Talk to me, Cora. You need a friend."

Cora looked away. Was this how these people saw her? Lonely? Burdened? She'd spent her life hiding her emotions, steeling her resolve. Yet these people, with their backward ways and unending hospitality, saw right through her.

Not the impression she wanted to give.

Cora turned and looked at Leona, who was leaning on her cane. "It won't be long before I'll need one of those."

"*Mei* Ephraim made this." Leona ran her hand across the smooth wood. "Before he passed. He never used one. I didn't really need it until a few years ago. Still, I used it even before that." She rested her hand on the top of the handle. "Makes me feel closer to him."

"Your husband was a woodworker, then?"

Leona shook her head. "*Nee*. He fixed small engines mostly, but every once in a while he liked to work with wood."

"Sounds like he was a man with many talents."

"And your husband?" Leona pushed her wire-rimmed glasses up on her nose.

Cora leaned back against the pillows. Her ankle throbbed a little less now. The pain pill she took a short while ago must have kicked in. She tried to think of something she could say about her late husband, something that reflected the same devotion Leona felt for hers.

"Cora?"

"Sorry." She turned and looked at Leona. "Got lost in my thoughts for a minute."

"I know what you mean." Leona looked at her lap. "I miss *mei mann* every day, and he's been gone a long time."

"So has my husband." But she couldn't say she'd thought of him every day. Or that their relationship had always been a good one. "I do miss him, though."

"It's a hard thing to lose a loved one. You and I, we've lost several. I lost *mei sohn* and daughter in-law."

"And I lost Kerry." She looked at Leona. "I don't want to lose Sawyer too."

"You won't."

"I lost Kerry because I pushed too hard. I wanted her to be the woman I'd always expected her to be. I wanted her to be like— well, like me. But she wasn't. Oh, she was headstrong like me. But she didn't value the same things I did." Cora blinked back the tears. "In the end, she chose her husband over me."

"Perhaps that was God's plan."

Cora looked at her with disbelief. "He's not much of a God, then, is He?"

"His ways aren't our own. We don't always understand them, but that's no reason to dismiss or ignore His work in our lives."

Cora turned away. She had no idea what Leona was talking about. More Amish religious babble. "I've never had much use for God." She turned back to Leona. "Money has always sufficed."

"Has it?"

Cora felt herself wilting under Leona's scrutiny. She slowly shook her head. "Not in this case. And not with Kerry."

Suddenly she started to tremble as reality sank in. Money

wouldn't force Sawyer to be part of her life. He had made that clear. Money couldn't break Laura and Sawyer's bond, and in some ways money and business had driven Kerry away, although she had to take responsibility for that as well.

Most of all, money wouldn't cure her Parkinson's. It didn't matter if she possessed every cent on earth, there wouldn't be a cure. Not in her lifetime.

"Let me pray for you, Cora." Leona reached out and took Cora's hand.

Cora looked down at Leona's hand. It seemed frail, with its pale, transparent skin and blue veins showing through. Yet she could feel the strength in that grip. Not a physical strength, but something Cora had never felt before.

"Thank you," she said to Leona, her voice thick with tears. "No one's ever offered to pray for me before."

"Then it's time they did." Leona closed her eyes. Cora waited to hear her say something, but she remained silent. Finally Leona squeezed her hand and released it.

"That's it?"

Leona chuckled. "God knows your needs, Cora. Even without me speaking them. Or you speaking them. But He does like to hear us talk to Him. More than just at holidays or out of desperation."

They sat in silence for a couple of moments. "Leona?" Cora said at last.

"*Ya?*"

"Could you pray that Sawyer changes his mind?"

Leona didn't respond right away. "I will pray for God's

will. If it's God's will that Sawyer become Amish, I can't ask for something different to happen."

"I see." And she did. Maybe it was the medicine, or the prayer, or Leona's calming presence. But for the first time she did understand. She couldn't ask God to change Sawyer's mind any more than Sawyer could force her to stay here. New York was where she belonged. And Sawyer belonged here. With this family.

It was time she stopped fighting that.

The next day Sawyer went through the motions at work. Laura wasn't due back for a couple of days, and he missed her. Cora wasn't making things easier either. His grandmother had been quiet since Leona's visit. Too quiet, which had Sawyer worried. She hadn't asked to return to New York, and she hadn't mentioned anything to him about Laura or his baptism or the wedding. When he tried to talk to her last night, she shut him down.

Sawyer left work a little earlier than usual. Lukas had stayed behind to visit with his parents, who lived next door to the shop. As he drove home he prayed for God to take away his worries. If he was to fully pledge his faithfulness to the Lord, he had to turn everything over to Him—especially what he couldn't control. Bishop Esh had emphasized that during their first visit together, when Sawyer expressed his desire to join the church. Too bad he hadn't told Sawyer how difficult it would be.

He arrived home, took care of his horse, and went inside.

In the mudroom, he hung his hat on the hook and brushed the dust out of his hair, which now touched the back of his collar.

The house was unnaturally quiet. Anna must be out visiting, and Cora was probably still in her room. He started toward the storage room, when the sweetest voice he ever heard stopped him.

"Sawyer."

He turned and saw Laura behind him, smiling. He hurried toward her and gently, very gently, touched her face. Then she was in his arms, leaning her head on his shoulder. His pulse thrummed as he drew her closer. Kissed the top of her *kapp*. Held on to her as if he never wanted to let go. He kissed her tenderly. A short, sweet kiss that held the promise of more as he entwined his fingers with hers.

"I missed you," he whispered.

"I missed you too." She stepped away, a serious expression on her face. "We have a lot to talk about, but there's someone I want you to meet." She took his hand and led him to the living room, separating from him as they entered.

A plump, blond-haired woman with Laura's delicate features sat on the couch, talking to Anna. Laura said, *"Mamm."*

The woman stood. She was several inches shorter than Laura, and everything about her was round. Her blue eyes narrowed in scrutiny as she approached Sawyer. "So. This is him."

"Mamm, meet Sawyer."

He held out his hand. "Pleasure to meet you—"

"Ella." Her firm grip surprised him. "I was just visiting with your *mudder*."

"Adoptive mother."

Sawyer winced as everyone turned at the sound of Cora's voice. He glanced at Anna, who didn't react to his grandmother's correction. Instead, she went to her. "Cora. I'm glad you can join us. You remember Laura?"

Laura moved a little closer to Sawyer. Anna didn't know about Cora attempting to pay off Laura to leave him. It needed to stay that way.

"How could I forget?" Even on crutches, she managed to put on an air of dignity. Or snobbiness. Sawyer could rarely tell the difference with her.

"Why don't you sit down?" Anna moved one of the chairs closer to her. "I was about to get everyone something to drink."

Cora didn't reply—she just hobbled to the chair, leaned her crutches against the wall, and sat down. She kept her gaze fixed on Ella. The two women took each other's measure.

"You're not Amish," Ella said.

"How perceptive."

"Grandmother—" Sawyer said.

But Ella held up her hand. "Are you planning to join the church, like your grandson?"

"Heavens, no. As soon as I'm healed, I plan to return to my home in New York." She looked at him. "I had hoped to convince Sawyer to come with me, but—"

Sawyer frowned. Why had she stopped speaking? His gaze went to Ella, whose expression was cold enough to plunge the equator into a deep freeze. Now he knew why his grandmother had clammed up.

Laura was right, they did have a lot to talk about.

"Sawyer, could you *geh* to the ice machine for me?" Anna smiled but kept twisting the ribbons of her *kapp*, as if she also noticed the tension. "Laura, you could *geh* with him while I fix our guests a snack."

"Nothing for me," Cora said. She kept her attention on Ella.

"I'm fine." Ella seemed just as interested in Cora.

"We'd be happy to." Sawyer hardly thought they needed ice, given the climate in the room, but he was glad to get out of there. He whispered thanks to Anna as he and Laura hurried out of the living room.

As soon as they got outside, Sawyer turned to Laura. "Want to tell me what's going on?"

With everyone else gone, Cora continued to look at Ella. She didn't seem happy to be here, and unlike the other Amish Cora had met, she wasn't overly friendly. Ella Stutzman even seemed suspicious of Sawyer. Which was preposterous. She ought to be counting her lucky stars that Laura had nabbed a man as wonderful as her grandson.

Cora didn't appreciate Ella's attitude, but she thought she might be able to use it to her advantage. "I understand you hail from Tennessee?"

"Yes, ma'am." Her voice held a soft Southern twang, similar to Laura's. "And you're from New York."

"Manhattan. Upper west side." Cora lifted her chin.

Ella didn't reply.

Cora leaned forward. "Let's dispense with the chitchat, Ms. Stutzman."

"Mrs." She sat back, folding her hands over her large belly. "I can appreciate a plainspoken woman. I can also see you disapprove of my daughter."

"As you do my grandson."

"I don't disapprove of him. I just want Laura to be happy. I reckon she's runnin' into this marriage a mite too fast."

Cora adjusted her glasses, but inside she rejoiced. Finally, an ally. For the first time in months she thought she might have a real chance at convincing Sawyer to come home with her.

"Mrs. Stutzman, we have much to discuss."

After a quiet supper, Katherine approached her mother, who was darning a pair of her father's socks in the living room. She sat down on the edge of the couch. Even though she was tired, she couldn't go to bed yet.

"What did you say to Johnny when he dropped me off earlier?" she asked *Mamm*.

Her mother didn't look up from her sewing. "I told him he's not welcome here anymore."

Katherine twisted her fingers together. It wasn't like her mother to be so rude, even when she was upset with someone. "Why?"

"Because I'm tired of you being hurt. There are other men who are interested in you."

"Please don't mention David Esh."

"All right, perhaps I shouldn't have said anything to *Frau* Esh." She put down her sewing. "But there's also Isaac, who's written you three times in a little over a week."

"I don't even know him."

Mamm went back to her sewing. "These things take time to develop."

Katherine glanced away. "I think you don't trust *mei* decisions."

"The *bu* is fickle. You know that better than anyone. And don't you find it coincidental that he's suddenly showing up here, acting like he cares? You've gone through a major illness. By next week he'll be back to ignoring you."

Katherine looked away, tears pooling in her eyes. She didn't want her mother's words to make sense, but they did.

"I don't mean to be harsh, Katherine. But you need to forget about him. Once and for all."

The tears she'd been holding back spilled. "I don't know how."

"You find someone else. You pray for God to bring you the right *mann*."

"But what if He doesn't?" She wiped the tears from her face. "What if I never get married? It's all I ever wanted. A husband, *kinner*. A *familye* of *mei* own, like Mary Beth has. Like *mei schweschder* Leah does. What if I can't have that?"

Her mother didn't say anything for a long time. She looked down at *Daed's* socks in her lap. "Then God will give you another desire, *lieb*. One that will serve His purpose. You must be content with that."

CHAPTER 24

Johnny awoke after a restless night, still trying to figure out what to do about Katherine. He couldn't show up at her house anymore, her mother had made that crystal clear.

But what about Katherine's father? He hadn't seemed upset with him when he came to pick Katherine up yesterday. Maybe *Herr* Yoder could get through to his wife. It was worth a try. But they didn't have a phone. And he didn't dare risk sneaking over there.

He sat up in bed. Before getting dressed, he went downstairs and searched his junk drawer in the kitchen for a pencil and some paper. He scribbled a note to Katherine's father, then ran back upstairs, dressed, and headed back to the kitchen. He was about to leave the house when his cell phone rang. Since he hadn't heard it ring for days, the noise made him jump.

"Hello?"

"John?" James Wagner's voice bellowed through the speaker. "How have you been, son?"

Johnny froze. He hadn't even thought about the Wagners, except when Katie had picked up the drawing yesterday. "I'm fine."

"Good to hear. Just checking in to see when we can draw up that partnership paperwork. Lois is eager to get started with her plans."

"I really haven't had a chance to think about it."

"Son, we've given you two days. That's plenty of time to decide."

Johnny shoved his hat on his head. "I've been caught up in a couple of things. Can I get back to you next week?"

"No. I need to know your decision now."

Johnny sat down at the table. He paused, wrestling with the decision.

He took a deep breath. "All right, Wagner," he said, "let's talk."

After his conversation with the Wagners, Johnny left the farm and went to his parents' house. As he pulled into the drive, he thought about everything that had happened since he moved out—most of it things his folks had no clue about. But despite his desire for independence, he felt an odd sense of separation from them. He hadn't thought he'd miss their closeness, not this soon. Not this much.

He put that out of his mind and searched for Caleb. He found his brother chopping wood behind the house. He approached him quietly, not wanting to startle him. When Caleb reached for another chunk of wood, Johnny spoke.

"Hey."

Caleb looked up and grinned. "You came to help me with the wood?"

"*Nee*. I believe that's your job."

Caleb placed the piece on the level stump. "I don't suppose there's some way I can convince you to give me a hand? It will take me all day to get this pile done. I need the time to look for a job."

Johnny nodded. "I'll help. But I need you to do me a favor first." He pulled the folded note out of the pocket of his jacket. Today had been hotter than the past week, almost like August instead of June. That's the way Ohio summers were—never could predict the weather from one day to the next. Johnny might say the same thing about life too.

"What's this?" Caleb put down his ax and walked over to Johnny.

"I need you to give it to Katherine's *daed*. To him only. And don't let Katherine or her mother know it's from me."

"Okay." His brother tilted his head to the side. "Can I ask why?"

"I don't want to *geh* into it. But if you can get this to him now, I'll work on the wood while you're gone."

Caleb didn't hesitate. "Deal." He took off his hat and wiped his damp forehead with the back of his hand. He took the letter. "Mind if I use your buggy?"

"*Geh* ahead." Johnny turned and picked up the ax.

"How's the farm going?"

"Haven't gotten very far. Some stuff has happened."

Caleb looked at him. "You're not giving up, are you?"

Johnny looked at the letter in Caleb's hand. "*Nee*. I'm not giving up. Just changing plans."

By the time Caleb returned, Johnny had finished half of the wood. His shirt was soaked with sweat. Once he got started, he worked at a furious pace, taking out his frustration on the wood.

Caleb parked Johnny's buggy in the driveway and got out. Katherine's father exited the passenger side. Johnny took off his hat and slicked back his damp hair. He put down the ax and met them halfway.

"*Danki* for coming out," he said. "And thanks, Caleb."

His brother nodded, then slipped past him and went back to the woodpile. He grinned as he saw the pile of split wood.

"You wanted to talk?" Katherine's dad looked him square in the eye. She favored her father more than her mother. Hopefully her father would be more understanding too.

"*Ya*. You want to sit down on the porch?"

"*Nee*. We're *gut* here. I have a question for you."

"What's that?"

"Why are you being so secretive? I don't like doing things behind *mei frau's* back."

"I know, and I'm sorry I'm putting you in that position. But I didn't know who else to talk to."

"About Katherine?"

Johnny nodded. "*Ya*. I've messed up, *Herr* Yoder."

"Call me Thomas."

"Thomas, I hurt your *dochder*, and I'm truly sorry for that. I want you to know that I care for her."

"You have a strange way of showing it." He wiped a bead of sweat off his forehead. "Then again, *mei* Katherine hasn't gone about things the right way either."

"This isn't her fault. I should have been honest with her from the beginning."

"The beginning?"

Johnny hedged. "Well, not exactly the beginning. But I know what a wonderful *maedel* she is now." He blew out a breath. "I also have to be honest with you. Up until today, I didn't have much to offer her."

"What's changed?"

He gave a brief explanation about his deal with the Wagners, leaving out the part about the Amish tourist trap. And that they weren't Amish. He'd deal with that later.

"So you're trying to make a case for yourself."

Johnny started to pace. "Your *frau* is mad at me, with *gut* reason. And Katherine doesn't believe I've changed *mei* mind." He stopped and looked at Thomas Yoder. Apparently he wasn't doing such a bang-up job explaining himself. "Maybe I shouldn't have sent Caleb."

"Now, hold on." Thomas put his hand on Johnny's shoulder. "I'm here, aren't I? And I wouldn't have come if I didn't think you were *gut* for *mei dochder*."

"But what about *Frau* Yoder?"

"I love Margaret, but we've been known to butt heads on occasion. This is one of them. Normally I stay out of this type of thing, but in this case I think you need a helping hand. You've been telling me how you feel about Katherine. Now you have to show her."

"I tried to help her get her memory back."

"That's not what I mean, John. You have to be honest with her, like you said. But completely honest. You have to tell her the real reason you've been pushing her away all these years."

Johnny took off his hat and tapped the dust and wood chips from it. "What if I don't know the real reason?"

"You do. Your pride is keeping you from admitting it."

Pride again. His father had accused him of being prideful about buying the horse farm. And looking back on it, he had to admit that his *daed* might be right. Did he really need a huge farm? Had he bought it to be boastful? Had he agreed to the Wagners' investment because it was the best plan?

Or was it all about being worthy?

"Search your heart, John. Pray about what to say to her."

"How can I talk to her? I'm not exactly welcomed at your *haus*."

"You let me take care of that." He smiled. "Then the rest is up to you."

⁂

"I think we both agree Sawyer and Laura are an ill match." Out of habit, Cora crossed her leg, accidentally jarring her injured ankle.

"Are you okay?" Ella asked. "That looks painful."

"It's fine." She straightened her posture. "Back to the

business at hand. I've been trying to convince Sawyer to change his mind about the wedding." She didn't add anything about the church. One problem at a time.

"Why? You don't think my daughter is *gut* enough for him?"

Cora swallowed. "No, that's not the case at all. She's a . . . a charming young woman."

"You don't know much about her, do you? Just like I don't know anythin' about Sawyer. That's why I came back with Laura. To find out what it is about this fella that has her so head-over-heels."

"Well, he is an exemplary young man. Anyone can see that."

"I'll reserve my opinion right now."

The woman's soft matronly appearance masked a strong personality. Impressive. But not intimidating. "Mrs. Stutzman, Sawyer has gone through a difficult time. Due to circumstances I'd rather not discuss at the moment, he hasn't had a chance to fully appreciate his legacy."

"*Geh* on."

"I'm the owner and CEO of a Fortune 500 company."

Ella cracked her first smile. "Then we have something in common. *Mei* Matthew and I run our own bakery."

"An interesting comparison." Cora had to struggle not to scoff that a tiny bakery could compare to her massive business domain. "Thus, as business owners, you know you have a responsibility to your financial interests. Sawyer is the one and only heir of my considerable assets." She adjusted the cuff of her cashmere sweater. "However, I cannot groom him for the business if he marries your daughter."

"Or joins the church."

"Precisely. He's giving up experiences he can only dream of on a mere religious whim and the delusion that he's in love with Laura."

Ella removed her hands from her stomach and leaned forward. Her small feet clad in plain black shoes barely reached the ground. She stared at Cora for a moment. Finally she spoke. "How much money are we talkin' about?"

"More than one billion dollars."

Her eyes widened. "That can't be right."

"I assure you, I'm not exaggerating. Not about something this important."

"Let me get this straight. Sawyer knows how much is involved here?"

"He does."

"And he's givin' all that up to become Amish?"

"Unfortunately, yes."

Ella leaned back against the couch. With one finger she wiped underneath her eye. "Unbelievable."

"Pardon me?"

She got up, walked over to Cora, and took her hand. "I was so worried after I heard what Mark did to her. When she told me about Sawyer, I thought she was—what's it called? When you fall for someone else because you're hurtin' inside?"

"Rebounding?"

"*Ya*, that." She smiled. "But from what you've told me, I can see that's not true. Your grandson is truly special."

"But—"

"Who's ready for some cold iced tea and oatmeal cookies?" Anna came into the living room carrying a tray laden with the goodies.

"Oh, that looks yummy." Ella took two cookies and sat back down. She bit into the cookie and nodded. "*Gut*, Anna. Worthy of our bakery, if you don't mind me sayin'."

Anna smiled. "I don't mind at all. Sawyer and Laura will be here in a minute with the ice."

"Great. I'll just grab me another one of these cookies while we wait." She looked at Cora. "I'm glad we had that talk, Cora. I feel like we're *familye* already."

"I, uh—" Cora sputtered.

"What's that about *familye*?" Sawyer walked in carrying a large metal bowl filled with chipped ice.

Ella stood. Walked to Sawyer and put her hand on his arm. "Your grandmother has been telling me all about you."

"She has?" Sawyer's eyes widened as he looked at Cora. "Hope it was all good."

Ella gripped Laura's hand and grinned. "Trust me, it was."

Cora sat back and watched in shock as the one person she thought could help her cause welcomed her grandson with chubby, open arms.

CHAPTER 25

"This is a surprise," Katherine said as her father drove the buggy out of the driveway. After a hot day, the sun glowed low in the sky. The sound of cicadas and bullfrogs surrounded them as they made their way down the road.

"We haven't been for a drive in a long time." Her father turned and smiled. "With you going back to work soon, I imagine you'll be really busy again. I figured tonight would be a *gut* night to bring back some memories."

Katherine leaned back in the seat and smiled. When she and her sisters were younger, their father would take them for evening drives. At the time she thought it was her father's way of rewarding all of them for good behavior. She found out later it was more to give their mother a break from three little girls.

But the reason didn't matter. Katherine cherished those drives together, watching the landscape pass by as their father, with an almost saintly patience, answered their questions about everything they could think of.

Yet right now she valued the quiet. The past couple of days, since she'd seen Johnny and talked with her mother, had been difficult. She tried to keep her mind off everything by working on a baby quilt she had started before she'd gotten sick. Bekah had to remind her who it was for. Although it had only been a little more than a week since she lost her memory, Katherine had accepted that she probably wouldn't get it back. And she realized her father was right—it didn't make a difference. The present counted, as did the future.

She'd also made some decisions during that time alone with her quilt, praying as she stitched. If she wasn't meant to marry, her heart would eventually heal. God would fill her with something else. A yearning she didn't know she had, and one that would be in accordance with God's will.

Wasn't that what she should have prayed for all along? Not for Johnny to love her, or for her to let him go. But for God's will to reign in her life. Her selfish desires had caused her to neglect Him.

"You feeling okay?" her father asked as he directed the buggy down Hayes Road.

"I'm fine." At his dubious look she added, "Really, I am."

"I believe you. You seem more peaceful than I've seen you in a long time."

"I am. You were right about the memories. They don't matter. Just like *Mamm* was right about Johnny."

"So you don't think he matters?"

"A part of me will always care for him, *Daed*. But I think I've finally reached the point where I can let him *geh*."

"I see." Her father didn't say anything else. He had no reaction at all, even when they pulled into Johnny's driveway.

"What are we doing here?"

Her father brought the horse to a halt. "I'm giving you the chance to let him *geh*. But hear him out first. And really listen to him, Katherine, before you make your final decision."

She heard the squeak of a door hinge. Johnny came out on the sagging front porch, his hands clasped behind his back. He wasn't wearing a hat, and he had suspenders on over his light green shirt. She hadn't seen him wear suspenders in a long time, other than at church. She turned to her father.

"I suppose you're not coming inside?"

"Nope."

"Does *Mamm* know you did this?"

"Nope." He smirked. "But she will. Eventually. Now get out. John's waiting for you."

Katherine couldn't move. Her stomach roiled, and her body was a jangle of sharp nerves. She wasn't prepared for this. Her mother had orchestrated things so she wouldn't have to see him again, other than at church functions, where he'd always made it a point to avoid her in the past. The idea of letting him go seemed easier that way. She hadn't thought she'd have to do it face-to-face.

"Katherine."

She couldn't ignore her father's command. She stepped out of the buggy and looked at Johnny. Her father turned the horse and pulled out of the driveway. Hopefully he would be back soon; she didn't intend to stay here long. The buggy rolled down the street, and the *clip-clop* of the horse's hooves disappeared in the distance before she'd taken a single step.

Johnny walked toward her. He put his hands in his pockets. When he reached her, he stopped a few feet away. *"Danki* for coming."

"I didn't have much choice." She blurted out the words, and for once didn't care. *"Mei daed* didn't tell me he was bringing me here."

"Would you have come if he had?"

She looked away, willing herself to say no. Instead, she said the truth. "I don't know."

"Can we *geh* inside? I want to talk to you."

"Maybe we should just talk out here."

"Can we compromise? Sit on the front porch at least?"

"Do you think it will hold us?"

He gave her slender frame a once-over, then smiled. "I'm pretty sure it will." He rushed to the house and went inside as she headed for the porch. By the time she reached the top step he'd brought out two very worn kitchen chairs. He set them down and gestured to one.

She sat down and looked at the front yard. She frowned.

"What is it?"

"I'm trying to picture a horse farm."

"And you can't?"

"Not right now."

He stared at the peeling porch boards. "Yeah, it takes a lot of imagination." Then he grinned. "But I found an investor."

"You did?"

"Ya. Soon enough I'll have the funds to do whatever I want with this place."

"Like raise horses?"

"And other things."

"Is that really what you want?" she asked.

"Why wouldn't it be?"

"You need to be sure, don't you think?"

"That doesn't matter right now." He looked at her intently, making her heart flutter. "I know you don't trust me. I've been terrible to you over the years, and I'm sorry." He turned in the chair, shortening the distance between them. "But I meant what I said the other day. I care about you."

She threaded her fingers together. "If it's out of guilt, you can let that *geh*. You don't have to feel guilty about arguing with me."

"Arguing? What are you talking about?"

"*Mamm* said we were arguing in the living room right before I passed out. It doesn't matter what we were fighting about. I realize I probably won't get my memories back from that time. I'm okay with that. I remember what's important."

"But we weren't fighting."

She frowned. "We weren't?"

He shook his head. "I can see why your *mamm* might have thought we were. I'd stopped by to give you the bag you left at my *haus*. And I had promised myself I was going to tell you the truth. To finally be honest about my feelings for you."

"And?"

"And—well, I told you. Then you fainted." He smiled ruefully. "Wasn't exactly the reaction I was expecting. But you were really sick."

"*Mei mamm* said you upset me."

"I thought I might have." He shrugged and stared at the porch again. "I probably did."

"But since I don't remember, we'll never know." She sighed. "Johnny. Look at me."

He turned, his expression the most serious she'd ever seen. "I've loved you for years, Johnny. You ignored me for almost as long."

He swallowed, his eyes turning glassy. "I know. And there's only one reason for it. I've been a coward. You put me on a pedestal so high, I was afraid of falling off."

She drew back. "So it's *mei* fault?"

"Nee." He rubbed his forehead with his palm. "That's not what I mean. I didn't think I was worthy of you. You deserve so much more than me."

She couldn't believe he was saying this. "Why would you think that?"

"Because I'm nothing special." He shrugged. "I'm not saying that because I feel sorry for myself, or because I'm fishing for compliments. It's the truth."

"You really believe that?"

"I'm just a simple *mann.*" He took her hands in his. "I'm sorry I took you for granted. I assumed you would always be there whenever I got my act together. But you became sick, and I realized I could lose you. And that Isaac guy showed up at the diner that day. I could see you were moving on. You had a right to. But things are different now."

"How?"

"I have this place." He gestured to the farm. "A way to make a *gut* living. I'm ready to settle down. With you."

"Johnny." She pulled her hands from his. "I appreciate you telling me this."

His face fell. "Appreciate?"

"I'm glad you finally told me."

"But?"

She crossed her arms. "This doesn't change anything."

He gaped. "It doesn't?"

"I'm different, Johnny. I don't know if it's because of the illness or just me finally understanding what I've been missing. I thought if you loved me, if we were together, then everything in *mei* life would be *perfekt*. I put *mei* faith in you."

"And I failed."

"It was an unfair burden. I wasn't putting my faith in God. All *mei* prayers were centered around you. Either asking Him to make you love me, or asking Him to make me fall out of love with you. Not once did I ask Him what His will was. Or what He wanted me to do for Him." She looked at him. "It was all about me, Johnny. It wasn't even about you."

He got up, paced across the porch, then returned and sat down in the chair. "What does that mean for us?"

"It means we have to let *geh* of each other. For *gut*."

Johnny's heart ached at Katherine's words. He had her within reach. Now she wanted him to let her go. Not because she was angry with him, or because she had found someone else.

Because of God. The last thing he expected. "It doesn't have to be like this," he pleaded. "Whatever you need me to do, I'll do it."

"*Ya*, it does." She stood. "This isn't the time for us."

He shot up from the chair. "God told you that?"

"He didn't have to. I've always put you first in my life, in my thoughts, in my heart. It's time for me to do that with God." Her gaze was so bittersweet it tore at his heart.

"So you're saying we'll never have a chance?"

"Only if it's God's will." She stepped down from the porch steps.

He watched as she walked away. He fought for a way to change her mind. But the words wouldn't come. They couldn't, because he knew she was right.

Yet he didn't want it to end like this. "Can I at least drive you home?"

She shook her head. "I'll walk."

She was determined. And he didn't follow her. Even though his heart lay bleeding in his hands, he stayed rooted to the porch.

He wouldn't beg. Wouldn't try to manipulate her. Because she was doing something that made him fall in love with her even more.

She was becoming a woman of God.

⁂

"I can't believe you went behind *mei* back, Thomas."

Thomas sat on the cedar hope chest at the end of their bed and watched Margaret's nostrils flare, as they always did when she was upset. And she was hopping mad right now. He'd expected it. And this talk was long overdue.

"You were being unfair to the *bu*," he said. "You know that."

Margaret whirled around. "Exactly when was he fair to our *dochder*? He's done *nix* but hurt her. And what do you do? Drop her off at his doorstep when she's most vulnerable."

"She seemed fine to me."

"She lost her memory!"

Thomas patted the empty space next to him. "Margaret. Sit down."

She crossed her arms. Gave him her hardest look, then plopped beside him.

"We have to accept that Katherine may never regain that time she lost. But she's going to be all right."

"As long as she stays away from Johnny."

"He's made plenty of mistakes, that's for sure." Thomas took her hand. "I did too, if you remember."

She looked away. "I hadn't thought about that in a long time."

"Because you forgave me for being a *dummkopf*."

"We were sixteen. It wasn't like we were engaged. You could see whoever you wanted."

"But I still hurt you. You wouldn't talk to me for weeks after I started dating other *maed*." He rubbed the back of her hand with his thumb. "But you forgave me when I apologized."

She sighed. "I know where you're going with this."

"*Gut*. We have to show John mercy. We have to respect Katherine's decision about him, and any other beau she might have. We can't control her life."

Margaret leaned her head on his shoulder. "I'm tired of seeing her hurt."

He kissed her temple. "Just remember, God loves her more than we do. When she hurts, He hurts for her. But He also knows what's best. You've always taught our *kinner* to rely on God."

"Time to follow *mei* own advice."

"*Ya, lieb*. It's all we can do."

CHAPTER 26

The day after Katherine left, Johnny sat on his front porch waiting for the Wagners to show up. They were running late. He didn't care. He'd spent all last night thinking about what Katherine had said and examining his own life.

Had he measured his choices against what God wanted? He had no idea, because like Katherine, he hadn't put God first. He'd shoved Him far down on the list. Now he was about to sign a contract that would change his life forever. And for the first time he truly asked God if he was making the right decision.

The Wagners approached in their fancy car. Until the moment he saw them exit their vehicle, he'd been a jangle of nerves. Suddenly, calm washed over him as a verse he'd heard long ago during a church sermon came into his mind:

Be filled with the knowledge of his will in all wisdom and spiritual understanding; that ye might walk worthy of the Lord unto all pleasing, being fruitful in every good work, and increasing in the knowledge of God . . .

He had only been worried about being worthy of Katie. Worthy of his family. But not once had he thought about what he had to do to be worthy of the Lord.

His father was right. Katherine was right. Everything he'd done, from buying the land to working with the Wagners, was impulsive. And as James and Lois Wagner reached his porch, he knew what he had to do.

"John," Wagner said, extending his hand as Johnny stood up from the old kitchen chair. "Good to see you again."

Johnny shook his hand but didn't respond. He looked at Lois, who was fixated on the house, probably making mental notes about the bed-and-breakfast she'd create.

"Lois and I are excited about this opportunity." He lifted his black leather briefcase. "I have all the paperwork right here."

"Yeah," Johnny said, putting his hands in his pockets. "About that. I've been doing some more praying"—he looked Wagner directly in the eye—"and this isn't going to work."

Lois snapped to attention. "What?"

"I'm sorry you had to drive all the way out here, but I can't be your partner. I'm not supposed to."

Wagner's eyes narrowed. "What are you talking about?"

"I'm talking about doing the right thing." He let out a long breath. It was early morning, but the sun was already heating up. Or something else was making him sweat. "There's nothing wrong with the idea you've proposed, but—"

"It's a perfect idea," Lois said, stepping in front of her husband.

"Not for me. I want a simple horse farm."

"We already said you could have your little farm." Lois crossed her thin arms. "We even put that in the contract."

"I'm sorry." What more could he say? How could he make them understand, when he was just now beginning to understand it himself? "The answer is no."

"You can't build your farm without our help," Wagner said. "Not even a little horse farm."

"You'll end up with nothing," Lois added.

"Maybe that's the point."

Wagner glared at him. "You're making a big mistake."

"Not to mention wasting a huge chunk of our time," Lois added.

"I apologize—"

"You know what you can do with your apologies," Lois said. "You'll regret this decision. We'll invest somewhere else. And we'll be successful. We always are."

Johnny nodded. "Then I wish you luck."

As the Wagners peeled out of his dirt driveway, Johnny plopped down on the chair.

They were right—he had nothing.

Except God and family. And right now, that's all he needed.

⚬⚬⚬

"I thought you weren't allowed to drive a car."

Sawyer glanced at Cora as he guided the midsized dark green sedan out of the Bylers' driveway. "I'm not a member of the church yet. I can drive. I just choose not to."

"Until now." His grandmother shifted in the passenger seat. "Where did you get the car?"

"Rental."

"Maybe you can rent it again when you take me to the airport."

Sawyer held in a sigh. After visiting with Laura's mother, Cora was more withdrawn than ever. And more determined to go back to New York. But he wanted to give her one more chance to change her mind—not about leaving Middlefield, but about rejecting it and the people who lived there.

"How did you manage to get a day off?" she asked.

"It helps that work is slow right now."

That gained a little of her interest. "Is the business in trouble?"

He shook his head. "It has its ups and downs. Like any business. I'm sure you understand."

She gave him a brief nod, looked outside the passenger window, and said nothing else.

This is going to be a long drive. "You asked me back at the house where we were going. I want to show you around."

"I'm not interested."

He expected her answer, which was why he didn't tell her the purpose of the trip. "You needed to get out of the house."

"I need to go home."

"You've said that." *A million times.* "When we return to the house, I'll call the airline. Or your travel agent. Whatever you need. We'll get you home."

A pause. "Thank you."

"In the meantime, I thought you should see *my* city. Cities, actually. I wanted to give you a little tour of the area. We can stop for lunch at Mary Yoder's—"

"I'm not hungry."

"Or not."

Sawyer left it at that. Despite his grandmother's sour mood, it was a beautiful day for a drive. Women were out hanging their laundry on the line—and not just the Amish, but Yankees too. The sun's golden rays warmed the interior of the car.

As he drove down Route 87, he saw an Amish farmer standing on his plow, directing a pair of huge Belgian horses as they broke up a patch of grassy field. It was a little late to plant summer vegetables. Maybe he was preparing a pumpkin patch.

Sawyer realized he was lost in his thoughts, drawn to the countryside as he wished Cora could be. But he wouldn't force anything on her. He also wouldn't let her leave without seeing where he and Laura would spend the rest of their lives.

Cora folded her hands in her lap, trying to ignore her grandson's incessant chatter. He was like a tour guide, pointing out different attractions and businesses as they traveled, explaining which friends lived where, even drawing her attention to "an authentic Amish schoolhouse."

As if she cared about any of this. All she could think about was her bleak future and limited choices.

A few words stood out as he talked, mostly names of places.

Mesopotamia. West Farmington. Parkman. Geauga County. It all meant nothing.

Everyone else, including Laura's mother, was overjoyed about Sawyer joining the church and getting married. They'd gotten what they wanted. She'd gotten nothing.

It was past noon by the time they were finished with the tour. Sawyer pulled up at a red light. A black buggy stopped next to them. Sawyer waved, and the Amish man driving the buggy waved back. Cora's hands remained clenched.

"So what did you think?" Sawyer asked as the light turned green and he propelled the car forward.

"Not much to recommend it. As I thought."

"Everyone's entitled to their opinion," Sawyer said, his voice sounding tight.

Cora looked at him. "I don't know what you hoped to accomplish. Were you hoping that once I saw green fields and horses and a cheese factory that I would suddenly accept everything that's happened?"

He shook his head. "I only wanted to show you a part of my life you hadn't seen before."

"I saw it. Let's go."

Before she turned away she saw Sawyer grip the steering wheel. A sudden and unfamiliar twinge of guilt battered her conscience. He was trying. But he didn't understand how bitter defeat tasted.

More importantly, he had no idea how much she would miss him.

He might not embrace her values, but she couldn't dismiss

that he was exactly what she'd told Ella Stutzman—an excellent young man. For a few brief moments, when she could get her mind off her own disappointment, she could see that he was successful on his own terms. And happy, so very happy. Wasn't that what she'd wanted for Kerry when she was young? For her daughter to be happy?

Something along the way interfered with that wish. Something had changed her definition of bliss and made her put wealth and status before her only child. Now she had tried without ceasing to do the same to her grandson. Like Kerry, he would have none of it.

Couldn't she be satisfied with his decision? Or was choosing pride, prestige, and money over another family member worth it?

"I have one more stop to make," Sawyer said, turning down a dusty gravel road. "It will only take a minute."

She nodded but didn't speak. A thick knob blocked her throat. A swelling rose in her chest. She fought the sudden tears that stung her eyes. How she despised sentimentality! Yet she was unable to control the emotions surging through her.

They pulled into the driveway of the saddest piece of property she'd ever seen. The yard was shorn and neat, but the house and barn were on the verge of collapse. A young man wearing a straw hat, a pale yellow short-sleeved shirt, and the same kind of blue denim pegged pants she'd seen all the Amish men wear was hammering a handmade sign at the street edge of the front lawn.

She peered at the lettering: FOR SALE.

Sawyer frowned. "What's he doing?" He got out of the car and walked over to the man. They talked for several moments, Sawyer clapping him on the shoulder in a sympathetic gesture. But he seemed more upset than the young man did. They parted and Sawyer went back to the car, but he didn't put it in reverse right away.

"Can't believe it," he said.

Cora's curiosity led her to speak. "What?"

"My friend. He's lost his farm."

"Oh. Sorry to hear that."

"That's not all. He told me he's also lost his girl, and a few weeks ago he lost his job." Sawyer shook his head.

"He's lost everything?" She frowned, compassion niggling. "How tragic."

"That's what I said. But he's okay with all of it. He said he has God. His family." He turned to Cora. "And then he said that's all that mattered." Sawyer put the car in reverse. "You'll be happy to know we're heading home now."

But Cora's mind was still on the young man. "Will he be okay?"

"He already is."

She glanced in the side-view mirror as the decrepit farm shrank from view. A memory, sharp and clear—and one she hadn't thought of in years—entered her mind. More than fifty years ago, when she and her husband first married, they had started a business, a simple print shop in a depressed area of New York City. They were so full of excitement and promise. Within six months the shop nearly failed.

Then they received an investment tip from a friend and put the rest of their meager savings toward it. The stock turned out to be a sure thing, and before the year was over they had sold their shop and started their own investment firm—one of many different businesses currently under her conglomerate.

A tip from a friend was all it took to change their fortune. She couldn't remember if she'd even thanked the man.

When they reached the Bylers', Cora turned to Sawyer. "What is your friend's name?"

"Johnny Mullet. Why do you ask?"

"Just curious."

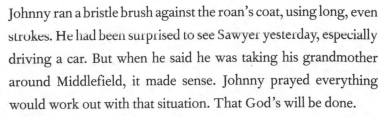

Johnny ran a bristle brush against the roan's coat, using long, even strokes. He had been surprised to see Sawyer yesterday, especially driving a car. But when he said he was taking his grandmother around Middlefield, it made sense. Johnny prayed everything would work out with that situation. That God's will be done.

Last night, as he sat in his empty house, the silence chilled him. He didn't belong here, not right now. Not with all the manipulation he'd done to obtain the farm and keep it. His drive to succeed had caused him to ignore his family and community and go outside his faith for help. What had that gotten him?

Nothing.

After a restless night, he rose early and started on his chores, his mind buzzing with thoughts. Not about the farm, but about Katherine.

He missed her, wanted things to be different between them. But she had been right. He had to strip away his pride, layer by painful layer, and get over himself. The only way to do that was to focus on what God wanted from him. Not on his own desires— whether those included Katherine or a farm or anything else.

"*Sohn?*"

Johnny looked up to see his father coming into the barn. "Hi," he said, stuffing down his turmoil. "I'm surprised to see you here."

"Considering you never invite me over, I can see why."

The comment stung. But his father was right. Since that first day when he'd showed his *daed* the property, he hadn't asked his father to come back. Mostly because he had so little to show for himself.

"I understand you've been having a pretty rough time." His father picked up an extra brush. "Mind if I help?"

Johnny shook his head. The two men combed the roan, not saying anything for a few moments.

"Why didn't you tell me you lost your job?"

Johnny looked at the ground. He shook the hay off his boots. "I was embarrassed." He glanced up at his *daed*. "You were right. I never should have bought this place."

"Is that why there's a For Sale sign out front?"

He nodded. "*Ya.*"

"I see." His father stroked one of the horse's withers. "I didn't think you would give up that easily."

"I don't really have a choice."

Might as well confess everything. He told his father about

the Wagners. About their plan for the fake Amish playground. About how he almost gave in to the temptation, all for the sake of his pride.

Daed's shoulders slumped. "*Sohn*, I really wish you'd come to us."

"You and *Mamm* don't have the money."

"We could have gone to anyone in the district. You know that."

Johnny put the brush back in its holder on the wall. "I wanted to do this myself. Now I know I can't."

"Do you think the place will sell?"

"I'm praying it will. I don't need the farm. Not right now. I'm starting to see things clearly for the first time in a long while." He opened the stall door, and his father followed him out into the middle of the barn.

"I suppose this new clarity includes Katherine Yoder?" *Daed* asked.

"Let me guess. Mary Beth." He'd confided in his sister yesterday, shortly after Sawyer left.

His father chuckled. He had grayed early, and the silvery strands in his beard and hair made him seem older than his years. "She's concerned about you. We've all been. But we also respect your right to your privacy."

"I appreciate that. But there's nothing private anymore." He held out his empty hands. "*Nee* farm, *nee maedel*, *nee* job. I've got *nix*."

"Nice wallowing you're doing there."

"It's not pity, *Daed*. I don't feel sorry for myself. *Ya*, I'm upset at some of the foolish stuff I've done. But I'm on the path to fixing all of that."

"All by yourself?"

"With God's help."

His father moved closer to him. "How about some help from your *familye* too?"

"Other than buying this farm or giving me a job, I'm not sure what you could do."

"We'll figure something out." He clasped Johnny's shoulder. "In the meantime, are you ready to come home?"

Johnny's chin twitched. Even after he'd abruptly left home and failed, his father still wanted him back, welcoming him with open arms. A jagged, broken dam burst inside of Johnny, the stress of the past month pouring out in a deluge. "*Ya,*" he said, choking back tears. "I'm ready to come home."

Several days had passed since Katherine had last seen Johnny. Her father hadn't asked any questions when she returned home on foot. He had simply given her a look, then went back to reading his paper. He hadn't mentioned Johnny again, and neither had her mother.

She had worked two part-time shifts at Mary Yoder's, getting back into the swing of things at work. It seemed that everything was back to normal.

Except nothing felt normal at all. There was a peace in her soul, one she hadn't felt in a long time. She didn't doubt her decision about Johnny. He didn't plague her thoughts or make her feel guilty or inconsequential. Instead, she felt free.

Bekah walked into the living room and plopped onto a chair. "Don't your eyes get tired from looking at that crazy pattern?"

Katherine looked up from the partially finished afghan. She was using primary colors in a zigzag pattern. She had to admit it was bright, not at all what she was used to making. "I like these colors. And the pattern." She looked at her sister. "I could easily say the same thing about you reading books all the time."

"Won't have much time to read."

"Why is that?" Katherine went back to crocheting.

"I got a job." She grinned. "I'll be working at Middlefield Cheese."

"Yum." Katherine smiled. "When do you start?"

"Next week." She folded her hands across her lap. "I feel bad for Caleb, though. He's still looking for work." She paused. "So is Johnny, from what I understand."

Katherine didn't look up from the afghan. "I'll pray he finds something soon."

"Or that he sells his property. No one seems interested in it."

"Sounds like you've been talking to Caleb recently."

"*Ya.*" Bekah didn't say anything for a long while. "Aren't you going to ask me how Johnny's doing?"

"You just told me."

"Don't you want to know if he was asking after you?"

"*Nee.*"

"Hmmph. He wasn't, by the way."

Katherine looped the yarn around her hook. "That's fine."

"Are you even listening? Katherine, put that yarn down and look at me."

She did as Bekah asked. "I'm looking. And I heard every word."

"Aren't you upset?"

"About Johnny? I'm not happy about his financial situation—"

"That's not what I'm talking about." Bekah lifted up her hands. "How can you fall out of love with him like that?"

"I haven't fallen out of love." She picked up the crochet hook again. "A part of me will always care about Johnny."

"Give me a break. That's not true and you know it."

"Bekah, it's true. If it's God's will for us to be together, He'll make it happen. I was trying too hard. Lately, so was Johnny. We have to wait on God. And we're both willing to do that."

"And you accept that?"

Katherine looked at her sister. "*Ya*. I do. For the first time, Bekah, I'm happy. I'm at peace. I'm looking at life and counting the blessings, not wishing for what was lacking. I'm finally *living*. And it's a *gut* feeling."

Bekah nodded. "I never thought I'd hear you say that, at least without Johnny being a part of it." She smiled. "But if you're happy, then I'm happy for you."

"*Danki*, Bekah. Now, you want me to show you how to crochet this stitch?"

"I'd rather read a book. Or plow a field. Or dunk *mei* head in cold water." She grinned. "Anything but yarn work."

After Bekah went upstairs, her father came into the room.

He sat across from her. Katherine put her crocheting down. Guess she wouldn't finish much of the afghan tonight.

"I heard what you told Bekah," he said. "Is that true? Are you happy?"

"I am." She touched her father's hand. "You don't have to worry about me anymore."

"I'll always worry about *mei dochders*. It's part of *mei* job." He sighed and looked at Katherine. "Johnny Mullet doesn't know what he's missing."

"I think he does, *Daed*. In fact, I'm sure of it."

CHAPTER 27

Sawyer paced the length of the Ottos' front porch. Laura watched him, worried. He hadn't said anything since he'd arrived a few minutes ago to pick her up and take her to work. Whatever was going on with him, she knew it had to do with Cora.

Finally he slowed his steps. Turned to her and grabbed her hand, still without speaking. Then he ran his thumb across her face, touching the raised ridges of her scars. She resisted the urge to turn away, knowing he would protest. He had told her not to be ashamed of them, and she wasn't, for the most part. But they were a reminder of her mistakes, of trying to take control of her life instead of letting God be in control. Her skin had healed from the cuts Mark had inflicted. But they would never fully disappear.

Sawyer leaned forward and kissed the raised ridge on her right cheek. His feathery touch made her smile. She brushed her hand over his homespun shirt, one Anna had made for him. One day she would be making his shirts.

"Are you going to tell me what's going on?" she asked, stepping away.

"You have to ask?"

"It's Cora."

He sighed and sat down in the wooden rocker on the porch. He squinted at the rising sun. "It's always Cora. A couple days ago I took her for a drive around Middlefield. When she got home she didn't say much, but at least she didn't ask me to call the airport. But this morning she wanted to go to the call box. She didn't tell me who she was calling, but I knew." He looked at her. "She's leaving."

"And you feel guilty about that."

"Yes. She's just now to the point where she doesn't need her crutches anymore. But she's frail. She's ill." He glanced away. "I can't force her to stay."

"Just like she can't force you to *geh*."

He nodded. "I'm worried about her. I'll keep worrying about her. I know I'm supposed to give this over to God—"

"But not overnight." She sat down next to him. Brushed a strand of his long brown hair from his forehead. "I'd like to talk to her."

"You won't change her mind."

"I know." But she had a debt to repay. She wasn't sure how she was going to do it with her meager salary at Byler and Sons. But she couldn't let Cora leave without promising to pay her back. And she wanted to reassure her that she and Sawyer wouldn't abandon her. Her mother had even liked the woman. "She's too fancy for her own *gut*," she'd said. "But she wants what's best for Sawyer. Anyone can see that, even if they don't agree with her."

"Do you mind if we go now?" Sawyer asked. "I can drop you off to visit with her on my way to work. Anna can bring you to the shop when you're done."

She smiled. "It's *gut* to be back at work."

He gave her a small smile. "Yes, it is."

A short while later Sawyer dropped Laura off at the Bylers'. She waved to him as he left for work and gave him a confident smile. Yet it wasn't long before she could feel the dread building in her stomach. The last time she saw Cora, the woman had tried to pay her to leave Sawyer. Laura figured she would try the same thing again. But she was Sawyer's grandmother, and she was struggling. If there was anything Laura could do to help, she would try.

After greeting Anna with a hug, she went back to Cora's room. She knocked on the door, softly at first. No answer. Maybe Cora was asleep. She knocked again, a bit louder.

"Yes?"

Laura opened the door, smiling. "Hello, Cora."

"Laura."

Cora was lying in the bed, her ankle propped up on pillows. She looked fatigued. Yet the glance she gave Laura was as cool as ever.

"Why are you here?" Cora asked.

"Sawyer told me about your ankle." She linked her fingers together, still standing by the doorway.

"And the Parkinson's, I'm sure."

"I came by to see how you were doing."

"I'm managing." She swung her legs over the side of the bed. She was dressed in light blue slacks and a long-sleeved white shirt with a wide collar.

"I'm sorry you're not feeling well."

"I don't need your sympathy. Or your pity."

The words stung, but Laura pressed on. "I know things didn't turn out the way you planned when you gave me that check. I'm not going to apologize for loving your grandson. I do apologize for taking your money, however. And I will pay you back."

"You don't have to."

"*Ya*, I do—"

"Laura."

Cora's tone softened, surprising Laura. "I won't accept your money. I have all the money I need."

"I know. But I always repay my debts."

"An admirable quality." Cora sighed. "I'll be returning to New York soon. You and Sawyer can get on with your lives."

"But we want you to be a part of ours."

"I don't see how that's possible."

"There are letters—"

"Letters. Of course. I guess I'll have to be satisfied with that. If he remembers to write."

"He won't forget you." She sat down next to Cora. "*We* won't forget you. We care about you."

She looked at Laura. "You care about each other more."

Laura didn't know how to answer that. But she could tell Cora what was on her heart. "I understand how important

Sawyer is to you. Even after we're married, he can visit. And you're always welcome to stay with us."

"Thank you for your generosity." Cora looked away.

Laura stood. She could see why Sawyer was worried. "The wedding is in November. I hope you will come."

Cora didn't say anything. Laura turned and walked toward the door. She was almost through the doorway when Cora's voice stopped her.

"If Sawyer had to marry an Amish woman, I'm glad it's you."

Laura smiled. It was as close to Cora's acceptance as she would get, and she was thankful for it.

Katherine returned from her first full day at Mary Yoder's tired but happy. She was glad to be back into a routine again. Instead of resenting what she didn't have, she was thankful for her job, and now the good health she had. Her friends at work were happy to see her, as were some of her regular customers. She had spent years seeking happiness and fulfillment from Johnny, and in the process had neglected to see that it was all around her.

As she pulled into the driveway, she saw an unfamiliar buggy. When she drew closer, a man about her age with blond hair got out. She pulled up beside him.

"Can I help you?"

He gave her a puzzled look. "Hi, Katherine." Then he smiled, revealing a dimple in his left cheek.

Her eyes widened. How did he know her? Then she

suddenly realized who he was—not from memory, but from his letters. "Isaac."

His grin widened. "For a minute there I thought you forgot who I was."

She put on a smile. "Let me take care of *mei* buggy and horse. I'll meet you on the porch."

"That's all right. I can help you."

"You don't have to."

But he was already leading the horse to the barn. Katherine got out of the buggy as Isaac unhitched the horse. She jumped out and took the reins. "I can get this. Really."

He gave her a doubtful look. "Okay."

He followed her into the barn. She put Chestnut into his stall, made sure he still had hay and water, then closed the stall door. Isaac stood right in front of her.

"I have to admit, I thought you'd be a little happier to see me." His smile faded. "Maybe I should have gotten the hint when you didn't write me back."

Katherine winced. "I'm sorry, Isaac. I didn't write you back because I was sick." She explained the meningitis and her memory problems.

That seemed to give him renewed hope. "Now it all makes sense." His blue eyes brightened. "I'm sorry you were ill. I didn't know meningitis could cause memory problems."

"Not always. In my case I can't remember the three weeks before I became ill."

"Then we should start over." He held out his hand. "I'm Isaac Troyer. Would you like to get a cup of *kaffee* somewhere?"

She looked at his hand, hesitating to accept it. Knots twisted in her stomach. "Isaac, a lot has happened while you were gone. There was a reason I didn't write you back. And it wasn't just because of my illness." She turned away from him. "I'm sorry, but we can't see each other."

"What?"

Katherine spun around at the frustration in his voice. His blue eyes, sparkling just a moment ago, now filled with emotional storm clouds. "I'm sorry, but—"

"You're *sorry?*" He glared at her. "I've spent the past five weeks on the road with *mei daed*, thinking about you, writing to you." The muscle in his jaw pulsed. "I even forgave you for not writing back. I couldn't wait to get back to see you, and now you're turning me down?"

Katherine took a step back. She hadn't expected him to get this angry. Was there more between them than his letters showed? "Isaac, were we dating before you left?"

"You said you'd *geh* to a singing with me." He folded his arms over his chest. "I consider that dating."

She considered it jumping to conclusions.

"Did you find someone else?" he asked. "Like that guy who was talking to you at Mary Yoder's?"

"I don't know what you're talking about."

"It doesn't matter." He unfolded his arms. "I thought you were a nice *maedel.* I didn't expect you to lead me on like this."

Her chin dipped to her chest. "I didn't mean to. Isaac, there's no one else. I'm not ready to date anyone right now."

"So when do you think you'll be ready?"

She shrank at his penetrating gaze. "I—I don't know. I'm leaving it up to God."

"And what if God is telling you to date me?"

"He will let me know."

Isaac flailed his arms. "So I'm just supposed to wait around for you to make up your mind?"

"*Nee.*" She went to him. "You have to live your life." She paused. "This sounds strange, but I know how you feel."

"You have *nee* idea how I feel." He walked away from her. "You wasted my time, Katherine. I won't be sticking around." He sneered. "You're not worth it."

Her cheeks heated from his insult. Moments later she heard him leave. Her father walked into the barn carrying a post-hole digger. "Who was that?"

"Isaac," she said weakly.

"Ah. He seemed to leave here in a huff."

"*Ya.* I hurt his feelings."

"I can't imagine you doing that, Katherine." Her father leaned the digger against the wall.

"Oh, I did."

"Seems the shoe's on the other foot now, *ya?*"

How right he was. She'd let Isaac down, even though she hadn't meant to. She not only understood his anger, but also realized how Johnny must have felt when he apologized to her. She could see both sides now, and she didn't like being on either one of them. She only hoped Isaac would be able to forgive her someday.

"I take it you told him the same thing you told Johnny?" her father asked.

"Not in so many words, but *ya*. I did. He wasn't too happy."

Her father put his arm around her shoulder. "Don't worry. You're doing the right thing, waiting on God. The right *mann* will understand that. And he will love you for it."

Katherine nodded. She didn't doubt her decision, but that didn't mean it was an easy one. "I hope so."

After work Laura, Sawyer, and Lukas headed home. Laura relaxed into the comfortable conversation, realizing that although she treasured her time in Ethridge, she had been right about Middlefield. It was her home.

"Will you stay for supper?" Lukas asked. "Sawyer can take you home later. I'm sure he wouldn't mind."

Laura chuckled at Sawyer's mischievous grin. "I don't think I'd mind either."

As they approached the Bylers', Laura saw a sleek black car parked in the driveway.

"That's weird," Sawyer said. "Wonder who's here?"

"*Geh* ahead inside," Lukas said. "I'll take care of the buggy."

When Sawyer and Laura entered the living room, they were surprised to see not only Cora sitting on the couch but a man seated next to her. Anna was nowhere in sight.

"Ah, Sawyer." Cora looked at him . . . and smiled.

Sawyer froze, and Laura understood why. Cora was smiling? She never smiled.

"You remember my attorney, Kenneth Jones?" Cora said.

Kenneth stood, smoothing his bright purple tie as he extended his hand to Sawyer. "Nice to see you again." He switched his gaze. "This must be Laura."

Sawyer nodded and moved closer to Laura. "My fiancée."

"I told him all about her," Cora said. "Your timing is perfect. Please, sit down."

"Where's Anna?"

"In the kitchen, working on supper. Smells delicious, don't you think?" She turned to her lawyer. "Now, Kenneth, where were we?"

"I should see if she needs help," Laura said.

"No, you should be here. This involves both you and Sawyer." She motioned to the two chairs near the couch. "Sit."

Sawyer and Laura exchanged a bewildered look and sat down.

"Kenneth and I were just discussing restructuring."

"Restructuring?" Sawyer asked.

"Yes." She looked at Laura, then at Sawyer. "I've realized something in my time here. I know you're resolute in your decision to stay. To become Amish. Nothing I can do or say can change your mind."

"Finally." Sawyer blew out a breath. "I'm glad you understand."

"I didn't say I understood. Just that I've accepted it." She paused, averting her gaze for a brief second. "I know your family is here."

"And you also have to know that you are part of that family now."

"Peripherally. And I . . . appreciate the inclusion. It's very unexpected."

"I'll say," Kenneth added. "I certainly didn't expect it."

"So what does this mean for your company?" Sawyer asked.

"Before I came to visit, I put Kenneth to work liquidating my assets."

Sawyer frowned. "Everything?"

Laura had no idea what liquidating assets meant, but Sawyer seemed to understand. "Once my shares of the company were sold," Cora continued, "along with my other investments, I had them put in a trust. For you," she said, looking at Sawyer.

"I can't take all that money," Sawyer said.

"I know. Even if you did, you'd probably give it all away. So I phoned Kenneth and changed my request. He will not only be managing my estate, he will also be the executor of my will." She looked at Kenneth. "He's the next best thing I have to family."

Kenneth cleared his throat. "Thank you, Cora. I'll do my best to manage your trust with integrity."

"I know you will." She turned back to Sawyer. "There's also a provision in the trust that if you change your mind, you will have access to the money."

"But what about you?" He leaned forward, casting a quick glance at Kenneth. "You have your own . . . expenses."

"Kenneth knows about the Parkinson's." She smiled again. Laura was surprised at how lovely it was. "But I appreciate your attempt at respecting my privacy. I will retain the penthouse and have an adequate monthly allowance that will cover all my expenses."

"Including travel," Kenneth added.

"Travel?"

"I will be visiting Middlefield from time to time." She looked at Sawyer. "I need to be with my family. And if my family won't come to me, I'll have to go to them."

"We've already talked about it," Anna said, walking into the living room. She handed Kenneth a glass of iced tea. "I told her she is welcome to stay here as long as she wants to."

"But I'm not living here," Cora quickly added. "I need my comforts. Electricity, to start with."

Sawyer looked at Laura. They both smiled. "There are apartments here."

"An apartment?" She scoffed. "I'd rather build. I noticed during your little tour, Sawyer, that there were several parcels of land available."

"Like Johnny's?" he asked.

"Among others. I'm still in the process of finalizing decisions. Kenneth will be assisting me."

Sawyer grinned. "So you'll be here for the wedding?"

Cora sighed, but it didn't hold its usual disdain. "Yes. I'll be here for the wedding."

Laura jumped up from her chair and hugged Cora's thin shoulders. "Thank you," she whispered in her ear. "You've made Sawyer very happy." When she pulled away, she could see tears forming in Cora's eyes.

"It's time I made someone else happy for a change," Cora said. "It won't make up for Kerry—"

Sawyer nodded. "But it's a start."

Two days later Kenneth loaded Cora's bags into a taxi. She was finally leaving Middlefield. But instead of being thrilled at putting this backwater town behind her, she had mixed emotions. She was eager to be going back home. And she'd made an appointment to see Dr. Clemens again. If she would be traveling between New York and Middlefield, she'd have to keep up her health.

Her pity party was over.

Lukas had already gone to work. Laura and Leona had stopped over last night and said their good-byes. Only Anna and Sawyer were left.

"I'll wait in the car," Kenneth said.

Cora nodded, keeping her gaze on her grandson. Next time she saw him, he would be Amish. She still found that hard to comprehend, yet she now respected his choice.

Anna approached carrying a small plastic bag with a zipper seal. Inside were several half sheets of plain paper, a pen, envelopes, and stamps. "We'd like to hear from you often," she said, handing the homemade stationery to Cora.

Cora hadn't written a letter in years, not when she had secretaries to do it. Now there was e-mail and texting. Letter writing seemed so old-fashioned. But it was necessary. And strangely, she looked forward to it.

"Thank you. I'll write to you as soon as I get back."

Anna smiled and stepped away. Sawyer came forward.

"Can't wait to see you again," he said.

"I think you really mean that."

"Of course I do." He looked at her. Then to her surprise, he put his arms around her. "I love you."

With shaking arms that had nothing to do with Parkinson's, she hugged him back. Tears stung her eyes. "I . . . I love you too."

As she and Kenneth were on the way to the airport, Cora leaned forward and passed a slip of paper to the taxi driver. "I'd like to stop here first."

"Sure thing, ma'am."

Cora settled back in her seat. She turned to see Kenneth looking at her. "I thought you were in a hurry to get home," he said.

"I have some business to attend to."

A short while later they pulled into the driveway of a modest Amish home. "I'll be right back," Cora said, opening the passenger door.

"Do you want me to go with you?" Kenneth asked.

"No. I need to do this myself."

With careful steps she started toward the front porch, but stopped when she saw someone come out of the barn. Sawyer's friend, Johnny Mullet. Just the man she wanted to talk to.

CHAPTER 28

Katherine sat in the church service, trying to concentrate on the minister's sermon. She'd been blessed by the past couple of services, yet today her attention strayed. The coolness of Gabriel Miller's barn offset the heat of summer. Bright sunbeams crept through the wooden slats. Above the voice of one of the ministers she could hear the twittering of barn swallows in the rafters.

Summer reflecting the warmth of God's love. She used to sit in services searching for Johnny, thinking about him, praying for things to be different. Now her heart was free to be filled with something else.

The service ended, and she walked outside into the enveloping sunlight. She spoke to a few of her friends as she walked by, and then she saw Laura Stutzman approach. When Laura was injured in the fire, Katherine had sewn a prayer quilt for her. Since then the two had formed a friendship. But she hadn't seen Laura in quite a while.

"Katherine." Laura smiled and touched her friend's hand. "I'm glad to see you."

"Me too." She leaned forward. "I hear you've been busy planning a wedding."

"No secrets around here." Her blue eyes danced.

Katherine grinned. At one time she would have been envious despite her happiness for Laura and Sawyer. Now she was simply happy. "All secrets come out eventually. When is the wedding date?"

"We moved it up to the beginning of October. *Mei* parents are able to come then, as will Sawyer's *Englisch* grandmother. You knew she was building a *haus* in Middlefield, *ya?*"

"*Nee*. Where?"

"She bought some property nearby." Laura took both Katherine's hands. "How are you doing? I heard about your memory loss during your illness. If you don't mind me asking, have your memories returned?"

Katherine shook her head. "The doctor says if they haven't by now, they probably won't. But I'm fine with that."

"You're content, then?"

She thought about everything that had happened the past few months. How she'd decided to put God first and let her desire for Johnny go. And she'd done just that. She couldn't say she didn't miss him, but she didn't ache for him like she did before. And he had respected her request for distance—they hadn't talked since that day at his farm. Even Mary Beth didn't bring the subject up anymore. Neither did her mother.

"I am, Laura. I can honestly say I'm truly at peace."

Laura grinned, took Katherine's hand, and squeezed it. "You deserve it. That and so much more."

"Katherine?"

A sudden lightness appeared in her chest at the sound of Johnny's voice. She turned slightly to see him standing behind her.

"Could I talk to you for a minute?"

Laura looked at him, then at Katherine. "I was just about to go look for Emma." She let go of Katherine's hand and glanced at him. "Hello, Johnny."

"Hi, Laura."

She faced Katherine again. "I'll see you later."

Katherine waved good-bye, then slowly turned toward him. It was the first time she'd been close to him in weeks. He was as handsome as ever. She had always especially liked him in his Sunday clothes, the cut of his black vest and crisp white shirt complementing his lean frame.

Today, however, there was something different about him. She met his gaze, seeing the familiar fringe of dark hair above his chocolate-brown eyes. But instead of the strain, worry, and at times even fear she'd seen there over the years, there was something else she saw.

Peace.

He pulled a folded piece of paper out of the pocket of his black pants. "I know I said I wouldn't bother you. This will only take a minute." He handed her the note. "For you."

He'd never written to her before. "What is this?"

"Read it and you'll understand." He held it out to her, his eyes pleading with her to accept the letter.

Reluctantly she took it from his hand. Then, without another word, he turned around and walked toward his buggy.

She looked at the letter but didn't unfold it. Warmth flooded through her, not only from the sun, but from deep inside her soul. She'd just thought about the peace she possessed from being free of Johnny, of envy, of perceived unfairness and unanswered prayer.

Now he'd brought her back into his life.

But not forcefully. Not out of guilt or manipulation. She ran her fingers over the plain, folded paper. She could at least read the contents. But not now. She held it in her hand and looked for the rest of her family.

Later that afternoon, with her father dozing on the couch, her mother reading a copy of *Family Life*, and Bekah with her nose in another book, Katherine slipped outside. She walked away from the house to the field next door. As the sun set in the distance, streaking the cloudy sky with its beautiful golden color, she began to read the words on the paper. Johnny's words.

Dear Katie,

It's taken me a good long while to write this. I'm not great with words. You know that, since I've said some pretty dumb stuff to you before. I thought maybe if I wrote things down they would make more sense to you, and to me. Guess we'll have to see.

I'll just come right out and say it. Katie, I miss you. I know you want to wait on God's timing to see if there's a chance for us, and I agree. But I can't let things end between us the way they did. Not without telling you how much you mean to me. You always will, no matter what God decides. You are a beautiful, kind, loving woman. Any man would be blessed to have you as his wife.

I promise to honor your request to let you go. I won't bother you. I won't pursue you. But I will always keep you in my heart. You will always be my Katie.

Love, Johnny

Katherine folded the letter and pressed it against her chest. She smiled, tears streaming down her cheeks. Knowing Johnny loved her was one thing; knowing he respected God enough to allow Him to do His will in their lives made him even more special. She wiped away her tears and hurried into the house.

"Katherine?" her mother called from the living room. "Everything all right?"

Katherine came inside and paused at the bottom of the stairs. She looked at her mother and smiled. "Everything is wonderful!"

As she ran upstairs, she could hear her sister's voice. "What's gotten into her?" Bekah asked.

"I don't know," *Mamm* replied. "It doesn't matter. It's just *gut* to see her happy."

Once she reached the bedroom, Katherine sat on the edge of the bed and read Johnny's letter again. She folded it and put it on her nightstand. She knelt beside her bed and pulled out a small wooden box, the one her father had given to her for Christmas years ago. She opened it. Inside were a few keepsakes—her first crocheted granny square, a bookmark she made when she was in kindergarten, the leaf Johnny had brushed off her shoulder the day he pushed her in the tire swing so long ago. She placed Johnny's letter in the box and slid it back under her bed.

Then she opened the drawer in her nightstand and pulled out a small notebook and pen. She sat down on the floor, leaned back against the bed, and opened the notebook.

Dear Johnny . . .

EPILOGUE

October

Katherine stood in the corner of the Ottos' living room, watching the mass of people as they congratulated Sawyer and Laura on their wedding. Across the crowded living room she saw Laura's parents seated at a long table, visiting with her own folks, her mother and father making sure the Stutzmans felt welcome.

In another corner of the living room she saw Leona seated next to Cora and Emma Byler, Lukas's mother. Sawyer's grandmother looked out of place, covered in sparkly jewelry, wearing a black sweater with a fur-lined collar that Katherine suspected was real. The contrast between the three women was startling, yet they spoke to each other as if they were old friends. Cora didn't seem the least bit uncomfortable with her flashy presence. She even used a sleek wood cane Sawyer had made for her in the workshop, painted a shiny black. His wedding gift to her, Laura had explained a few days ago. Cora gripped it tightly, as if she would never let it go.

Katherine sighed and leaned against the wall, content for her friends. For the first time, she attended a wedding where she didn't feel the sting of jealousy. The grip of pity. The yearning for a man who would never care for her as much as she cared for him.

Everything was different now. She had put God first in her life. And she knew she had Johnny's love. That was all that mattered.

She continued to scan the room, looking at family and friends dressed in their Sunday best, enjoying the fellowship. Her sister Bekah was talking not only to Melvin but to Caleb too. Katherine was pretty sure both young men were smitten with her. But typical of Bekah, she didn't seem to notice.

As people meandered through the crowd, the room began to feel a bit stifling. Katherine had started for the back door when a little girl in a plum dress and black *kapp* tapped her on the arm. It was little Velda Miller, Moriah and Gabriel Miller's oldest daughter.

"I'm supposed to give you this." She handed Katherine a tiny folded piece of paper.

Katherine accepted it. She crouched down to Velda's level. "Who is it from?"

"Can't tell." Velda leaned forward. "It's a secret."

"And you're *gut* at keeping secrets?"

"If it means I get candy." She held up a peppermint stick, stuck it in her mouth, and walked away.

Laughing, Katherine opened the paper.

Meet me outside, by the barn.

She frowned, folded the paper, and stepped outside on the back deck. The crisp October air held a fall chill, and a cool wind lifted her *kapp* ribbons. She stepped down from the deck and walked across the Ottos' backyard. Past the animal shelter, past the energetic barking of dogs well cared for. All the way out to the far reaches of the yard, where a grove of trees brimming with autumn color surrounded an old oak barn.

Then she saw him, right before he disappeared behind the barn. She looked around to see if anyone was watching. The few people outside were mostly kids getting ready to play a game of baseball on the other side of the Ottos' house. She rushed to the barn and turned the corner, expecting to see him there.

She was alone.

"Psst."

Katherine spun around and saw his hand poking out of the barn's open back door. He motioned for her to come inside. When she entered, she shivered, still cold from the chilly air outside.

He appeared in the center of the barn, his jacket slung over one shoulder. He didn't move toward her, didn't say anything. Just stood there, looking at her. Then he smiled.

And something inside her shifted.

She gasped, the sensation so strong, so real, she couldn't

describe it. An emotion she'd never felt before. Her hand rested on her chest, feeling her pulse thrum beneath it.

"Hi, Katie."

"Hello, Johnny."

"I see you got my anonymous note."

She chuckled. "Not very anonymous. I can tell your handwriting anywhere."

"Well, we've been writing to each other for months now." The smile never left his face.

Katherine grinned. Since he'd sent her that letter in July, they wrote each other at least once a week. Through his letters she found out that Cora Easley had purchased his farm, offering to rent it back to him, with him eventually owning it outright. He had taken her up on the offer, but instead of moving back into the run-down house, he stayed at home, doing some part-time work for Byler and Sons and picking up a few jobs at Gabriel Miller's blacksmith shop. Gradually he was fixing up the place, making it his own.

I'm going to do this right, he wrote to her shortly after signing the deal with Cora. *That house isn't going anywhere.*

"I wasn't sure you'd come," he said.

They gazed at each other for a moment. Katherine could barely stem the emotions running through her. She felt as if she were looking at Johnny Mullet through new eyes—and indeed, she was. But he was different too. His last few letters had detailed how he was forging ahead with the life God wanted him to lead. She hadn't realized how afraid and insecure he was until they spent time apart, getting to know each other all over again through their constant stream of correspondence.

She looked at him. The *bu* she thought she loved all these years had become a *mann*. A man of God.

And suddenly she *knew*.

"Johnny—" She choked on his name.

He nodded and closed the distance between them. He draped his black jacket over her shoulders, swallowing her in its warmth. Then he held out his arms and she stepped into them.

This was what she had wanted all along—the security of Johnny's love. Until now he couldn't offer it. Until now she couldn't accept it. They had to be apart and discover who they were as God's children before they could be together.

He moved away but kept one arm around her waist, rubbing his fingertips over the small of her back. "Does this mean we can start over?"

She nodded. *"Ya."*

"There's a singing this Sunday . . ."

"I think we're a little bit past singings. Don't you?"

He stroked the top of her cheek with his thumb. "I suppose so." He gazed at her, dropping his hand from her cheek and removing his arm from her waist. "Then what should we do?"

"This." She took his face in her hands and drew his mouth to hers, his jacket slipping off her body and falling to the ground. When their lips touched, she closed her eyes. He pulled her against him.

After the kiss, his chest heaved. "I wasn't expecting that."

"Was it all right?"

He moaned and stepped away. "More than all right." He shook his head as if he was clearing it and picked up his jacket. This time he handed it to her, keeping his distance. "You never cease to surprise me."

She took the jacket and put it over her shoulders. "Sometimes I surprise myself."

Johnny laughed. Moved closer to her, but just out of reach. Then he took one more step and entwined his fingers with hers. "I love you, Katie."

"I love you too."

"The time is right, *ya?*" He grinned again.

Katherine gripped his hand. "*Ya.* It's exactly right."

DISCUSSION QUESTIONS

1. For years Katherine struggled with unrequited love. Have you ever yearned for something you couldn't have? How did you handle having a dream just out of your reach?

2. Did you find Johnny's actions impulsive? Do you understand why he refused his family's and community's help? Why or why not?

3. What do you think might have happened to Johnny and Katherine's relationship if he had told her about his feelings earlier? Would their relationship have lasted?

4. Sawyer had to convince several people he was serious about his faith—Laura, Cora, Laura's mother, the bishop, among others. Do you think he succeeded? Why or why not?

5. How do you think living in the Amish community will affect Cora? Do you think she'll ever understand the Amish faith?

6. Do you think Johnny made the right decision by turning down the Wagners' offer? What do you think would have happened if he had accepted it?

7. Can you relate to Katherine's struggle with letting God take the lead in her life? Are there areas in your life where God needs to take control?

8. In what ways do you seek God's will and timing for your life?

ACKNOWLEDGMENTS

I want to thank my editors Natalie Hanemann and Penelope Stokes, who always take my raw manuscripts and provide invaluable guidance to help me get them in shape. *Letters to Katie* is no exception. Thank you to the team at Thomas Nelson for their unwavering support during the writing of the Middlefield Family series. Thanks as well to my agent, Tamela Hancock Murray, for standing by me. And above all, my family, my friends, and my Lord—without whom I couldn't get through the day, much less write a book.

Enjoy
Kathleen Fuller's
Amish of Birch
Creek series!

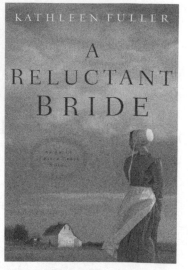

Available in print,
audio, and e-book.

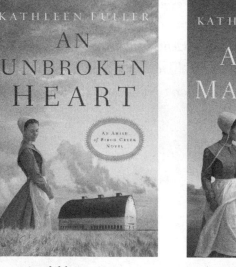

Available in print,
audio, and e-book.

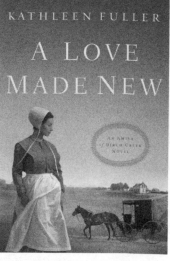

Available in print,
audio, and e-book.

ABOUT THE AUTHOR

Kathleen Fuller is the author of several bestselling novels, including *A Man of His Word* and *Treasuring Emma*, as well as a middle-grade Amish series, the Mysteries of Middlefield.

Visit her online at www.kathleenfuller.com

Twitter: @TheKatJam

Facebook: Kathleen Fuller